at

THRACKLEY

WEEKEND
at
THRACKLEY

Alan Melville

With an Introduction by
MARTIN EDWARDS

This edition published 2018 by
The British Library
96 Euston Road
London NW1 2DB

Originally published in 1934 by Skeffington & Son, Ltd

Cataloguing in Publication Data
A catalogue record for this publication is
available from the British Library

ISBN 978 0 7123 5211 6

Typeset by Tetragon, London
Printed and bound by TJ International, Padstow, Cornwall

WEEKEND
at
THRACKLEY

INTRODUCTION

Weekend at Thrackley is a country house mystery in the classic tradition. Jim Henderson is a likeable young man typical of his time. Having left school to fight in the war, he has returned "with each limb intact but with neither business training nor experience." As the story begins, he's spent three years out of work before unexpectedly receiving an invitation to a country house party in Surrey.

The summons to Thrackley is slightly mysterious. Edwin Carson, who owns the old house, says he recently returned to England from abroad, and claims to have been a very close friend of Jim's father. In fact, Jim hasn't heard of him, but the prospect of "a free weekend with free food and free drink" proves irresistible, and he accepts.

Inevitably, this being a Golden Age mystery novel, Jim finds himself in the midst of a curiously assorted group of individuals, presided over by Carson and his sinister sidekick Jacobson. And it soon becomes clear that Carson's motives for assembling his guests are not purely social.

First published in 1934, *Weekend at Thrackley* was a debut novel, and—although the plot is very different—its style was clearly influenced by A.A. Milne's *The Red House Mystery*, which achieved enormous popularity after it appeared in 1922. Raymond Chandler, no less, described Milne's novel as "an agreeable book, light, amusing in the *Punch* style, written with a deceptive smoothness that is not as easy as it looks." Melville was aiming for something similar. He admired Milne's light touch as a writer, and says in his autobiography, *Merely Melville* (1970) that the only distinction of any kind that he achieved during his schooldays was winning a prize for English literature on the strength of a parody of Milne's works.

William Melville Caverhile (1910–83), who became much better known as Alan Melville, was born in Berwick-upon-Tweed. After leaving school, he started working for the family timber firm in Berwick. Hopelessly unsuited for business life, he showed stirrings of independence by deciding to move out of the family home and live in a local hotel, presided over by "an energetic saint called Miss Nellie Robinson", who may just have inspired his affectionate portrayal of Jim Henderson's landlady, Mrs Bertram, in this novel.

Melville yearned to go on the stage, but recognized that "as it seemed unlikely that I would ever go direct from a back room in the Waterloo Hotel, Berwick-upon-Tweed, to stardom in the West End, there was a possible side-entrance through writing… the thing was obviously money for old rope". He started to pound away on an old typewriter, working long into the night, much to the despair of commercial travellers in adjoining rooms who were trying to get some sleep. His earliest efforts, short stories for children, were accepted by the BBC, and Melville broadcast them himself. He followed up this initial success with a flurry of poems, stories, and news items for the Press, while continuing to work at the timber yard.

The part-time author's next venture was to write a whodunnit, and the result was *Weekend at Thrackley*. According to his light-hearted recollection, half a lifetime later, in *Merely Melville*, "it wasn't very good… but to my amazement it was accepted first time out by a subsidiary of Hutchinson, sold rather well, went into paperback, and was subsequently made into a film called, for no reason that I could fathom, *Hot Ice*. The film was quite terrible and bore no relation at all to the original masterpiece." This is not quite the full story, since the publisher, Skeffington, was a small independent firm, and Melville also wrote a play based on the book, which was then adapted for film. The movie, starring John Justin and Barbara Murray, was released in 1952, so in one guise or another, *Weekend at Thrackley* enjoyed a long life, although the original novel has been out of print for many years.

Melville was modest about his crime writing, but *Weekend at Thrackley* changed his life: "I had earned much more during the three months it had taken me to write the whodunit in my spare time than I could have earned in three years at my present emolument in the timber business." When his uncle proved reluctant to raise his pay, he resigned to become a freelance writer and performer. With the money from the sale of the film rights, he bought a bungalow, and called it Thrackley.

He rapidly wrote five more crime novels, including *Death of Anton* and *Quick Curtain*, both of which have been given fresh life in the British Library's Crime Classics series. But there were no more sales of film rights, and like many novelists before and since, he found that repeating an initial literary success, and earning a good long-term living from writing fiction, was at least as difficult as making the initial breakthrough. In 1936, he took a job as a scriptwriter in the Variety Department of the BBC, under Eric Maschwitz, who had himself dabbled with success in the crime genre, collaborating with Val Gielgud on several mysteries, the most successful of which was *Death at Broadcasting House*, published at around the same time as this book.

Like many people who tried their hand at crime writing during "the Golden Age of Murder" between the world wars, Melville had other priorities. For all his gifts in the field of light entertainment, he did not have the commitment to the genre necessary for a lengthy run as a published crime writer. But it didn't matter. After the Second World War, in addition to writing lyrics, plays and revues, he became a popular television personality. By then, *Weekend at Thrackley* was long forgotten. Its republication gives modern readers the chance to sample the first full-length novel by a young man who would, in later years, become a household name.

MARTIN EDWARDS

www.martinedwardsbooks.com

I

THE ALARM CLOCK AT MR. HENDERSON'S LEFT EAR GAVE A slight warning twitch and then went off with all its customary punctuality and power. It had not cost a great deal of money (to be exact, three shillings and elevenpence), but for all that it had a good bullying ring which could be calculated to waken most of Mrs. Bertram's lodgers. Not, however, Mr. Henderson. In the flat below, Mrs. Twist heard the sound of the alarm and dispatched her several offsprings to their several schools. Even nearer the bowels of the earth, in the very bottom flat, Mr. Jackson started at the sound, bolted his second egg and his third cup of tea, snatched his umbrella and bowler hat from their places on the hallstand, kissed a good-bye to his wife, and departed at a steady trot in the direction of the 8.25 to town. But the alarm had very little effect on the person nearest to it. It rang uninterrupted for nearly a minute, and then a hand appeared slowly from beneath the bedclothes, stretched itself out in the direction of the clock, waggled for a second or two until it found the alarm-pointer, and disappeared again beneath the sheets. A strange stillness settled once more on Number 34, Ardgowan Mansions, N. And Jim Henderson turned over on his other side and went to sleep.

His landlady, Mrs. Bertram, knew her business. Jim had given her strict orders on the early-morning procedure. At eight-fifteen, alarms but no excursions. At nine, breakfast. In the sitting-room if the sensational happened and Jim rallied to the alarm's ringing. In bed if he didn't. During his three years' stay at Mrs. Bertram's "establishment" (which was the official description given to the place whenever Mrs. Bertram put a two-line advertisement in the evening papers), Jim had had breakfast thrice in the sitting-room. Once out of sheer necessity in order to catch a train. Twice when the three-and-elevenpenny alarm clock had made unfortunate blots on its otherwise excellent record. On all other mornings, breakfast was brought to him in bed. It was brought there this morning.

Mrs. Bertram brought it herself. A large and benevolent soul, this Mrs. Bertram; a woman who talked a great deal more than was necessary and who read the newspapers rather more than was good for her. Mrs. Bertram thrived on news. Each morning, before she began her round of duties in the house, she consumed the more important portions of three of the morning dailies. And then to each of her four lodgers she passed on those portions, amended and exaggerated as she thought fit, as a kind of free gift with their breakfast trays. On Christmas Day and Easter Monday and other paperless occasions Mrs. Bertram pined in agony from the lack of news. Breakfast served neat, without a spot of morning scandal, seemed a futile affair altogether.

She laid Jim's tray down on the table beside his bed, crossed to the window and pulled back the curtains. The sunlight had more effect on Mr. Henderson than the alarm clock, for he sat up in bed, propped himself on one elbow, and blinked first at his breakfast and then at Mrs. Bertram.

"'Morning, Mr. Henderson," said Mrs. Bertram. "Lovely morning. Sun and everything. Regular summer's day, it is."

Mr. Henderson grunted.

"There's your breakfast, dearie. Kippers again, I'm afraid. Price of eggs is something shocking. It's this here government with their tariffs and their duties and their whatnots."

Mr. Henderson thought for a moment of asking for further particulars of a government's whatnots. Instead of doing which he grunted again.

"And there's the morning paper for you. Nothing much in it. Some sort of a how-d'you-do in Borneo, and a typist in Manchester got strangled coming home from a dance. That conference has bust up without doing nothing, as usual. And Lady Carter—her that was the actress—has had another baby. Five, that is. And that horse you gave me for the three o'clock yesterday was last by a quarter of a furlong."

Mr. Henderson (give the man his due) roused himself at this last piece of news. He said: "That's a pity, Mrs. Bertram."

"It's more than a pity, Mr. Henderson. Thank heaven I don't know how long a furlong is—that's some consolation."

"Any letters, Mrs. Bertram?"

"Three. On top of your kippers, dearie."

"Thanks."

And Mrs. Bertram steered her large frame across the room and closed the door behind her. She scuttled back to the armchair at the side of the kitchen fireplace, found her spectacles, and continued the *Daily Standard's* unnecessarily full details (with photograph on back page and cross marking the spot) of the Manchester strangle. She had not had time to digest the thing fully before the bells started ringing for their shaving-water. Done in with a length of picture cord, she was, poor girl. And such a nice-looking girl, too. Really nowadays you never could tell.

In his bedroom Jim Henderson poured out coffee and began an attack on his kippers in a depressed silence. Usually at this time of the day he indulged in a fit of the blues. He reviewed the situation as he had done a hundred times before. Out of work. Been so for

three years. And with every possibility of remaining so for the rest
of his days. He had left school to join in the war, during which his
mother had died. Had returned from the war with each limb intact
but with neither business training nor experience. And since then
things had not stopped going wrong. Letters, crisp and typewritten
("we regret very much that we are unable to accept your applica-
tion for this post, but we have been forced to fill the vacancy with
a rather more experienced man") became as frequent as rejection
slips to the budding author. He got a job, and very promptly lost
it through telling the managing director, with a commendable
but very rash frankness, exactly what he thought of him. And
after that jobs were even harder to get. "So," said Jim Henderson,
picking the last vestiges of edible matter from his second kipper,
"so here we are. Pleasant and extremely good-looking young man,
aged thirty-four, possessing no talents or accomplishments beyond
being able to give an imitation of Gracie Fields giving an imitation
of Galli-Curci, with no relations and practically no money, seeks
job." He told himself that the subject of the sentence was much
too far away from the verb to make the thing at all pleasant to the
ear, and then proceeded to open his morning's mail.

Mrs. Bertram had been perfectly right when she said that there
were three letters. She might, of course, have added that two of
the three bore only halfpenny stamps, thus considerably reducing
their interest. But the third was a real, live, honest affair with the
full three-halfpenceworth of stampage in its top right-hand corner.
Jim inspected it thoroughly. Felt it. Smelt it. Decided that he didn't
know the handwriting, and that he had never heard of the post-
mark. And then laid it down beside the remains of his kippers. Best
to keep a thing like that to the last; much more satisfactory to deal
with the riff-raff first. He dealt with the riff-raff. In the very remote

chance of being able to get odds against one of the two halfpenny letters being a bill, Jim would have made money. A bill it certainly was. From Messrs. Smith, Hopkinson and Trevor, Ltd. "To account rendered, one lounge suit, £8 8s. od." Jim swore, under his breath at first and then audibly. The other was an appeal from the old boys' association of the public school at which he had learned the finer points of Rugby football. Mr. James Lockhart, M.A., was resigning his post of Senior Science Master at the end of the summer term, and it was felt that all old boys should be given the opportunity of subscribing to some small token of their appreciation of Mr. Lockhart's long and valued services. Jim swore, audibly at first and then under his breath, and remembered the classic occasion when he had lathered the seat of old Lockjaw's desk with soft soap. He passed on to the third letter.

He read it slowly, took a sip of his coffee, and read it again. He laid it down for a moment beside his coffee-cup and lay back to contemplate his bedroom ceiling. The ceiling was in need of dusting and whitewashing, and the soot from the gas-jet had made a dark circle in one corner. But for once Jim did not notice these things. He poured himself out a further supply of coffee while reading the letter for the third time, and sent most of the coffee into his saucer and very little into the cup. The amazing thing was that the letter read exactly the same each time. He read:

Thrackley,
nr. Adderly, Surrey.
21st.

Dear Captain Henderson,

    I am not quite sure whether you will know me. I was a very close friend of your father and lived with him in

South Africa for many years before he died. I met you once or twice in England when you were very young. I have recently returned to England from abroad and have taken this house in Surrey for a while. I wonder if you would care to come down next weekend and join in a little unofficial house-warming?

I can promise you excellent fishing and fair shooting, and the company will be nearer your age than mine, so you need not worry on that account. There is an extremely bad train which leaves St. Pancras at 3.20, getting to Adderly at a quarter-past four. May I expect you down next Friday? I can send the car to meet you at Adderly station, if you will let me know when you are coming. I hope that I may have the pleasure of seeing you again.

Yours very sincerely,

EDWIN CARSON.

"Well," said Jim. "Never heard of the fellow in my life." He pushed the bedclothes back, threw his legs over the side of the bed, and stretched himself. Then he crossed to his dressing-table and looked at his reflection in the mirror. He mentioned casually to the reflection that it would have been much better if he had been very fair instead of very dark, passed his hand over the offending scrubbiness of his chin, and said "What about it?"

"What about what?" said the reflection.

"This Thrackley business, of course."

"Oh, that," said the reflection. "Accept it, you fool. You'll probably be bored stiff, but it's a free weekend with free food and free drink. You might even be able to get twelve-and-six knocked off

Mother Bertram's monthly bill for board, lodgings, and services. So why not?"

"Very well," said Jim Henderson. "Very well, Mr. Carson, whoever you are, we shall be pleased to accept your kind invitation for Friday next. Now where in the name of heaven is my shaving water?"

II

AN ANNUAL SUBSCRIPTION TO GRAHAM'S WAS ONE OF THE few luxuries which Jim Henderson permitted himself. It was, he felt, money well spent. Most people know Graham's. You enter it from the Strand, and its interior makes up for all that the exterior lacks. At Graham's you may obtain a cocktail which is really much the same as the best cocktail in any of the other London clubs, but which has just an extra something which makes it far superior and leaves the others lagging miserably behind. At Graham's, too, you can get a very fine *omelette aux champignons*, so light and airy that you have to be ready to bolt it the very minute it arrives on its heated pewter dish; if you are not, the wretched thing falls flat like a burst balloon and sags despondently all over your plate. At Graham's—well, in any case, Graham's is certainly worth its fifteen guineas a year membership fee. No matter how hard it is for you to scrape together the said fifteen.

When Jim entered the club shortly after eleven that morning he found the usual before-lunch crowd in their usual places in the lounge. Derek Simpson astride an armchair, his long legs swinging over the leather arms, his group of satellites listening to Derek Simpson's opinions of Derek Simpson's acting in the new thing at the Alhambra. John Fletcher and old Angus and some of the more elderly members in their corner, drinking Bacardis and bemoaning the new level to which rubber had fallen. Someone whom Jim remembered as having played for Oxford at something (squash, he imagined) relating, with a wealth of detail, his experiences of a recent Channel crossing. A large gentleman in plus fours practising chip shots on the lounge carpet, with the screwed-up front page of *The Times* as a ball and an empty beer tankard as the hole. And in the cocktail bar through the swing doors the Honourable Freddie Usher was laughing.

No other person in the world laughed quite like Freddie Usher. Mercifully so. Large and oily film-directors, ever ready to jar their talking-picture audiences with a new and devastating noise, offered the most amazing terms for the inclusion of half-a-minute of Freddie Usher's laugh in their latest productions. There were no half-hearted methods adopted when Freddie Usher became amused. No discreetness. No lack of abandon. No thought for the ear-drums of those in the next street but two. No… Freddie Usher threw back his chest, opened his mouth to a distressing width, slapped his thighs and all thighs within reach, and announced his amusement to the world.

Jim pushed open the heavy swing doors which led from the lounge to the bar. He stood at the doors for a moment, realizing that conversation was out of the question until the Honourable Freddie had recovered from his mirth.

"'Morning, everybody," he said at last. "'Morning, Freddie."

"James!" said Freddie, cutting short the last diminuendoes of the cackle. "Dear old James! What is it?"

"Gin-and-ginger, please, Freddie."

"So be it. Make it two, Edward. Double ones."

"What on earth were you making that fiendish din about?"

The Honourable Freddie looked puzzled.

"Din?" he asked. "Din? Did I hear you correctly? Was I making a din?"

"You certainly were."

"Really. Well, I forget why. Some little thing someone said about something, I suppose."

He handed Jim his drink and pulled two chairs close to each other in a corner of the bar.

"Just a minute," said Jim. "I want a word with you, Freddie. Let's go into the lounge where it's quieter."

"As you say, James."

They left the crowd in the bar and entered the comparative peace of the lounge. Jim looked round. In one of the window corners two chairs stood invitingly empty. There was no one within a dozen yards with the exception of Sir Reginald Forrest, M.P. And the prospects of being disturbed by Sir Reginald seemed rather remote, for that eminent financial expert was in a very undignified and almost horizontal position, *The Times* over the upper quarter of his face, his mouth open and sagging, his arms clasped contentedly over that portion of his being where presumably his breakfast lay.

"Over there," said Jim.

"Righto. But why this air of mystery? Why this come-hither-where-no-alien-ear-may-lurk attitude?"

"Stop prattling, Freddie. And park yourself in that chair."

They sat down, drew their chairs together and took a sip of their drinks.

"Well?" said the Honourable Freddie.

"This morning I had a letter."

"A letter?"

"A letter."

"Just fancy that. A letter. Well, well, well. Most remarkable. So far as I can remember, I had eleven. Three from charitable institutions, one account rendered for a pair of singularly snappy silk pyjamas which I've never quite had the face to wear, one kind offer from a Mr. Andrew Isaacs with absolutely no security, a picture-postcard from my Aunt Florence, who—funnily enough—is in Florence, and—"

"For heaven's sake shut up."

"My celebrated imitation of a deaf and dumb oyster sent to Coventry," said the Honourable Freddie, and subsided into his gin-and-ginger.

"A letter from someone I've never seen or heard of before. The question is, can I get into your dress trousers?"

"I beg your pardon?"

"Will I fit your evening clothes? You're lending them to me, you see. For next weekend. I can't possibly go and stay at a very superior country house in a navy blue serge suit that's slightly shiny at all the obvious places. They're bound to dress for dinner and observe all these quaint medieval customs. He's even threatened fishing."

"Sorry, old man. It's impossible."

"But, Freddie…"

"Impossible. Quite imposs."

"Remember we were at school together."

"Which merely shows a lack of discretion on the part of my parents, and has nothing whatever to do with the present question."

"And I promise to take terribly good care of them, and not to spill the Mulligatawny down your white waistcoat."

"I tell you, Jim, I can't lend you the damned things. I'm using them myself."

"You are?"

"I, too, have received the call to the wide open spaces next weekend. Down to a house-party in Surrey."

"Surrey?"

"Surrey. Don't dither your lower lip at me like that, Jim. You've heard of Surrey before, surely? Percy Fender used to captain it at cricket."

"Freddie, are you invited to a place called Thrackley by a bloke called Carson?"

"How the blazes did you know?"

"Intuition, my boy. Sheer intuition. That's the place where I was going to parade in your tails."

"You've been asked down to Thrackley? Jim, this is splendid. Here have I been looking forward to the most ghastly weekend, with long walks and tapioca pudding and redoubling four spades and going three light, and possibly slipping away on the milk train in the grey dawn of Sunday morning. But if you're coming down there's a chance that it may not be quite so mouldy."

"Thanks very much. But what about the dress suit? We'd be apt to look odd if you wore trousers and I contented myself with the jacket."

"True. Jim, this is a time when personal sacrifices must be made. You shall have Number Two suit. It's all right—a bit moth-ballish, perhaps, but quite good enough for the wilds of Surrey."

"Thanks very much."

Jim called to the passing waiter and muttered something concerning the same again, please.

"The thing I'm trying to get at," he said, "is who the devil is Edwin Carson? Never heard of the fellow in my life."

The Honourable Freddie thought for several seconds before answering.

"Edwin Carson," he said at last, "is a rum bird. A bird, Jim, of extreme rumness. The pater used to know him well, but I've only met him once or twice. He's been abroad for years, I believe. India, someone told me. Probably spending weekends with the ruling princes and picking neat little holes in their crowns."

"What d'you mean?"

"Edwin Carson is the greatest living authority on precious stones in the world. The only reason why he isn't acclaimed as such in public and in the Press is that his methods of collecting his jewels—he's got an amazing collection, I believe—is not supposed to be all that it might be. Comrade Carson is a person with a past. He was out in South Africa years ago—"

"I wonder if that was where he met my father? Dad died out there, you know, when I was just a kid. He said in his letter that he was an old friend of Father."

"Maybe. In any case, he collected a pretty fat fortune for himself out there, and since those days he's lived half in England and half abroad."

"And what's the idea in asking us down? Ordinary hospitality?"

"When you meet friend Carson, you'll realize that he's not at all the sort of fellow who might be expected to ooze with good old English hospitality. No… the object in asking me down is the Usher diamonds."

Jim stopped his second gin-and-ginger half-way on its journey to his mouth, stared at Freddie, and said "Uck?"

"The Usher diamonds. Carson wants me to bring the damned things down. Wants to compare them with some in his own collection."

"You're not going to?"

"If I can get them out of pawn and give them a wash and brush up in time. Why not?"

"Of all the blithering, nit-witted—"

"Don't you worry. I can take care of them all right. Besides, old Carson's a reformed character now. A bit potty, one hears, but otherwise quite harmless."

"And why d'you think he wants me to join the party?"

"I've been trying to think that out. You haven't a collar-stud or anything like that that's a priceless heirloom?"

"I wish to heaven I had."

"Then he's probably trying to get his daughter married. Obviously the man hasn't heard of your murky past."

"There's a daughter, then?"

"There certainly is. And if my informants are correct, the said daughter is just about the gem of the entire collection."

The two men rose and crossed the lounge to the cloak-room to collect their gloves and hats.

"By the way," said the Honourable Freddie, "I suppose you still happen to have a revolver lying about the house somewhere?"

"A revolver?"

"Yes. I'm packing one beside my razor blades and toothbrush next weekend. Just for fun, of course."

"You're... what?"

"I'm taking a revolver to Thrackley. You never know with blokes like Carson. A bit potty, but otherwise quite harmless. And I hate these harmless, potty people. They're always up to something."

"Why not take those new pyjamas you were talking about? A much more deadly weapon."

"These broad attempts at humour do not come naturally from you, James. And that looks to me remarkably like a taxi. *Taxi!*"

They had stopped on the steps of the club, before being lost in the traffic of the Strand.

"I'll run you down on Friday, Jim," said the Honourable Freddie. "Fishing, you said, didn't you?"

"Excellent fishing," said Jim. "And fair shooting."

"Only fair? What a pity!"

And Mr. Usher disappeared head first into his taxi.

III

THE HOUSE CALLED THRACKLEY STANDS ABOUT THREE MILES south of the village of Adderly. It lies, comfortably but damply, in a dip of the surrounding hills. Tall pine-trees close it in on all sides, and the motorist travelling along the road from Adderly village sees very little of the house itself. A glimpse of two high turrets above the tips of the pines, a pair of heavy iron gates hung on massive stone pillars... and that is just about all. The house itself forms the main source of gossip in the thirty-odd private and the three public houses of Adderly. When the other affairs of the outside world have been settled, when the government has been given what it damned well deserves, when the prospects of the local football team for a week come Saturday have been thoroughly discussed, and the state of the country and the weather and the crops and the beer have all been debated, then the villagers of Adderly hark back to their favourite topic. The goings-on at Thrackley.

For years Thrackley had stood silent and empty. The former tenant had found his pocket insufficiently large to keep the big house going, and when it was put into the market there was no buyer to be found. People nowadays were buying maisonettes or semi-detached villas with neat little imitation oak trolleys instead of heavy mahogany sideboards and almost transparent wallboards instead of good stone walls. So for years no one lived in Thrackley, and the once immaculate drive became first coated with a thin covering of green, and then turned itself into quite a respectable hay-field, and finally allowed two healthy alder-bushes and a young laburnum to sprout in the middle of a track intended only for Rolls-Royces and Bentleys. And the ivy, which had always been a fairly strong feature of Thrackley's exterior decoration, spread itself madly in all directions, and even forced an entrance into the house through a lavatory window and festooned itself gaily round the hot-water tap of a bath.

And then suddenly, without warning, things began to happen at Thrackley. Things like plumbers and masons and joiners; van-loads of furniture, and painters and gardeners and under-gardeners. They whirled through Adderly village and on to Thrackley without even stopping at the Hen and Chickens for a quick one; and the inhabitants of Adderly were very annoyed at all this taking place without any of them knowing exactly what was going on. They sat at their windows, or in the bar-parlour of the Hen and Chickens, and mournfully watched each item of the procession, and said to each other: "Another one of them there furniture lorries. The fifth since a week past Thursday. Beats me, it does."

Then there was a short interval when nothing happened at Thrackley. And then the place became inhabited.

There was no doubt about it. The big iron gates (which had been scraped and polished and their gilt tops regilded) were pushed open, and shiny saloon cars began to purr up the drive (which had also been scraped and polished, and the odd alders and laburnums removed, and had been covered with a thick layer of pebbles which gave out satisfying crunches when a pair of feet walked on them). And smoke made its appearance out of each of the many chimney-pots and curled slowly out over the tops of the pine-trees. And at night lights twinkled in nearly all of Thrackley's windows. All this was noted by the inhabitants of Adderly: the shiny saloon cars by all of them, the smoke by nearly all, the lights by one adventurous soul whose curiosity carried him to the gates of the house after dark one evening.

But Adderly (again very much to its annoyance) never saw the new tenant of Thrackley. Never so much as a glimpse of the fellow's back view. The navy saloon car purred out through the iron gates every now and then, but whoever was sitting on the cushions of the rear seat sat well back and occasionally even drew the pale cream curtains to foil Adderly's interest in the matter. And the staff at Thrackley (for presumably, as Adderly argued to itself, there must be a staff: butlers and things like that) seemed to share their master's fondness for the beauties of home life. Did they mingle with the villagers? They did not. Did they patronize the Hen and Chickens, the Brown Bear, or the King George the Fifth Inn? Not on your life. Did they make a single purchase at the village general stores, that marvel of variety where corsets and picture-postcards of the Royal Family rubbed shoulders on the counter? They did no such thing. Over its early-evening pint of ale, Adderly decided that the new occupant of Thrackley was a lunatic. Or an invalid. Or a nervous wreck. Or (a little later in the evening, in a flight of imagination just before closing-time) the head of a powerful gang of counterfeiters. In any case, it was all very perplexing.

To the few who had yet seen it, the interior of the house was surprising. You drove up the long drive, flanked on each side by the dark green of the pine-trees, and as you rounded the last curve a sense of gloom settled firmly upon you. This, you decided, would be a house of damp walls, cobwebs in corners, obsolete sanitations, rats (or at least mice), and prunes and rice for dessert. Even when you stepped from your car and looked the heavy door square in its ugly face, the sense of gloom showed no sign of disappearing. The house was large, built of a dark grey stone, and mostly hidden beneath a wealth of ivy which seemed badly in need of a few hours with a vacuum cleaner. The pines effectively did their job of keeping away any sunlight which may have expressed a desire to shine upon the house called Thrackley; only one window, and that a microscopic affair at the top of the house, seemed to have a sporting chance of getting any of the sun's rays. (And that window, as a matter of fact, belonged to a small and very dirty box-room which had not been opened for years.) Otherwise the trees completely blotted out the light from the house, leaving it grey, cheerless, drab. Inside was a very different matter...

Once you entered the lounge hall of Thrackley you were forced to forget about the unpleasantness which you had left behind. Beautiful furniture everywhere. Thick pile carpets into which your shoes sank luxuriously. The latest in fireplace designs, in curtains and hangings, in wallpaper and friezes. Very few pictures on the walls, but those in excellent taste—a group of etchings in one room, a couple of modern watercolours in another, a trio of unframed woodcuts in a third. The owner of Thrackley and the army of workmen who had so puzzled and annoyed the village of Adderly had certainly done their job well.

The beauty of the house, unfortunately, was lost on Jacobson. Perhaps because his own lack of beauty made him unappreciative of the things beautiful. There was no doubt at all about it, Jacobson was not a pleasant-looking individual. He was tall, very thin, with a crop of closely cut greying hair. It had been pointed out to Jacobson on several occasions that his face might very well have been his fortune if only he had removed it from its present job to Hollywood or Elstree and spent the rest of his days portraying those characters which are known in the film world as "thugs". And at each of these suggestions Jacobson had contorted his face into what, in another set of features, might have been recognized as a smile, and had socked the suggester firmly and squarely on the jaw. For Jacobson preferred his present occupation. Wisely so, perhaps. Officially he was Edwin Carson's butler. Unofficially he was Edwin Carson's confidant, adviser, right-hand man. The relationship between the two was a thing which often puzzled even Jacobson himself. Often he wondered whether he really held the upper hand with Carson... or whether (unpleasant thought) it was the other way about.

He walked silently across the heavy carpet in the lounge hall, and laid Carson's morning mail at his place at the breakfast-table. He looked over the table to see that all had been set in order, took a slice of toast from the electric rack and spread it liberally with butter. Then he crossed to the chair beside the fireplace, attacked the toast wetly and rather noisily, and settled down to read the racing page of the morning paper. It was not altogether pleasant reading, and Jacobson's face became, if anything, a shade less easy to look at. Fizzy Lizzy, which had been printed in large lettering as the Best Thing of the Day, and alongside whom the Man on the Spot had affixed three large-sized stars (signifying that Fizzy Lizzy was a pinch, a cert, a snip and a walk-over), had refused to over-exert herself in the two-thirty and had been beaten by half a length by Maiden's Passion. And Two's Company (concerning whom the *Daily Clarion* Racing Correspondent had said: "If Undertaker is still unfit, and the Buckenthirst stable do not put forward a candidate for the race, I should strongly recommend this promising filly as an each-way investment")—Two's Company, blast its soul, had been last by a quarter of a furlong, having on its way thrown its jockey, crossed its forelegs twice, and stopped to inspect a bookmaker at the rails. (The same unhappy brute, be it noted, which Jim Henderson "gave" to Mrs. Bertram, and on whom Mrs. Bertram placed her modest bob each way.) Jacobson read the sad tidings uninterrupted for five minutes, and then...

"Jacobson!"

The butler leapt from his chair and stared at the speaker. He dropped the newspaper which he had been reading, and his hand, when he raised it to wipe a few buttery remains of toast from around his mouth, was shaking slightly. Even though he had known him for years, a sudden confronting of Edwin Carson always gave Jacobson what he described as a "turn". Carson stood half-way down the wide flight of stairs which led from the first floor into the lounge; the light from the landing window behind him fell on his bald pate and made it shine like a highly polished melon. He was small, almost hunchbacked, and completely bald save for a few rather dirty vestiges of grey hair which hovered around his ears. But the most arresting feature of Edwin Carson's face was his eyes. No one ever actually saw Edwin Carson's eyes. They were hidden by steel-rimmed spectacles, the lenses of which were so thick and so powerful that they made the eyes behind them almost invisible. Somehow one felt, rather than saw, the eyes of Edwin Carson. Jacobson always felt at a cruel disadvantage when talking to him: like a mouse being watched by a cat in the dark, unable to see the thing that was staring at it, conscious all the time that every movement was being watched.

"What the devil are you doing here?"

"Waiting for you."

The little man came slowly down into the room. He was still staring at the butler.

"The kitchen is the proper place for that. The kitchen, do you understand? That's your place. And when I want you, I ring, you see? And you come then... when I ring."

"Listen to me, you—"

"This room is where I belong... and the kitchen where you belong."

"Oh, for Gawd's sake—"

"Jacobson!..."

He spoke quietly, with a soft, cultured accent. But the butler, after looking at him for a second, shrugged his shoulders and turned to leave the room. Edwin Carson raised his hand as he reached the door at the other end of the room.

"Just a minute, Jacobson. Where are my letters?"

"Are you blind? Beside your plate."

"M'm... well, wait until I open them and you shall hear the news. Yes, come and hear the news. Pour yourself out a cup of coffee, Jacobson, and sit down... you're not angry with me, are you, Jacobson?"

The butler grunted.

"That's right," said Carson. "That's right. I don't know what I'd do without you, you know. Really, I don't know..."

He bent down over the back of his chair and picked up the four letters with his thin, bony fingers. He held up the envelopes in front of Jacobson's face, smiled as he waved them in front of the butler. He inspected each before opening them, smelt one with apparent satisfaction, then slit the four open with a butter knife picked up from the table.

"The Honourable Frederick Usher... yes, very pleased... the Bramptons... yes... Catherine Lady Stone... yes, delighted..."

He spoke half to himself, and then turned to the butler.

"So far, extremely satisfactory, Jacobson, Always remember, if ever you should be inviting people down to spend a weekend at a country house, always remember to invite only the people whom you would think to be too wealthy and too busy and too important to accept. They're the very ones who will jump at the chance of a free weekend. Curious, but true, Jacobson. It's a useful tip, though you'll probably never have the opportunity to make use of it."

"Thank you all the same, Carson," said the butler.

The little man turned to the last of the four letters. He read:

34, Ardgowan Mansions,
London, N.W.I.

Dear Mr. Carson,

Many thanks for your very kind invitation for next weekend which I shall be delighted to accept. I am afraid I must plead either to never having known you, or else to the worse crime of having forgotten you. However, I am looking forward very much to meeting an old friend of my father.

I understand that Mr. Usher is to be a guest at Thrackley next weekend, and as he has offered me a lift down in his car, there is no need for you to meet me at Adderly as you kindly promised. We expect to arrive somewhere about five o'clock on Friday evening.

Thanking you again for your kindness.

Yours sincerely,
James Henderson.

The little man smiled again. Jacobson felt that behind the heavy glasses his eyes were twinkling.

"And Captain James Henderson, M.C.... splendid. Absolutely splendid. A most enjoyable weekend, I should imagine. And... profitable, perhaps, eh, Jacobson?"

And for the second time Jacobson did the smiling act with his features.

"And our arrangements?" said the little man. "Everything in order?"

"Everything all right, Carson."

"There must be no mistakes this time, Jacobson. I can't have mistakes… can't tolerate mistakes. Unpardonable things. You understand?"

"There won't be any mistakes this time, Carson."

"Right. Now you can get out."

The butler turned to go, then hesitated for a moment before laying his hand on the handle of the door.

"Well? What the devil are you waiting for? Get out, I said… get out!"

"Just a minute, Carson."

"What is it?"

"I know why all these other blokes are coming here next week-end. But this Henderson bird. What's he being brought in for?"

The little man looked up from his chair at the breakfast-table.

"I wish," he said, "that you would stop referring to my guests as 'birds' and 'blokes', Jacobson. Don't you realize that most of them are members of the richest and most exclusive set in England?"

"Exclusive my aunt Emma! What's the idea in getting Henderson here? He's no gold-mine, from all accounts."

"No, Jacobson," said Edwin Carson. "Captain Henderson is, as you say, no gold-mine. Not worth a penny, I should imagine."

"Then why the hell—?"

Edwin Carson smiled. Not an attractive smile.

"Captain Henderson is visiting us, Jacobson, for a very differ-ent reason to our other guests." He patted his serviette neatly into his lap and poured out a cup of steaming coffee. "A very different reason," he repeated.

And Jacobson, as all good butlers should do when their masters make remarks which they do not quite understand, shrugged his shoulders and closed the door softly behind him.

"If only," said Edwin Carson to himself, "I could get him to call me 'sir'. Hopeless, I suppose…"

IV

A ROLLS-ROYCE WAS SO MUCH OF A RARITY IN THE NEIGH-bourhood of Ardgowan Mansions, N., that the appearance of Freddie Usher's long-nosed yellow tourer caused quite a flutter of excitement. The traffic in Ardgowan Mansions consisted mostly of obsolete types which rattled noisily from house to house delivering specimens of butchery and bakery. With the exception of a couple of very secondhand baby Austins, the car as a pleasure vehicle was unknown to the district. Hence the quite excusable sensation when Freddie's tourer purred round the corner from Ardgowan Crescent, along Ardgowan Place, and into the straight of Ardgowan Mansions. Rupert, a message-boy in the employ of Messrs. Parkinson Bros., Fruiterers, Florists and Greengrocers, was the first to notice the car. He could scarcely have been in a finer position for his noticing, for Rupert was freewheeling along the wrong side of Ardgowan Mansions road with a fourpenny novelette in one hand and a quarter-stone of potatoes, half a dozen leeks and a few similar items dangling from his handlebars. The driver of the Rolls gave a long, unmusical toot and Rupert left his novelette in mid-sentence. He did not return to it. He said "Gosh!" referring not to the fact that he had nearly read his last fourpenny but rather to the lines of the car in front of him. And then Rupert got busy. This, he felt, was a thing that ought not to be kept to oneself. And Rupert became possessed with this very laudable sentiment of sharing a good thing with his fellow-creatures and set off to spread the glad tidings throughout the neighbourhood. When Mrs. Bertram looked down from her third-storey window on to the scene at her front door she threw her arms heavenwards (a very difficult feat when half of your anatomy is sticking over a window-sill and the other half is still in your sitting-room), decided that at last there had been a Young Girl Murdered by Unknown Assassin Sensation in Ardgowan Mansions, and rushed to tell Jim. And when Jim put his head out of his own window, he saw an elegant Rolls-Royce car surrounded by seventeen message-boys, eleven message-boys' friends, eight of the unemployed of the district, five housewives and two policemen. And, in the middle of it all, the Honourable Frederick Usher.

"Hoi!" said Jim.

"Hoi!" said Freddie, brushing off a couple of message-boys from his rear off mudguard. "Nearly ready?"

"Be with you in a couple of shakes!" said Jim, and banged his head on the sash of the window as he vanished into the room.

He slammed the window behind him and cast a thoughtful eye over his suitcase. Pyjamas. Dressing-gown. Handkerchiefs and collars. Bedroom slippers. Brushes and comb and razor and shaving-soap. And tooth-brush and tooth-paste. And an evening suit in Freddie's car. Everything appeared to be in order. He sat on the suitcase and locked it with difficulty. Mrs. Bertram hovered fussily around the room, and asked him if he was sure he'd remembered everything, and wouldn't he need this, or this, or at any rate those? For it must be admitted that in Mrs. Bertram's estimation Jim had behaved like a helicopter in the last few days. As she had pointed out to the lady over the fence during the previous Tuesday's hanging of the washing, Mrs. Bertram had a lodger who received invitations for weekends at country houses. And as she would also point out to the same lady at the first opportunity, she had also a lodger who had Rolls-Royces coming for him at the front door. (But when

Mrs. Bertram did mention this fact to the lady over the fence, that worthy merely said: "Not Rolls-Royces, my dear. Just one Rolls-Royce. And a 1930 model at that, so my Alfred tells me!" which took a considerable amount of wind out of Mrs. Bertram's sails.)

"Good-bye, Mrs. Bertram," said Jim. "See you Monday some time, I expect."

"Good-bye, dearie," said Mrs. Bertram. "Take care of yourself, now." (For if half of what you read in the papers were true, you never could tell with these house-parties.)

Jim took the stairs three at a time and arrived at the front door slightly out of breath. He pushed his way through the multitude and placed his suitcase in the back seat and himself in the front beside Freddie. The car gave a snort, a powerful roar, a second snort, and then slid down Ardgowan Mansions and round the pillar-box into Ardgowan Place and past the rubbish-bin into Ardgowan Crescent. Mrs. Bertram waved to the number-plate of the car as it swung round the corner of the road, and then went back to the society column of her morning newspaper and learned all about what the charming Lady Anne Beaulieu (who was, of course, Miss Anne Dudley-Dempster) was wearing at the Trocadero on the previous evening. The eight unemployed went back to their favourite corner and resumed their favourite sport of spitting across the full width of their favourite pavement. The five housewives suddenly remembered that they had left their five lunches on the boil and rushed off ovenwards. And Rupert the message-boy mounted his bicycle, rearranged his potatoes and his leeks over the handlebars, found his place in the novelette, and set off to deliver the goods to Number Seventy-two. Ardgowan Mansions, its little slice of excitement over, settled down once again to its normal and remarkably uneventful life.

And the Rolls purred contentedly out of Ardgowan Crescent, and along Pillington Road East, and along Pillington Road West, and through all the rest of the suburban streets until it reached the city. And at last, outside the placarded walls of the Alhambra, a traffic block stopped its purring progress.

"Seen this show?" said Freddie.

"No. Derek Simpson's in it, isn't he? I heard him telling some people at the club how good he was."

The Honourable Freddie made a noise which seemed to indicate that he thought nothing or possibly less of Mr. Simpson.

"Only one person in that show," he said. "Only one. This Argentine dancer, Raoul. The most marvellous, gifted, amazing, beautiful woman I've ever seen. What features! What a figure!"

"I can see that from here without having to pay fifteen bob for a stall."

"Posters?" said Freddie, and snorted at the idea. "Posters! My good man, those things in front of you are rank insults to the woman. She'd win an action for libel any day against them. Or are posters slander? And, mind you, no scenery to help her. No costumes. Well, hardly any costumes. Of all the…"

"Get on with it—the signal's changed."

"Eh? Oh, all right!"

Once out of London, Freddie put his foot on the accelerator and kept it there. Jim took off his hat and let the wind rush through his hair. Conversation resolved itself into a bawled "Wass-itsay on that signpost?" and a yelled "Dunno, couldn't see!" Villages appeared in the distance, tore towards them, flashed past in split-second impressions of hens and dogs and oldest inhabitants jumping indignantly from in front of the car's bonnet. The sport of passing the car in front became monotonous through repetition. The long yellow Rolls gave a toot of annoyance, the car in front waved a slightly peevish hand, the Rolls sailed past in a swirl of dust and gave a second toot of victory. In less than half an hour the village of Adderly presented itself through the frame of the windscreen.

The village of Adderly looked, as always, particularly charming. True, the owners of the cottages had been somewhat conservative in the planting of their gardens, and Dorothy Perkins seemed to have a complete monopoly where climbing over wire arches was concerned. But a monopoly of Dorothy Perkins is just about as good a monopoly as you will find anywhere, and the general effect of Adderly's gardens was good to the eye. Adderly village is one of those delightfully lop-sided affairs where one house has been added to its neighbour at random and at the angle which suited the builder's frame of mind at the time. The road through Adderly twists and turns and reverses and takes sudden impulses; all of which is no doubt picturesque but at the same time is very difficult for the motorist who is passing through the village in order to be at a certain place in time for tea. The Rolls negotiated the twists and the impulses fairly well, coming at last to a fork in the road. Freddie said: "This way?"

"No," said Jim. "That way."

"Up there, I'm sure."

"Down here, I should think."

And Freddie, having said "Very well, then," turned the nose of the car in the direction which he himself thought was fit and proper, accelerated, and hit a girl on a bicycle.

The girl had picked herself up before Freddie brought the car to a standstill. She was small and fair-complexioned, and her age, one imagined, was considerably less than that of the bicycle which she had been riding. Jim had a feeling that in other circumstances she might have been classed as good-looking. Very good-looking, in fact. But just now her hat was on at a rakish angle and covered half of her face, and there was a large smudge of dirt on the rest of the face, and altogether it could not be truthfully said that she was looking her best. Girls rarely, of course, look their best immediately after they have been knocked down by large Rolls-Royce cars. The bicycle had landed in the ditch by the side of the road, and a rather pathetic rear wheel stuck heavenward out of the grass. Jim jumped out of the car, and set it on its feet again.

"Thank you," said the girl. "I'm really awfully sorry—it was my fault absolutely."

"I don't think so."

"Oh, yes it was. Only somehow I never expected a car to be coming down this road."

"Isn't this the main road?" said Jim.

"This road leads to a pigsty, a large heap of manure, and a duckpond with three ducks." And the girl swung a shapely leg on to her bicycle and vanished in a slightly wobbling manner round the corner.

"Well!" said Jim.

"I told you it was the other way," said Freddie. "Just as well we hit the girl. We might have gone on to the duckpond."

Jim got into his seat again, and the Rolls went through a series of very complicated manœuvres and finally backed itself clear of all danger of duckponds.

"Rather nice-looking girl, that," said Jim. "Eh?"

"I said that that was rather a nice-looking girl."

"Nobbad. Hope we're in time for tea after all this."

And the car left Adderly village, and climbed a fairly steep hill, and then swooped down into the little valley in which the house called Thrackley lay. From the top of the hill they could see just as much as was ever seen of Thrackley by the outside world… the two turrets standing out grey in the mass of dark green pines. "There it is," said Freddie.

"Thrackley?"

"Thrackley in person. Situated in the midst of densely wooded countryside, and possessing the finest dry-rot in the kingdom."

The iron gates were open when they reached them, and they drove slowly through and up the drive. And the usual thing happened: the thing which happens always when a car drives up to Thrackley for the first time. The supply of sunlight seemed suddenly to have been cut off as though they had been shockingly behind with their payments for the same; the temperature cooled under the shade of the pines; the colour scheme, which up to now had been a pleasant affair of golds and light browns and bright greens and blues became at once a sordid affair of dark greens and darker greys. As the car crunched along the gravel of the drive, Jim had a very disturbing mental picture of night at Thrackley, with the pine-trees tenanted by a crowd of nasty, hooting owls and a quantity of whining wind, of himself bathing in tepid water and finding no hot-water bottle between his sheets and no reading-lamp beside his bed, and an annotated copy of the New Testament lying at his bedside, and the prospects of porridge and prunes for breakfast at seventy-thirty, and… "Hell!" he said.

"What's the matter?" said Freddie.

"I've a sickening sensation that this is going to be one of the world's worst weekends."

"Me, too. Listen, Jim."

"Yes?"

"If to-night turns out to be absolutely mouldy, have you any objection to receiving a sudden call from a sick aunt in town?"

"If you only knew the number of aunts I left on their death-beds."

"And spending the weekend with me at my flat, and having a nice little dinner at the club, and paying a return visit to Raoul at the Alhambra, and—"

"There are times," said Jim, "when I'm convinced that you were given some sort of a brain after all."

The car turned round the last bend in the drive and came in view of the front of the house. And wobbled. And nearly stopped. And drew two of its four wheels across a neatly planted flower-bed, putting an effective amen to a dozen and a half Coltness dahlias. Simply because the Honourable Freddie Usher had lost control of the steering-wheel. His mouth had dropped open, and he gaped rudely at the figure standing at Thrackley's ivy-draped front door.

An immaculate figure, superbly dressed. Raoul the dancer, in fact.

V

B Y THE TIME FREDDIE USHER HAD REGAINED CONTROL OF
himself and of the steering-wheel, had persuaded the tyres
of his car to finish their caressing of the dahlias, had applied the
brakes and stepped out on to the gravel in front of Thrackley's
front door—by the time all that had happened, the elegant figure
of Raoul the dancer had moved up the few steps which led to the
door and had disappeared into the house. The performance was
not unlike those party occasions when something very desirable
is dangled before one's eyes, removed almost immediately, and an
oily voice is heard to remark: "Now, if you're very good you shall
have it." Except, of course, that in this case one had to imagine the
oily voice and its pleasant promise. Freddie Usher shoved his long
legs out of his even longer car, stretched himself, and said quietly:
"Did you see what I saw?"

"Yes," said Jim.

"And did you know who it was that we both saw?"

"Yes."

"Very well, then. It strikes me that that milk train may carry
only milk after all. Come on."

The bell at the side of Thrackley's front door was one of a rapidly disappearing breed: the species that you disentangle from the
surrounding ivy, pull towards you in a series of stiff and creaking
jerks, release suddenly and wait patiently until a deep rumble is
heard far away in the bowels of the house. Thrackley's bell did not
tinkle; no one could say that it even rang. It gave (if you pulled the
thing far enough out of its socket) a dull, gong-like boom—very

much the same unpleasant sort of sound as that made by Dr. Fu Manchu and other Oriental sinners when about to distribute cups of poisoned tea, make a couple of lengthy vows to their ancestors, or commit *hari-kari*. The boom which followed Freddie's heave went a fair distance in cancelling the cheering effect which Raoul had produced. And when the front door of Thrackley opened and Jacobson inserted his set of features between it and the wall, Raoul might just as well never have happened.

"Good afternoon," said Freddie.

He had expected something at least to happen to the features following this remark. Anything, he felt, would necessarily be a change for the better. But Jacobson remained still and silent and kept the door open just enough to fit his face.

"Er... good afternoon," said Jim. "Is Mr. Carson at home? My name is Henderson. This is Mr. Usher. Mr. Carson is expecting us."

Having delivered himself of this speech, there seemed very little to add. Fortunately the speech seemed to have had some effect on Jacobson, for he moved his mouth a little to the west (Jim was later to recognize this movement as a smile of welcome and good cheer), bowed slightly, and opened the door a full three inches farther to allow them to pass in.

"If you will wait here, sir," said Jacobson, "I will tell Mr. Carson that you have arrived." But there was no need for this: mine host himself appeared at a door at the far end of the lounge hall and came at a steady canter to meet them. It surprised Jim to come across such a surfeit of ugliness at once; he remembered a certain evening in Paris when on leave during the war when, at a quarter to twelve, he had seen definitely the Most Beautiful Girl in the World (a blonde) and a little later, at half-past one or so, he had come face to face with positively the Most Beautiful Girl in the

World (but this time a brunette). It had always seemed to him bad staff management that the two could not have been spread over at least a couple of evenings. Jacobson and Edwin Carson were very much the same: too much of a bad thing to take in at one gulp.

Mr. Carson stretched forth the hand of welcome to Freddie first. "I'm so glad you were able to come, Mr. Usher," he said. "A popular young fellow like you, you know—you're paying a great compliment to me by burying yourself in the backwoods for a whole weekend."

"Not at all," said Freddie. "In any case, it'll be a new one on my creditors."

"Quite," said Mr. Carson. He turned to Jim. "And this is Captain Henderson. Well well, well. I'm glad to see you, Henderson. Very glad indeed."

The handshake, Jim felt, was a shade over-hearty for so small a man. And (or was it only his imagination?) he felt that his host was scrutinizing him very carefully indeed in the few moments of shaking hands. Mr. James Lockhart, M.A., had had, many years before, an irritating habit of peering in silence at any small boy who had failed to prepare preparation or who got his cotangents mixed up with his tangents—a long, silent scrutiny, taking in every despicable detail from head to foot, and during which the object of the gaze grew steadily smaller and smaller, pinker and pinker, and hotter and hotter. And mine host Carson, damn him, had exactly the same disturbing effect. He stared and continued to stare, much as though Jim were the bearded lady of a circus or some newly discovered skeleton of a prehistoric mammal. Well, thought Jim, might as well have my hand back if he's quite finished with it... "Very glad to be able to come, Mr. Carson," he said politely.

"You have luggage in the car? Yes—Jacobson, attend to Mr. Henderson's and Mr. Usher's luggage. Come along, gentlemen, I'll show you your rooms. This way. I'm afraid you'll find this place very dull after London—very dull indeed. You have a gay time of it in London, eh, Henderson?"

"Occasionally I go out and watch the electric signs in Piccadilly."

"Now, now—I know you young fellows. I hope you won't be bored at Thrackley. We have a tennis-court—not a very good one, I'm told, too many worm-holes in it, I believe—and the stream near here is supposed to be over-stocked with trout, though I've never seen a single one myself. D'you fish, Henderson? Your father was a great man with a rod. Oh, that's your room, Mr. Usher—go in and make yourself at home. Now, my dear Henderson…"

It was a considerably long time since anyone had paid so much attention to Jim. He turned back over his shoulder and smiled at the forlorn way in which Freddie was entering his room after being dismissed (no other word for it) by mine host. This was all contrary to expectations. Jim had expected to be a definite back-number of the Thrackley house-party—invited to it mainly out of charity and the memory of a chance acquaintanceship between his father and this ugly little Mr. Carson. But… "And this is your room, Henderson, my boy—best in the house, in my opinion, but that's for you to say yourself. Bathroom next door. And just give the bell a ring whenever you want anything. I do hope you'll be comfortable." Well, if that was the way of it, so be it. And very nice, too.

"This is great, Mr. Carson. It's really damned good of you to ask me down here this weekend."

"Not a bit of it. Best friend I ever had, your father was. No reason why his son shouldn't be the same, eh?"

Perhaps not, thought Jim; but very difficult getting so friendly with a face like that.

"Right. I'll leave you. Tea's ready—come down when you are."

"Thanks."

"Oh—and, Captain Henderson…"

"Yes?"

"Perhaps you might do me a favour and have tea with me in my study. Just the two of us. I'd like so much to have a chat with you about your father."

"Why, certainly, Mr. Carson—but Freddie… Mr. Usher…"

"That's all right. Two of my other guests are to be in for tea… the rest are out walking. I'll introduce Usher to them. They're both very charming ladies—he'll get along splendidly with them. My study, then, when you're ready. First door on the right at the foot of the stairs. Jacobson will show you."

And Mr. Carson bared what remained of his unclean and uneven teeth in another smile of welcome, and closed the door softly behind him.

Jim took a look round. He quite believed Mr. Carson when he said that the room was the best in the house. Not that Jim supposed there would be much opportunity for comparing other bedrooms with his own; but, at any rate, any improvements on the room which he had been given would have to be pretty carefully thought out. The room was large (from the glance he had had as he passed along the corridor, it was about three times as big as Freddie's). It was beautifully furnished. The bed, the dressing-table and wardrobe, the easy chairs and the little settee were all of a finely grained and unstained walnut. There were, as the hotel advertisements tersely put it, all mod. cons.—electric fire, h. and c. pouring when necessary into a rose-coloured wash-basin, telephone by the bedside, reading lamp above the bed. The usual collection of bedside books (the New Testament, Bunyan's *Pilgrim's Progress*, *Little Lord Fauntleroy*, and an annotated autobiography of Archimedes) were conspicuous by their absence; instead there were a couple of what looked to be promising thrillers, a book of modern poems, two Oscar Wilde plays and some selections from the diaries of Mr. Pepys. The walls were mercifully bare of oleographs of Queen Victoria or prints of Diana in the Forest. There was no regrettable affair on the mantelpiece informing one when breakfast, lunch, dinner and the last post happened. In short, the room was perfect—except for one thing only. The view. The trouble with which being that there was none. A dense barricade of thick pine branches two feet away from your windows—you cannot by any stretch of imagination call that a view. Jim crossed to the window and lit a cigarette. "Even if it breezes," he said to himself, "those things will swish all night, and if it blows a gale there'll be a hell of a row." And, hearing outside his door what could be fairly described by the last phrase of these thoughts, he added aloud, "Come in!"

The hell of a row proved to be Jacobson juggling with luggage and door handles. When Jim's suitcase had been safely landed on the settee, and the butler satisfied that he could be of no further assistance at the moment, and that Mr. Henderson preferred always to unpack himself (a quaint Henderson custom, but necessary with superior country-house butlers when one has re-cuffed shorts and rather over-darned socks), Jacobson bowed his trim little bow and made for the door.

"Jacobson, just a minute," said Jim.

"Sir?"

"Are there many guests here this weekend?"

"Six, sir. Mr. and Miss Brampton, Lady Stone, a Miss Raoul—an actress person, I believe, sir—and Mr. Usher and yourself."

"I see. Been here long, Jacobson?"

"Since Mr. Carson bought the house, sir. But I have been in Mr. Carson's service for a good many years now, sir."

"Decent sort of bloke?"

"Mr. Carson, sir? The very best, sir. One of the kindest of men. I only hope you will find him so, sir."

And that, thought Jim as the door closed, was a dashed peculiar sort of remark for a butler to make to a newborn guest. He unlocked his suit-case, spreadeagled a few garments over the room, felt at the foot of his case for the hard lump which marked the resting-place of the old army revolver—incidentally unloaded and with no ammunition supply. He smiled again at Freddie Usher's idea of bringing guns to Thrackley and went off to see how that gentleman's unpacking was getting along.

"Small but adequate, I suppose," he said as he entered Freddie's room. "Mine is about four times as large and has a much better bed. But then I expect you're used to roughing it, old man."

Freddie removed the notorious pyjamas from his case and laid them reverently on his bed.

"I suppose you've got the bridal suite," he said. "Old man Carson seems to have taken to you all right. Quite the pet of the party, aren't you? I must be losing my sex appeal, I suppose."

"Honestly, Freddie, I can't make it out. He's running round me as though I were a long-lost relative."

"It's the daughter, I expect."

"I'll let you know about that when I see her, thank you. Anyway, I've got to have tea with the old geyser in his private sanctum. You're having it with Raoul, God help her. Good luck."

First door on the right at the bottom of the stairs, Carson had said. Edwin Carson's voice said "Come in" almost before he had knocked. The study was a small room, overfilled with furniture: a big desk, a table, a heavy bookcase, many chairs. Somehow the room seemed out of place when one compared it with the rest of Thrackley. Rather cheaper and not so genuinely old. When Jim walked into the room, Edwin Carson was sitting at the desk; tea had already been laid out on the table.

"Well, my boy," said Carson, "everything to your liking?"

"Thank you, yes."

"Fine. Now come and sit down and have some tea. You know, this is the realization of one of my ambitions—to get in touch with the son of my old friend, Edward Henderson."

"Did you know my father very well, Mr. Carson?"

"He was my best friend. We met in prison."

"I beg your pardon?"

"I said we met in prison. I think, don't you, that friendships formed under circumstances like that are often the most lasting? You take sugar? And cream?… Yes, he was in for two years… I was reaching the end of a rather longer term."

"Are you trying to tell me that my father was in gaol?"

"Why, yes. You never knew? Most of the men like your father and myself found themselves on the wrong side of prison bars in those days, you know. The arm of the law wasn't a very long arm in South Africa then. But occasionally it caught you up. I.D.B.—you know. Your father, Jim—I may call you Jim, mayn't I?—your father wasn't such a clever man as I, I'm afraid. Perhaps I should say he wasn't such a good criminal, eh? That term of imprisonment was the only one I ever served out there… your father wasn't so fortunate."

"You mean—he went back to gaol?"

"That's where he died. Johannesburg gaol. And so I lost the best friend I had in that country. A clever man, your father, Jim—good thinker, cool plotter, brave as they make them. I remember the second time they got him—"

"I'm afraid I'm not interested, Mr. Carson. We won't discuss my father any more, d'you mind?"

"I'm sorry. I imagined that you knew—"

"I don't really want to, thank you."

"If that's the way you feel, my boy… certainly. A piece of this cake? Home-made, I understand, but quite edible."

"Thank you."

"Er… the walks round here are particularly fine… I'm sure you'll enjoy them… and then the fishing in the little stream…"

And a quarter of an hour later, when a rather puzzled Jim left the study of Thrackley, Edwin Carson pulled open a drawer of the big desk and brought out an envelope that was dirty and very obviously suffering from senile decay. He took out the photographs and peered at them for a long time through his thick glasses. Four small prints and an enlargement. The prints were of a child whose sex and features had been effectively disguised in the regrettable clothes which the parents of 1900 thrust on their long-suffering children. The larger photograph was of a young, attractive-looking man in the uniform of a second-lieutenant. The subject of the small photographs was unrecognizable. Mercifully so, no doubt. But the enlargement was, without any doubt whatever, a photograph of the member of the Thrackley house-party who had just left the study.

Edwin Carson put them all carefully back in their old yellow envelope. Perhaps a little later in the weekend, he thought…

VI

A T EIGHT O'CLOCK PRECISELY JACOBSON, THE BUTLER, opened the swing doors which led from the lounge to the dining-room and said: "Dinner is served, sir."

It must be admitted that Jacobson said it just as it should be said. With exactly the correct intonation. With exactly the right bearing. With just that amount of insinuation which makes the hearers of such a remark sit up in their chairs and mutter: "Now, if I'm not mistaken, this is going to be a damned good dinner." Exactly, in fact, as the perfect butler breaks this perfect news in the talking pictures or on the stage. Catherine Lady Stone thought to herself that this Carson person had collected a remarkably efficient staff around him, and wondered where the devil he'd found them, for she had had three cooks through her kitchen within the last month. Marilyn Brampton thought to herself how nice it would be to have a butler like that, instead of messing with sausages in a modern flat and being called "artistic". Henry Brampton thought to himself that eight o'clock was much too late an hour for dinner when the last time one's stomach had been attended to was one-thirty. Raoul the dancer thought to herself how different this was to her last house-party (where each of the guests had taken a piece of wild duck on to the carpet and worked away quietly at it with their teeth)... for the English people seemed to be very varied in their behaviour. Freddie Usher thought to himself that Jacobson, if anything, beat Edwin Carson for ugliness by a short (and very unpleasant) head. And Jim Henderson thought that if Carson's daughter didn't put in an appearance within the next few minutes he would have quite a lot to say to Freddie Usher about false pretences.

And Catherine Lady Stone gathered around her the various odd ends of her evening gown, and took Edwin Carson's arm and led the procession to the dining-room. Marilyn Brampton and Henry Brampton removed their cigarette-holders from their mouths, and their cigarette-stumps from their cigarette-holders, and threw the stumps into the fire, and marched off to the first respectable meal they had eaten since Henry sold his last painting. And Raoul the dancer rose, slowly and magnificently as always, patted her hair carefully without moving it in the slightest, glanced at herself in the mirror for an instant, and followed the Bramptons to food. With Freddie and Jim on either side of her, feeling both a trifle embarrassed at being there. And Jacobson the butler sniffed at the amount of brown back which the lines of Raoul's gold *lamé* gown revealed, and closed the swing doors when the last inch of the *lamé* had trailed itself slowly into the dining-room.

The dining-room at Thrackley was shaded in warm tones of browns and golds. Two trios of gold-coloured candles stood on the table. The silver, the crystal of the glasses and decanters, the choice and cooking of the food—each showed that here at Thrackley existed that rare combination of money and good taste.

Caviar. Brought by Jacobson in a hollowed-out block of ice, the roe fresh and perfect and not the sad, clinging variety which one usually meets in restaurants. Jim spread butter on the wafer of toast on his plate, lathered the caviar on richly, cut the toast into six delightful mouthfuls. And studied the other members of the Thrackley house-party.

Catherine Lady Stone, for instance. Sitting at the other end of the table next to Edwin Carson, gushing at her host and refusing this exquisite caviar because it disagreed with her and made her rumble in her bed. Fat and fifty, he put Catherine down as. Or fat and sixty? Yes, more probably sixty, even at the sacrifice of the alliteration. A dangerous type of woman. The type that spends her days and other people's days in Getting Up Things; on fifty-three committees, he had heard, and perpetually organizing charity matinées and midnight cabarets and chain teas for vague and unknown institutions. The kind of woman who would—

(Soup. A clear soup, nameless and almost colourless. Amazing how something which looked like slightly dirty water should have such a taste...)

Marilyn Brampton, too. Sitting next to Freddie Usher and explaining to him, in bored and condescending tones, why Clair was so much finer a director than Lubitsch. Which, in its way, was amusing, since Freddie's favourite film was, and always had been *The Gold Diggers of Broadway*. Jim had heard of Marilyn. Not so often, perhaps, as Mrs. Bertram, his landlady, who read the gossip columns more thoroughly than he; but still he knew quite a lot about the lady. Twins, weren't they?... Marilyn and Henry... the famous Brampton twins. Son and daughter of Brampton, the art connoisseur. Artistic blokes, who had left their home and set out to make a living for themselves... Marilyn with a series of grimly sexy novels, Henry with a succession of violently modern paintings. Rather hard up, he imagined, though they must still have a number of the priceless things which old man Brampton left when he died three years ago. That rope of pearls, for instance, twining three times round Marilyn's neck as a collar, and then falling down her back until it touched the chair on which she sat... how like Marilyn Brampton to wear them that idiotic way. Just the sort of thing which showed that—

(Fish. A boiled turbot, pure white, which slid into neat flakes when you touched it with your fork. Served in a nest of custard flavoured with one kind of light wine, and covered with a sauce tasting of another... and how the two blended!...)

Then Henry Brampton. Sitting on Jim's right, and giving rude and very pointless retorts when he tried to make conversation. A nasty piece of work, this Brampton fellow. Spoiled. Too unaccountably popular. And the clothes he wore: that double-breasted waistcoat, for instance... folding so perfectly around his absurd waist. Corsets, in all probability, beneath the damned thing. And side-whiskers, an abominable disease at the best of times, became twice abominable when they curled sleekly down in front of Henry Brampton's ears. The things he painted, too... square women and hexagonal horses positioned grotesquely in puce fields. Yes, a nasty piece of work. The kind of fellow who might very well—

(Entrée. A small portion of veal, cooked à l'espagnol, carefully browned to amber, topped with a little island of lemon sprinkled with something which he couldn't name. Delicious...)

And Raoul the dancer. The star turn of the house-party. He looked across the table at her: a picture of brown and black and gold which toned perfectly with the room where she sat. He thought that in all probability Raoul would always tone exactly with her surroundings. Or was it that her own personality was strong enough to force those surroundings to fall in with her scheme of colouring? Hair of jet black, parted down the centre of her scalp, drawn tightly to each side to end in a single wave around her ears. Dark brown skin against which her teeth and eyes shone brilliantly in their respective red and black frames. And that dress... showing every line of her body, moving with her as though it were a part of her. He wondered how on earth a dress like that managed to cling so closely to such a woman… as though the wearer had been poured into a coating of boiling gilt and then allowed to cool. Or, more probably, there was a subtle Zipp fastener about it somewhere which Raoul would pull when she reached her bedroom and cause the coating of *lamé* to go "zoomph!" and leave her naked. A marvellous woman. But for all that a woman who—

(Quail. Half a dozen of them on a huge ashet. Served with another of Thrackley's remarkable sauces, with potatoes crisp and buttered and thin as wafers, with juicy young green peas which squelched when you pressed them with your fork. Unlike Mrs. Bertram's green peas, which came out of a tall round cardboard packet, and leapt briskly from the prongs of your fork to hit you in the face…)

And at the head of the table, Edwin Carson. Freddie had been right when he said "a rum bird". Though, so far, Carson had been merely the perfect host. A trifle too hospitable, a trifle too greasy, a trifle too attentive. But otherwise a charming old man with the misfortune of possessing a particularly repulsive face. A man, obviously, of good taste and discrimination. A man obsessed by his hobby—for he had talked of nothing but jewels since they had arrived at Thrackley: the jewels his guests were wearing, the latest additions to his own collection, the terrible imitation which people twined about their necks nowadays, and so on. Curious eyes, he had… the light from the candles twinkled on his glasses as he bent over his plate. Really you couldn't see the man's eyes at all… and Jim began to think that he had never actually seen the eyes of Edwin Carson. Yes, a rum bird. But, as Freddie Usher had pointed out, not the sort of man who would—

(*Crêpes Suzettes*. Cooked by Jacobson over a flame on the big oak sideboard, piping hot, wallowing in a juice of maple syrup. Magnificent…)

Finally, the empty chair. Separating Catherine Lady Stone (now busy telling Edwin Carson of her plans for the All-Star Matinée in aid of the Unemployed Cottonworkers' Relief Fund)—separating her from Marilyn Brampton (still talking to Freddie Usher about camera angles and the effects of synchronization in emotional scenes). Who was to have occupied that chair? Edwin Carson's daughter, he supposed. Well, then, why the devil hadn't she? And having failed to put in an appearance at dinner, to-night, would she turn up at breakfast to-morrow? Or lunch, or tea, or dinner to-morrow night? Carson had never even mentioned her. Had Freddie Usher been romancing when he said that Edwin Carson possessed such a thing as a daughter? But, dash it all, the place was there, opposite him, ready and set for someone.

He stared at the vacant place all through the excellent *crêpes Suzettes.*

Through the savoury.

And the coffee and the *friandises* in their little paper frills and the expensive cigar and the very expensive port which followed.

And when they filed back into the lounge, contented with life and filled with the fullness thereof, Edwin Carson's daughter was waiting for them, silhouetted against the light of the fire. A small girl, fair-complexioned and with blonde, lightly waved hair; dressed in a gown of white silk, cut on expensively simple lines. Rather a nice-looking girl, Jim thought. And unmistakably the girl whom the Rolls had removed from her bicycle.

Edwin Carson was going through a series of introductions. "My little girl... Mary... Mary, this is Lady Stone... and Miss Marilyn Brampton... and her brother, Henry... and Captain Henderson... his father was an old friend of mine, Mary..."

"Well!" said Jim. "But we've—"

And then stopped suddenly. For the hand which Mary Carson had stretched out to him fastened round his own in a most surprising grip, and the expression in her eyes as she looked up at Jim Henderson was one of real fear.

"What d'you say, Henderson?" said Carson.

"Nothing," said Jim. "I was rather surprised for a moment. Your daughter's so terribly like someone I used to know."

"But, my good man," said the Honourable Freddie Usher. "This is the—"

One of Jim Henderson's large feet placed itself in position on top of one of Freddie Usher's equally large feet, and pressed firmly until both had almost disappeared in the pile of the carpet. "You saw the likeness, too?" said Jim.

"Y—yes. Amazing, isn't it?"

"The living image."

"The dead spit."

From the background Henry Brampton murmured how odd it was that two such inane expressions should mean the same thing.

And Mary Carson smiled twice. A smile of polite attention to Mr. Brampton, and a smile of intense relief to Jim.

VII

Edwin Carson looked round his collection of guests and smiled. A perfect collection, he thought: moderately well-behaved, easily entertained, and with practically one exception only, all pleasantly rich. Near the fire Catherine Lady Stone pushed her horn-rimmed spectacles up the short stump which passed for her nose, inspected the thirteen cards which had been dealt out to her, said "My God!" under her breath and "Two Clubs" above it. On her left Freddie Usher sighed, and muttered "No bid" for what seemed the fiftieth time. Opposite Lady Stone, Jim Henderson stared at the seven clubs in his hand and wondered if anyone had ever told his partner that clubs were those black curly things. And, next to him, Marilyn Brampton removed her cigarette-holder again from between her lips, blew a long column of smoke down her nose so that it hit the green baize of the table and ricocheted up into Freddie Usher's face, and said slowly "Two Spades". And Catherine Lady Stone snorted slightly, and inspected her hand once more. Let a mere chicken like this Brampton girl get away with a paltry couple of spades? Not on your life. "Three Clubs," said Catherine Lady Stone, trusting in Providence and her partner.

At the piano Raoul was playing soft improvisations—snatches of the tunes to which she danced in *Soft Sugar*, fragments of South American songs which she had learned years ago, bits of modern musical comedies and revues in which she had played. Arched over the piano and gazing alternately at her fingers and her face, Henry Brampton listened in silence. It was only very rarely that Henry Brampton allowed himself to enthuse over anything (except

possibly his own paintings and the virtues of any art critic who
happened to praise them) but at the first sight of Raoul he had
fallen, as the Americans put it, good and hard. The somewhat sappy
expression of a young man in love registered itself all over Henry
Brampton's face, down even to the lowest hair on the obnoxiously
curving side-whiskers. "Exquisite," he said. "Play it again."

And sitting on one of the padded seats fitted in the wall at each
side of the fireplace, Mary Carson paid a polite attention to the
game of bridge, and said "Well played" and "Bad luck. One down,
were you?" and "If only you'd had the king" at suitable intervals at
the end of each hand. Once she had smiled to Jim when he brought
off what he himself considered a particularly snappy finesse; and
Jim had smiled back and put his king on Lady Stone's queen and
revoked twice. Lovely teeth she has when she smiles—he thought—
and what the hell are trumps?

So Edwin Carson looked round the lounge-hall and its occupants and murmured a few words of excusal, and slid noiselessly
from the room. He crossed the wide passage outside and opened
the door of his study. He did not switch on the light, but walked
across the room in darkness until he came to a recess in the wall
opposite. Here he fumbled in his pockets until he found a tiny
electric torch, switched it on, and ran the circle of light down
the panelling in front of him. He stretched out his other hand
and pressed the moulding of the panels with his fingers. Silence
for a moment, and then a faint whirr... and the panels in front
of him parted and he stepped inside. Again the faint whirr... and
when the panels had closed behind him, Edwin Carson felt for a
switch and turned on the light. And then he pulled the lever in
the wall in front of him and felt himself moving slowly down
to his cellars.

His own idea, this lift. And a remarkably good idea, though he said so himself. A lift which no one except his staff knew of, which could only be controlled when once you were safely inside it, which formed the one and only entrance and exit to the cellars where Edwin Carson's whole life lay. He had had it built in two sections: half of the cage ran from the panelled recess in his study, the other half from a corresponding panelled cupboard in the kitchen which adjoined the study. But the two halves could not be raised or lowered separately. No, no. He had to come down to these cellars of his himself first, and then send up the lift and allow anyone who had orders to come down to do so. And even when they did descend in their half of the lift, they could only get out into the cellars when he opened the door of their cage from the outside. No unwelcome callers to the cellars of Thrackley. If there should be such things, then they would simply remain shut in the half of the lift which had brought them down. And standing upright in a cage four feet by three with a total lack of ventilation and light, is not just an ideal way of spending a pleasant evening. Silly, of course, all these precautions. Very silly. But here in these cellars Edwin Carson had collected so much that was priceless and amazing and (much better to admit it and be done with it) incriminating, that an ordinary flight of slippery stone steps would not have done at all as an entrance.

He stepped from the cage when it stopped its descent, and the two halves of the door met and locked themselves behind him. He switched on his torch again and threw the light up the wall at his side until it fell on an electric switch. He turned on the light and gloated (as he always did) at the sight in front of him. For the cellars of Thrackley were no ordinary cellars. None of your damp, cobweb-covered affairs where lie the usual couple of tons of coal, and the bowls in which next season's selection of hyacinths and narcissi will be planted. Not even one of those smaller, but more interesting, affairs which are neatly stacked with a careful selection of sherries and hocks and brandies and the like. Far from it. The cellars which stretched themselves out under Thrackley were long and narrow. Their roof was low, so that when even an undersized man like Edwin Carson stood upright in them there was only a bare two feet between the ceiling and the shiny dome of his bald head. And round the walls of the cellars perhaps twenty long showcases had been fitted; they were built back fully eighteen inches in the solid wall, and protected by a thick shield of plate glass and an outer covering of steel wire. And then, when necessary, they could be covered a third time by the coating of artificial stone which slid over them and made them look only part of a grey and uninteresting stone wall. Each separate case was fitted with a concealed point of electric light, and each case sparkled with a selection of Edwin Carson's collection of jewels. There was no need for other lighting in the cellars themselves: the oblongs of the cases shone out through their glass and wire shields and the jewels inside flashed and sparkled as their facets caught the light.

Edwin Carson walked slowly round the cases and peered into each. The lights twinkled on his heavy glasses, turning the lenses from gold to palest green and on again to the colour of the rubies at which he was staring. A magnificent collection—carefully planned, artistically presented... a pity that it could not be shown in some more accessible spot. No, not such a pity, thought Edwin Carson; for it would be agony to see these gems paraded in some museum or art collection for all the idiots in Christendom to peer at, to poke their umbrellas at, to mutter "Isn't it *lovely*?" or "Aren't they marvellous?" Much better for the pleasure of it to be reserved for him, Edwin Carson—who knew every millimetre of every facet of these stones, who understood them and appreciated them as no other person in the world could do. And, incidentally, much safer to keep a collection like this in a cellar whose entrance very few persons knew. Very much safer indeed.

It took him quite a while to walk round the cases and examine the contents of each. He stopped for a minute before the case where a dozen pearls lay on a cloth of dark blue velvet, bathed in a soft white light. And he thought of Marilyn Brampton playing bridge upstairs, and of a spot far down her back where the triple rope of pearls which she wore twined round her neck and falling down her back ended in a large and perfect specimen. And, thinking of Marilyn's back, he remembered also that he was host to what he hoped was a charming weekend house-party, and told himself that he had better get on with the arrangements before his guests upstairs became fidgety in his absence.

At the end of the long narrow room stood a heavy oak desk. He crossed to it, pushed his finger on one of the several little discs inlaid in the side of the desk, and picked up the receiver of the telephone in front of him. In the kitchen above him Jacobson the butler looked up from the paragraph headed "The Above Have Arrived", said, ungrammatically and unattractively, "Hell! That's him!" and crossed to the the dresser where the telephone stood.

"That you, Jacobson?" said the voice of Edwin Carson.

"Yes."

"I want you to come down to the cellar for a minute."

"You down there? Here... you're supposed to be playing Up Jenkins with the guests, aren't you?"

"Shut your mouth, Jacobson. Come down here at once, and bring the rest with you."

"All right."

And Jacobson banged the receiver back in its holder and turned towards the other occupants of the kitchen.

"Downstairs. All of you," he said. "Toot sweet."

"The lot of us?"

"That's what I said. Where the hell's Burroughs? Always off by himself, that bloke. Washing the car, I suppose... God help his babies if ever he has any."

At his desk downstairs Edwin Carson waited for five minutes. Then a bulb in the wall at the other end of the cellar showed itself in a red light. He pressed another of the tiny discs at his side, and listened again to the faint whirr of the lift. When it stopped he stretched out his fingers and pressed... the doors of the lift slid open and Jacobson and the other three servants stepped out.

"Come over here," said Edwin Carson.

They crossed the room and stood in front of the desk, staring at the little man behind it. The staff of Thrackley numbered four and were all of the stronger sex. When Thrackley became inhabited again, George, the son and heir to the Hen and Chickens, had given generous odds to all in the bar-parlour that he would be on walking-out terms with the new housemaid within a week. George, being, much to the worry of his father and to the detriment of the Hen and Chickens' business, that kind of a lad. It was a pity that none of the bar-parlour habitués accepted George's odds, but then they had known the lad since he was so high and had learned to appreciate his powers where women were concerned. If, of course, they had seen the staff of Thrackley as Edwin Carson was seeing them now, they would have jumped at even shorter odds, for young George was not the one to waste his summer evenings meandering through Adderly woods with his arm round the waist of a six-foot-three bruiser with a club foot. Such being the person who carried out most of the household duties at Thrackley. And carried them out surprisingly well, as Catherine Lady Stone herself admitted when she found her suitcases unpacked and her weekend's luggage neatly folded away or carefully swinging from clotheshangers. And those excellent sauces which had accompanied that admirable dinner had been made, too, by another of the bruisers. (Had Lady Stone known this she would, in all probability, have eaten considerably less at dinner; which would have been all to the good, for the veal *à l'espagnol* was beginning to have words with the savoury and to have an effect on her bidding.) The chauffeur, Burroughs, completed the quartet standing in front of Edwin Carson. Perhaps the best-looking of the four, though that might still be taken as an insult rather than a compliment. A tall, thin man with powerful muscles and an intense love of taking risks... whether in passing the car in front in a traffic-laden street or in any of the other duties which he had to perform at Thrackley. The kind of man that suited Edwin Carson.

"Kept me waiting down here for five minutes... where the devil have you all been?"

The thick lenses of Carson's spectacles turned and shone up at Jacobson.

"Burroughs was out in the garage," he answered. "Had to go and find him."

"At this time of night? Doing what, Burroughs?"

"Something wrong with the carburettor, sir. I was getting it fixed in case any of the visitors wanted the car to-morrow."

(The only one of the four who used that word "sir". A good man, this Burroughs...)

"That's all right, then. Now, about to-night."

The four men edged a little closer to the desk. "Lady Stone… you all know which is her room?… opposite the stairs leading to the main landing on the second floor… what I want to… borrow… is a ruby set as the centre stone of a choker necklace. She was wearing it at dinner to-night. A beautiful stone, perfect… quite perfect. You noticed it, Jacobson?"

"I saw it."

"Splendid… now… I should imagine that my guests will retire round about midnight. I'll get them off earlier than that if I can. Jacobson, you will get that necklace from Lady Stone's room. She uses an old-fashioned jewel-case, I believe; probably she'll lock it and sleep with the key under her pillow. She's that kind of a woman."

"Nasty suspicious type," said Burroughs.

"Exactly. You'll have to bring the whole case with you, Jacobson."

"Right."

"You, Kenrick, will stay on the second landing and see that everything is all right up there. Burroughs, you further along the passage at the other side of the house—keep a look-out for those two Bramptons. You down here, Adams, with everything ready. Understand?"

Four nods.

"If anyone turns up or anything goes wrong, signal to me from your nearest point. I'll give the warning to Jacobson."

The four stood in silence for a minute. Then Jacobson spoke.

"What about the girl?"

"Mary? I'll take care of her. Now, everything clear, Jacobson?"

"Yes."

"Kenrick?"

"Yes."

"All clear, Adams?"

"Yes."

"And you, Burroughs?"

"Yes, sir."

"Right," said Edwin Carson. "And now I must be getting back to my guests. Very thoughtless of me to desert them like this... very thoughtless indeed. What will they be thinking of me?... dear, dear, dear..."

And the little man led the way back to the lift.

VIII

AT PRECISELY SIX MINUTES BEFORE MIDNIGHT CATHERINE
Lady Stone laid her four remaining cards on to the table
with a flourish. "The last heart," she said. "And those three on
the table. A very nice little helping hand, that was, Captain
Henderson." And Jim picked up the marker and pencil, and
decided that the guardian angel who hovered over bridge tables
must have a peculiarly warped mentality to allow Lady Stone
to get away with it as she had done all evening. "Forty below,"
he said. "And twenty-four above. And two-fifty for the rubber...
check that, will you, Freddie?" And the Honourable Freddie Usher
roused himself from the stupor in which he had been following
suit and throwing away and losing his queens in his opponents'
finesses, licked the point of his pencil and made a few gestures
which he hoped would give the impression of an addition, and
said, "Quite right. Nine hundred down." Addition: at this time
of night!... "Nine hundred, Lady Stone," said Jim. "That's four
and sixpence."

"Splendid," said Lady Stone, and gloated at the thought of it.
"Damn!" thought Marilyn Brampton, and fumbled in her pochette,
and vowed that she would never lift another card during her visit
to Thrackley, and hoped devoutly that this Usher ass would have
the decency to run Henry and herself back to town and so save
thirteen shillings and eightpence train fare. "And now I must really
get off to bed," said Catherine Lady Stone. "It's so rarely that I get
a chance of being in bed early—so many things to attend to in the
evenings, you know—and I want so much to be up early to-morrow

morning and go for a nice long walk before breakfast. So very good for one... don't you think so, Mr. Usher?"

"Eh? Oh! Ah!" said Freddie, rallying suddenly. "Quite. Exactly."

"Then perhaps I shan't need to go alone? Nothing like having a companion on a long walk. Makes the miles simply fly. And I do so want you to hear all about the little garden-party that I'm getting up for the Disabled Seamen's Children's Fund. Lady Plumb-Drummond and I are doing the organizing of it, you know. And dear Raoul has promised to come and dance for us if her manager or whoever it is will allow her... such a deserving cause... a quarter to eight, shall we say?"

And Lady Stone collected her spectacles and spectacle-case and her diamanté bag and her two handkerchiefs and heaved herself from her chair.

"Going off so soon?" said Edwin Carson. "But it's early yet."

"If you don't mind, Mr. Carson. I'm really very tired... the country air, I think... and I had a very heavy day in town before I left... three committee meetings... and dear Mr. Usher has insisted that I go for a long walk with him before breakfast to-morrow. So..."

"Well, if you must leave us, then... But the rest—you're not all going to bed so soon, are you?"

But the rest were all going to bed so soon, as it happened. For Raoul had got just a little tired of this Brampton thing staring at her, and the Brampton thing's back was aching rather badly with keeping up the adoring position into which he had curved himself over the piano. And Marilyn Brampton had no desire to lose anything more at sixpence a hundred. So Edwin Carson led his guests from the lounge and up the wide staircase and to their various rooms. Again Mr. Carson behaved as all perfect hosts should behave: hoping that they would sleep well, that their beds would be comfortable, that the noise of the pine-trees outside their windows would not be disturbing, that they would not hesitate to ring if they required anything, that they would rise in the morning just whenever they wished and not a moment earlier. Breakfast, he assured them all, was an elastic affair starting... shall we say?... at eight-thirty and available until... well... elevenish. "Good night, then, Lady Stone," said Edwin Carson.

"Good night, dear Mr. Carson," said Lady Stone. And feeling that something of the kind was called for, she added vaguely: "And thank you terribly for everything."

"Good night, Miss Brampton."

"Good night."

"Good night, Mr. Brampton."

"'Night."

And Edwin Carson took Raoul's arm and led her off along the corridor to show her to her room. And took, Jim noticed, a remarkably long time in doing so.

He turned to say good night to Carson's daughter before he and Freddie went on to the third floor where their bedrooms were. "Good night, Miss Carson," he said.

"Good night... and thank you."

"Thank you? For what?"

"For not giving me away—about being in the village."

"Oh, that. But, listen, Miss Carson, surely you're—"

"Good night."

And within a few minutes half a dozen doors had closed behind the half-dozen guests of Thrackley, and there was a brief period of activity followed by silence and stillness. Catherine Lady Stone squatted on the edge of her bed, and kicked off her evening slippers and wiggled her toes and ran her fingers over her tired feet.

She found her spectacles and her diary and her fountain-pen and she entered up the day's happenings in a microscopic and quite illegible handwriting. (A diary-keeping sort of woman, as well.) "At Henrietta's in the morning," she wrote, "re bridge drive for Wed. week. Lunch at Simpson's and then to S. about Dis. Seamen's. Children's garden-party. Left town at 4.15 for Thrackley—delightful place, looks damp but doesn't seem to be. Mr. Carson v. charming but v. ugly, promises subscription to Dis. Seamen before I leave. Raoul person from Alhambra among the guests—persuaded her to dance at g.-party if her manager allows her. Remember write Lady P.-D. about this in case she fixes up with Gertie Collins—no use having both and Raoul much better attraction. Won 9s. 9d. at bridge, auction, contract unknown here. V. excellent *crêpes Suzettes* for dinner."

And Lady Stone blotted and closed her diary and screwed the cap on to her fountain-pen and put both pen and diary back in her ample leather handbag. She stretched her fat arms heavenward and disappeared for quite a while in the folds of her black evening gown; when she emerged again she was rather redder in the face and just slightly out of breath. These modern dresses were the very devil to get in and out of if one didn't have a modern figure to match. And Lady Stone touched her hair in a few vital spots, causing whatever it was that was keeping it up to stop doing so, and the hair leapt down her back in thick black folds. She put it through a severe programme of combing and brushing, did some more attachments to it, and finally tucked it all away beneath a boudoir cap of pale pink silk. Then, with a good deal of groaning and gasping and blowing, she uncorsetted herself and peeled her stockings from her flabby legs, and threw various garments on various chairs until the bedroom looked very like the last day of a remnant sale at Pontings. She disappeared into a loose-fitting nightdress (embroidered around the neck with a border of extremely repellent violets), and shoved the hot-water bottle a little further down the bed so that both her feet and her posterior would hit a warm spot when at last she slid between the sheets. She took out her teeth and placed them carefully in a tumbler of water. She patted her pillows into her favourite position. She stretched out her hand to switch the main light off and the bed-reading-light on. And then she said "Oh!" and "God bless my soul!" For Catherine Lady Stone had almost forgotten to remove the priceless choker necklace that she was wearing. Almost forgotten—for the first time for years. Heavens! Imagine going to sleep with that necklace still around her neck. Supposing someone had come into the room during the night— just an ordinary burglar, say. And had seen it. And pinched it. Or, worse still, strangled her with it and *then* pinched it. Catherine Lady Stone went hot and then very cold at the thought, and took the necklace off carefully, and laid it on its bed of navy-blue velvet in the second compartment of her jewel box. She turned the key of the case, and pushed it under her pillow. Not that a burglar or anything like that would get into a place like Thrackley... but still, you never knew. And Lady Stone turned out the light, heaved herself into bed, sat for a moment and wondered if there was any chance of getting the Countess of Cranell to present the prizes at the bridge-drive on Wednesday week, and lay back on the pillows and stretched up her arm to turn off the bed-light. For five minutes the noise of the breeze feeling its way through the pines outside the bedroom window was the only sound in the room. Then the rhythmic beat of a heavy asthmatic breathing filled the room and made the swishing of the pine-branches a poor second. Catherine Lady Stone, it was fairly obvious, was asleep.

On the floor above, Jim Henderson undressed slowly and thought deeply on quite a number of things. Of Lady Stone, and what immense legs the woman had, and what foul calls she made at bridge. Of Raoul the dancer, and what a surprisingly long time had passed before he heard old man Carson returning from seeing her to her room. Of Edwin Carson, and the conversation they had had together in the study. Of Mary Carson, and what a damned good-looking girl she was even when you looked at her closely, and how she had behaved when Freddie and he were on the point of recognizing her as the girl on the bicycle. And why the devil shouldn't she want papa Carson to know that she was cycling through Adderly village? Had it been a surreptitious visit to some miserable male of whom Edwin Carson did not approve? An unpleasant thought. Though, if that were the case, he was quite in agreement with Edwin Carson's disapproval. Probably not at all the sort of fellow for a nice girl like that. A nasty greasy specimen, more than likely. Like Henry Brampton. Worse, perhaps.

He folded his trousers carefully and screwed them down between the jaws of the press which he had found in his wardrobe. He pulled the cord of his dressing-gown around him, and lit a last cigarette before going to bed. He selected one of the books by his bedside and sat down on the settee: a big, comfortable settee which, he imagined, would make dressing in the morning a slow and restful affair. He read for ten minutes, cackling occasionally at Oscar Wilde's epigrams, though he had read them many times before. And then he threw his cigarette-stump into the fireplace... a charming modern fire-place, in shaded tiles of blue, fitted with an imitation pile of wood logs as an electric fire. And...

There are quite a few things in life which one does without having very much idea why one is doing them. Jim Henderson did one of them now. He crossed to the fireplace and stared at the dummy logs. They were covered with a fall of soot. And yet the actual fire probably hadn't been lit since the beginning of summer. Funny... A bird, perhaps, nesting in the chimney cans. And then he noticed the three-quarters of an inch or so of fine wire which was showing just where the tiles met the chimney-piece. He looked at the wire for a minute, and then he bent down on his knees, cocked his head to an extremely uncomfortable angle, and peered up into the blackness of the chimney. And just stopped himself from giving a whistle of surprise.

For—much as he admired Edwin Carson's capabilities as a host—he felt that to suspend a microphone in the chimney of his guest's bedroom was really going a bit too far.

IX

JIM HENDERSON OPENED THE DOOR OF HIS BEDROOM AND stepped out into the darkness of the passage. He felt that the finding of a microphone in one's bedroom chimney was not the sort of thing to be kept to oneself; for all he knew there might be a similar instrument tucked in every bedroom of Thrackley. And if Freddie Usher started singing some of his not-so-drawing-room ballads then whoever was listening-in would get a series of very nasty surprises. So Jim crossed the landing and stopped outside the door of Freddie's room. He listened for a minute, and heard what suggested that Mr. Usher had only reached the trousers-pressing stage. He turned the door-handle and walked in.

"Hullo," said Freddie Usher.

Jim did not answer. Instead, he put his finger to his lips in the way which he had seen all suspicious characters do when they wished complete silence and attention. On the stage or the screen this simple little action had been always a total success; here in Freddie Usher's bedroom it was a complete fiasco. Mr. Usher stopped his screwing of the trousers-press, stared at Jim for quite a while, and then said: "What the hell do you think you're playing at?"

Still Mr. Usher's visitor did not speak. Instead, he waggled his forefinger at Freddie in a highly irritating manner and walked to the bedroom fireplace and kneeled down in front of the fireplace. Loopy, thought Mr. Usher, completely loopy; and as right as rain when they set out from London not ten hours before. The country air, he supposed, affecting the poor old Henderson brain. What other explanation could there be when a fellow walks into a fellow's bed-room at a quarter to one in the morning and behaves in this pathetic way, placing forefingers on lips and prostrating himself before fireplaces? And now the symptoms seemed, if anything, to be getting a shade worse; for the visitor had removed the electric fire from its usual position in the fireplace, and laid it carefully on the carpet, had shoved his face right into the fire-place and was now staring up the chimney and allowing a fair amount of soot to fall on various parts of his head and neck. Oh, yes; completely loopy, no question about it... he had withdrawn his face from the chimney-piece now and was fumbling among the contents of Mr. Usher's dressing-table. Much better, thought Mr. Usher, to humour the poor fellow: hadn't he read somewhere that people in this condition were less liable to become violent if left severely alone? Very well, then. But when Jim found what he was looking for, and dissembled the four parts of Freddie's safety razor, and returned to the fireplace with the razor-blade gripped firmly in his fingers, Mr. Usher began to edge towards the door and to wish that he was wearing a little more than a dress shirt and a pair of black silk socks.

Jim disappeared head first up the chimney again, and stayed there for quite a while working away with the hand that held the razor-blade. A very complicated and awkward way of committing suicide, thought Mr. Usher; for if you must cut your throat, why choose the foot of a chimney as a place to do so? But after a while Jim extracted himself from the fireplace (with his neck a great deal sootier but otherwise quite unharmed) and held up a round black metal object in his hand. And actually spoke. He said: "What d'you think of that, Freddie?"

"What is it?"

"It's a very good example of the species microphone. I've just removed one from my chimney and I thought I'd come to see if your bedroom had been fitted with all the modern comforts."

"D'you mean to say that everything I said would be heard by someone listening through that blessed little thing in the chimney?"

"Yes. But you needn't worry. You can go ahead and talk your tonsils out now. I'm afraid I've spoiled your razor-blade—you'll get a lovely stream-lined effect with that nick I've made in it. Who were you expecting to be talking to, anyway?"

"James!..."

"Oh, all right."

"But—where the devil do the wires from these damned pick-up things lead to? Who's doing the listening-in? Edwin Carson?"

"I suppose so."

"But why?"

"Haven't the foggiest. Except that it must be rather jolly to lean back in your study and listen to half of your guests telling the other half exactly what they think of you."

"And what a hell of a weekend it's going to be."

"And what a perfectly lousy dinner they had to eat."

"And—Jim!"

"What's the matter?"

"You don't think there's any chance of a second microphone hanging around anywhere? I mean to say, before I go on to give my personal opinion of Edwin Carson's face..."

"I shouldn't think so. Whoever did the microphone-furnishing in this house wouldn't expect to have to cope with my brains and powers of observation, Freddie."

"No. Of course not."

"What beats me is—why on earth Carson (if it is Carson) wants to hear all that goes on in the bedrooms of his house."

"A nasty suspicious mentality."

"You remember what you told me about his mania for getting hold of jewels—legally or otherwise?"

"Yes."

"And did you have a look at the brilliancy of the dinner-table to-night? Apart from my conversation, I mean? Lady Stone's necklace, that Brampton girl's pearls… you couldn't see Raoul for platinum and emeralds… and you've got your old family diamonds here with you, haven't you? You don't think that comrade Carson—"

"I think," said Freddie Usher, "that you've been reading too many detective novels, Jim. Not good for you at your age. Go away to bed and leave me in peace."

"Righto."

"Good night, then."

"I suppose those damned diamonds are locked up?"

"Good night."

"And don't forget your nice invigorating walk with Lady Stone before the grape-fruit to-morrow morning."

"Get out!"

"Oh, very well, then."

And Jim Henderson closed the door softly and set out on his return journey across the corridor to his own bedroom. He felt his way along the wall until it deserted him suddenly and he was left flapping his arms in mid-air. He took a few steps forward and his fingers touched the heavy mahogany newel post at the head of the staircase. He leaned up against it, tightened the cord of his dressing-gown, and took a mental bearing of his position. Six paces to the right, and then left turn… and then about four more paces…

and he would be at his bedroom door. He set out on the first of the six paces when something made him stop and peer over the balustrade down to the landing below.

A small circle of light was playing along the panelling of the landing. He watched it, intrigued. The circle seemed undecided about its movements. It ran along the wall, passed two bed-room doors and wavered at a third. Then it returned to the first of the doors. And flitted lightly over its four panels. And finally stopped moving and showed up in its round of white light the keyhole and handle of Catherine Lady Stone's bedroom door. The circle grew smaller until Jim could see the pin-point where the ray of light began. One of those tiny electric torches which can be focused to as large or as small a ray as you wish.

And then a hand appeared in the circle.

For a long time it seemed to be absolutely still. Then Jim realized that it was slowly moving... a fraction of an inch at a time... until at last the key which had been so silently inserted into the door's keyhole completed its turning, and gave a little snick of satisfaction. Silence again for a minute... then an almost inaudible crunch as the jamb of the door parted company with the coat of paint on the casing where it had been resting. Lady Stone's door opened an inch, two inches... six... and the circle of light vanished suddenly. From the landing above, Jim knew that someone had gone into Lady Stone's room...

He thought it over for a minute. Should he give the alarm or go back to his bed and persuade himself that he had dreamed the whole thing? Rather awkward if he roused the house-party to catch a burglar, and found that Lady Stone had been expecting the visitor with the electric torch. But Catherine Lady Stone (or so it seemed to Jim from the short time he had known the lady) was not that kind of girl. Far from it. A woman, this Catherine, who would wash and undress and clean her teeth and read a couple of chapters of some good, uplifting book, and turn off the light, and curl soundly off to sleep. Nothing more. No harm, then, in doing a little investigation into Lady Stone's visitor by himself? None at all. Right... He tiptoed slowly down the flight of stairs, thanking heaven that this was happening in a house whose floors and staircases were covered in a luxurious growth of carpets. A cold, bare linoleum would have been sheer hell in a situation like the present.

He reached the last step of the stairs and paused for a moment before setting out on the landing. He felt his way along, steering himself past the little oak table which stood to the left of Lady Stone's bedroom door. His fingers touched the panels of the door, and he bent down and listened. Not a sound. He tried the door with the tips of his fingers, and it gave slightly. He listened again... to the quiet movement of the trees outside the bedroom window... to another series of noises which he put down as a mixture of Lady Stone's breathing and Lady Stone's dinner rumbling around Lady Stone's stomach... to the slight but unmistakable sounds of a drawer handle being touched and a drawer pulled slowly out. No doubt about it: there was someone uninvited in Lady Stone's room. And Jim Henderson put his fingers round the handle of the door, pushed it silently open, and was on the point of following Lady Stone's first visitor into the room when a hand was placed lightly on his arm.

In other circumstances Jim would have said, in all probability, "Hoi!" Or "Who the devil's that?" Or something of the sort. Instead of which he kept his mouth shut and did not move. It was not a nice situation. He thought in a haphazard fashion of his small but comfortable bedroom at 34, Ardgowan Mansions, of Mrs. Bertram waving good-bye from the lavatory window and telling him to take care of himself, of Freddie Usher's description of Edwin Carson, of the revolver which Freddie had suggested he should include in his packing. He thought of all this, and still the hand rested on the same place on his arm. He stepped back from the bedroom doorway, and the hand gripped the sleeve of his dressing-gown and pulled him further away from the door. There seemed no option to going where the owner of the hand wished him to go: he allowed himself to be pulled by the sleeve along the landing and up the flight of stairs to the floor on which his own bedroom was situated. And then the hand released its hold on his sleeve. And "Thank heavens I saw you in time," said Mary Carson.

"You!... Miss Carson!..."

"Please don't make a noise. I don't want anyone to know I'm out of bed... or you either."

"Yes... but—"

"Captain Henderson—will you please go back to your room and stay there till morning?"

"But listen, there's someone just gone into Lady Stone's bedroom. It may be a burglar... or anything—"

"I know. That's all right."

"You know? Well, it's not all right. I'm dashed if I—"

"I can't explain everything here. Please go to your room. I promise that everything's all right. Please..."

"Oh, very well, if you say so. But..."

"Can I see you in the morning and talk to you about all this?"

"Of course."

"Thank you so much. And thank you again for keeping quiet about seeing me in Adderly. My father would have been fearfully angry if he'd known that I was down in the village."

"But why on earth shouldn't you go down to the village?"

"No questions, please... good night."

In the darkness Jim realized that Mary Carson was no longer beside him. He said "Good night" softly, and received no answer. He peered into the darkness and saw that she had brought him to within a foot of his own bedroom door. And now... what? Go and tell Freddie Usher what he had seen? Stay out for another quarter of an hour in this charming landing and see if Catherine Lady Stone's visitor reappeared? He remembered that he had promised Mary Carson to return to bed and stay there. He shrugged his shoulders, pushed his bedroom door open, switched on the light, and closed the door behind him.

And the tall thin man called Burroughs who had been watching this little performance smiled to himself and signalled to Edwin Carson that all was again quiet on the second floor of the house called Thrackley. And Edwin Carson said: "Good. Very good."

X

EDWIN CARSON, HAVING SEEN EACH OF HIS GUESTS DEPOSITED safely at their bed-room doors, having taken an affectionate but perhaps over-lengthy farewell to Raoul the dancer, having gone his usual rounds of the house and seen that the front door was bolted and barred, that the sherry was under lock and key, that any respectably sized lumps of coal had been taken from the fire in the lounge and laid on the tiles to be reinserted in the morning, having made sure that the burglar-alarms on each window were in their usual efficient working order—Edwin Carson, after all this, went to his study and pressed the moulding of the panelling in the little recess, and prepared to spend an entertaining night in the cellars below Thrackley. He settled himself at his desk, lit a cigar, took a sip of the double whisky which he had brought down from his study, drew open a drawer of the desk, and lifted from that drawer a pair of light silverized headphones. And Edwin Carson placed the headphones over his bald, shiny head, and adjusted the screws at each side until the earpieces fitted snugly but not too tightly on his own large ears. Then he rolled back a section of the desk, revealing a panel of switches, each with a round disc of ebonite at its side, and with each disc lettered in a neat black lettering: "A", "B", "C", up to "K"... and "1st Landing"... "2nd Landing"... "3rd Landing"... and "Kitchen"... "Lounge"... "Dining-Room"... "Garage".

He leaned back in his seat, so that he could just reach the double row of switches with the tip of his forefinger. He pressed the switch labelled "D" and it slid back into its socket with a click...

"... back to your room," Marilyn Brampton was saying. "I'm dead tired, and I want to get some sleep."

"Funny, isn't it?" said the voice of Henry Brampton. "If anyone in town suggested your going to bed at this hour you'd be tickled to death at the idea."

"All depends who did the suggesting. Give me another of those foul cigarettes, Henry."

The sound of a cigarette-case snapping open and then shutting. The scratching of a match. H'm... Mr. Brampton evidently preferred to throw his spent matches into the fireplace rather than use the ashtrays provided for the purpose: funny how loud these little things seemed to be when they happened within a foot or so of the microphone...

"Well... what's the verdict, Marilyn?" said Henry Brampton.

"Pretty foul, don't you think? What an odd collection of freaks he's got hold of... that Stone female makes me want to cry out loud. She cheated at bridge to-night—twice, did you notice?"

"I didn't see her."

"No. I didn't think you would."

"And how often did you cheat?"

"Thrice. I think the Henderson man saw both of us... you could play with twenty cards in your hand and that Usher object would see nothing wrong..."

"What d'you think of Carson?"

"Pretty foul."

(Edwin Carson shook the ash from his cigar and thought to himself that for a novelist Miss Brampton possessed a remarkably limited range of descriptions.)

"No... not exactly up to standard for the front row of Mr. Cochran's Young Gentlemen, is he? And did you notice the butler man? Just about as ugly as Carson."

"Wonder what he'll make us do to-morrow?"

"Oh, the usual… nice long walks, and a spot of shooting, and perhaps a really energetic game of tennis…"

"My God! The food's decent, though."

"And Raoul may help to liven things up… wonder how she's got off from her show?"

"The management's regrets that owing to the sudden indisposition… I suppose."

"Rather a nice girl."

"I noticed you'd noticed that."

"Well… what d'you think of her yourself?"

"Pretty foul, I should say."

And Edwin Carson stretched out his hand to the switch marked "D" and pulled it back to its original position. Going to be quite interesting, this. It was the first time that he had had an opportunity of really testing his microphones. Yes, quite interesting. Rather like those two-act sketches one used to see in concert-parties: the kind of thing where everyone said the correct and polite thing in the first act and then in the second just exactly what they thought of each other. He took the cigar from his mouth, and leaned forward to touch the next switch. "F"… young Henderson's room.

No talking. Obviously hadn't any visitors… sensible lad. But he wasn't in bed yet: he could hear him walking up and down picking up things and laying them down, shutting wardrobe doors and pulling open drawers. Whistling, too. Why on earth should a man whistle a tune like "Up in the Morning's No for Me" just before getting between the sheets? Edwin Carson closed his eyes and listened to the series of little sounds in the headphones. And pictured each action of Jim Henderson as clearly and as accurately as if he were in the room beside him. He was unscrewing the trouser-press now... now screwing it up again... placing it back on the low wooden shelf in that corner... taking something from the glass holders at the back of the dressing-table... yes, toothbrush, of course... cleaning them well, too... lighting a cigarette now... this last-minute-cigarette-before-we-turn-in idea seemed to be popular amongst his guests... thrown the match into the fireplace just as Henry Brampton had done... how careless people were... silence now... walking to just in front of the fireplace now... what the hell was he doing?... the sounds came down magnified, almost deafening... must be within inches of the microphone now... and then silence. Complete silence. Edwin Carson waited for over a minute. But the connection to room "F" had gone dead.

He took the headphones from his ears and swore. Several times. Just what had happened? Had the man in room "F" accidentally severed a connection while doing something or other near the fireplace? Or had he seen the microphone in the chimney, and cut the wire not at all accidentally but with a very definite purpose? Had that idiot, Burroughs, left a loose wire hanging down from the chimney-piece which might be noticed? Edwin Carson took out his silk handkerchief and dabbed his brow with it. Well, nothing could be done until the morning; then he would see for himself when Jim Henderson was safely out of reach of his bedroom. But... he might find out now whether the disconnecting of the microphone were intentional or accidental. What would young Henderson do now—supposing that he had, for some inane reason, looked up his bed-room chimney and discovered the microphone? No... almost certain that he would go to the room of his friend, Usher, and tell him about his find. Very well, then... the switch marked "G".

Freddie Usher, too, was whistling. Slightly off key, in a tune which might have been anything but was probably an improvised nothing. Moving slowly around the room, and throwing each layer of clothing on to various chairs as he discarded it... obviously a young man accustomed to the services of a valet. Silence for quite a while... probably wrestling with his collar... yes, he could just hear a muttered "Dammit! Damn the thing!" in the headphones. And then quite distinctly a knock at the door of the bedroom. Freddie Usher's voice saying, "Who's that?"... The microphone did not pick up the answer, but... "Oh, it's you, Jim—come in!" And as the door opened, Edwin Carson drummed with the fingers of both his hands on the desk in front of him: an action which meant only that he was angry and annoyed. Practically no doubt now that Henderson had seen the microphone and had come to tell Usher... but he would hear definitely when Jim Henderson spoke. But Jim Henderson did not speak. Freddie Usher said, "Hullo!" but there was no answer. Edwin Carson leaned forward In his chair and strained to catch the sounds in the phones at his ears. Still nothing audible happened in the room marked "G"... then the voice of Freddie Usher: "What the hell d'you think you're playing at?" A very pertinent question, thought Edwin Carson; and one which he would dearly love to be in a position to answer. And then... those same magnified sounds which meant that someone was moving very near to where the microphone had been placed... and finally the same little click followed by an absolute silence. Edwin Carson did not wait in the hope that the wire would come alive again; he knew exactly what had happened, and he took the headphones off his head and swore for the second time that night.

What an advantage these microphones were... and how utterly helpless one felt without them! What wouldn't he give to hear exactly what Jim Henderson was saying to Freddie Usher at this minute... oh, damn that fool, Burroughs! For it must have been that he had left a wire showing when he was fixing up the things... no normal guest goes to peer up his bed-room chimney when he retires for the night at one o'clock. Under the bed, perhaps. But up the chimney, definitely no. Hell!

Well, no use wasting any more time swearing about it. He pressed one of the tiny discs at the side of his desk, and picked up the receiver of the telephone. He heard Kenrick's voice whisper "Everything quiet—all O.K.", and he nodded to himself and then grunted into the receiver, and laid it back on its pedestal. And then he rose from his chair and crossed to the little table standing at the side of the desk, and poured himself out another whisky-and-soda in which the whisky predominated. Then he returned to his seat and put on the headphones again. To hear something worth hearing this time. Room "B"... where Catherine Lady Stone, bless her, was sleeping the sound sleep of the just.

Oh, yes; no doubt at all: Lady Stone was asleep. The sensitiveness of the microphone picked up her heavy breathing and sent the sounds down to Edwin Carson's ears like the noise of waves rushing in on the surf. No other sounds for quite a while... he sat back and sipped his drink. No need to rush things; let Jacobson take his own time and do the job in his own way. A good man, Jacobson. A man he could trust. At least he hoped so. And Jim Henderson must surely be back in his room by now. Yes, any time now... no need to wait any longer... why the devil?...

The door of Lady Stone's room gave a tiny click as it opened and an even fainter one as Jacobson closed it behind him. After that, not a sound. Somehow he knew that Jacobson was in the room, though. There, now... he was at the dressing-table now, from the sound of things. Another faint noise, and another... feeling his way over all Lady Stone's trinkets and powder-bowls and hairpins

and cold creams and vanishing creams and other impedimenta…
would he never lay hands on that jewel-case?

And then Edwin Carson jumped from his chair, and sent the
glass which had held his whisky flying with a movement of his
hand, and the dregs of his drink spilled themselves slowly over
the top of his desk.

The voice of Catherine Lady Stone rang out in the phones
on his ears. Almost deafening him, it seemed, after the silence of
the previous few minutes. Eight words only, in that shrill, decisive
voice of hers:

"Move away from that dressing-table, whoever it is…"

X I

THE HOUSE CALLED THRACKLEY, WITH ALL ITS GLUT OF
furniture and fittings and food, was completely lacking in
one thing. It possessed no alarm clock. Or, if it had such a thing,
it kept it hidden and muffled and well in the background. And Jim
Henderson, a bad riser at the best of times with a lusty three-and-
elevenpenny alarm next to his ear, was a total failure at getting
out of bed when there was nothing to go off with a loud com-
motion at eight-thirty. Which, no doubt, explains the fact that it
was dangerously near ten o'clock when he rose on the Saturday
morning. The pine-trees outside his window were another thing
which could possibly be made an excuse for the hour of his rising;
for in the bedroom at Mrs. Bertram's establishment there was
always a definite difference between day and night so far as the
lighting effects were concerned. When you opened your eyes for
the first time in the morning at Number 34, Ardgowan Mansions
you knew at once by the amount of light coming through the holes
in the cretonne curtains that it was getting near breakfast time
and certainly time you weren't lying there. Though, of course, on
some mornings the light in the curtains had less effect on you than
on other mornings; for when a November fog was wafting itself
about your window, then all you said was that it couldn't possibly
be a minute after six. And turned over on your other side and went
to sleep. But here at Thrackley there were no varying degrees of
light. Always the same half-darkness; always, if you cared to look,
the same dull shade of green framed in your window. No chance
of being able here to say: "What a perfectly glorious morning!

Criminal to miss a morning like this by frowsing here in bed!"
You cannot, however hard you may try, work up an enthusiasm
necessary to make you leave a warm feather mattress by merely
saying: "What a marvellously dirty shade of dark green the trees
are this morning!" Of course not.

Added to this there was no Mrs. Bertram to thump on the
bedroom door with a heavy hand, to rattle the handle and finally
to crash open the door with a jab of the breakfast-tray. For with all
her faults and her prattling of the murders and bankruptcies and
divorces of the day, there was this to be said for Mrs. Bertram: she
did wake you up. Now Jacobson, when he paid his early-morning
visit, left no impression on you at all. He knocked on the door (a
stealthy, slimy, half-nervous sort of knock), and he slid into the
room and drew back the curtains at the window slowly and with
a tenderness of touch which suggested that if he used any force
on the wretched things they would fall to pieces before his face.
Mrs. Bertram, when she drew the curtains of her bedroom (only
they went up at Ardgowan Mansions instead of sideways as at
Thrackley) did so with a flourish and a clatter, as if to say: "Well,
if you aren't awake yet, that ought to do the trick!" Mrs. Bertram,
too, was not above giving you a hefty shove or yelling a loud "Hi,
you!" in your ear. But Jacobson merely murmured "Good morning, sir" to the outline of what he presumed was Jim Henderson
underneath the sheets, and added in an even quieter whisper: "A
very nice morning, sir. Quite warm and pleasant, sir. Would you
be wishing a hot or cold bath, sir? And could I lay anything out for
you, sir? Breakfast will be ready just when you wish it, sir. In the
dining-room, sir," and receiving no answer to any of these remarks,
drifted silently from the room and closed the door after him, taking
quite half a minute to do so so as not to disturb the sleeper inside.

Again, no doubt, the perfect butler; but quite useless at making one realize that this was after nine o'clock on a Saturday morning, and what about it?

When at last he did waken it took Jim some time to realize that he had been sleeping in a very charming bedroom of a very delightful mansion in Surrey. He thought: now what will dear old Mrs. B. have to tell me this morning? A society scandal? Or a famous financier fraud sensation? Or a couple of meaty suicides? Rather pleasant to lie here and wait for the dear old thing with her morning's budget, knowing quite well that some morning she might open the door with Greta Garbo strangled or the Prime Minister swimming the Channel. And what for breakfast this morning? Not so wide a scope for speculation here, he remembered: kippers, hadn't it been these last few days, and all because of the government, poor souls. He blinked across at the window and came slowly to the conclusion that Mrs. Bertram had at last invested in new curtains. Not before time, either. And then he turned to see what the alarm clock had to say about it, and suddenly remembered: Thrackley!... Edwin Carson and Raoul and the Bramptons and Mary Carson and Lady Stone. Lady Stone... and the man who had gone into Lady Stone's bedroom last night... Heavens, yes!... and the microphone in his chimney. He threw his feet over the side of the bed, and fastened the sash of his dressing-gown around him, and collected his shaving-brush and his shaving-soap and his bath-towel and his face-towel, and disappeared to where he could hear the pleasing, gurgling sounds of water careering hotly through a tap.

Plus-fours, he thought: for hadn't someone suggested last night a game of tennis, and he had no intention of being involved in a mixed doubles with the Bramptons or the Raoul woman. A single against Mary Carson, certainly; but any other combination, definitely no. When he at last reached the dining-room he found the Bramptons busy with grape-fruit. There was no sign of any other members of the house-party.

"Good morning," he said.

"'Morning," said Marilyn Brampton. "You help yourself from the sideboard."

"Thanks," said Jim, and proceeded to do so. A pleasing selection of breakfast items, he reflected, and much to be preferred to the kippers of Ardgowan Mansions. The misbehavings of the government, as far as they affected the breakfast-table, had apparently no effect here at Thrackley. The grape-fruit was kept iced in a small refrigerator, the eggs and the sausages and the bacon and the rest of them still kept warm on their electric heaters. He poured out coffee for himself and for Marilyn Brampton ("while you're busy," she said, and stretched out a cup in his direction), and as he crossed to his seat at the table beside the Bramptons the door of the dining-room opened and Mary Carson came in. Thank God, he thought. (Now why should he think that, eh? Well, of course, breakfasting with the Bramptons would have been rather an ordeal without someone to help in the conversation. And Mary Carson was a remarkably nice girl. Funny, though, thinking that... not often that he took very much notice of the opposite sex. It must be, he supposed, that Mary Carson's attractions stood out in bold relief from those of the other females at Thrackley. Well, anyway, a remarkably nice girl.)

"Good morning, Miss Carson," he said.

"Good morning. I'm glad someone else is late for breakfast beside myself. Good morning, Miss Brampton. 'Morning, Mr. Brampton."

"'Morning."

Mr. Brampton had rather too much sausage in his mouth to answer. He nodded.

"Did you sleep all right?"

"Yes, thanks—fine," said Jim.

"Was it Noel Coward who said that he always considered that question an impertinence?" said Marilyn Brampton.

Henry Brampton swallowed the last of his sausage, and said: "No. Beverley Nichols."

"I'm sure it was Noel."

"Well, it wasn't. Pass the marmalade."

A very long pause in the conversation. "What about a walk after breakfast?" said Mary Carson. "The country at the back of the house is rather lovely."

"I never walk," said Henry Brampton.

"He means," said Marilyn, "that he never walks if there's a chance of going by car."

"I'll get Burroughs to get the car out, then."

"Personally," said Jim, "I never go by car if there's a chance of walking."

"Really?"

"Pass the toast, Marilyn."

"You're slightly nearer it than I am."

"Oh, all right…"

Another long pause.

"So if you could be bothered, Miss Carson," said Jim, warming to the point, "I'd very much like to see a bit of the country at the back of the house."

"I'd love to."

"Splendid."

"Right after breakfast, then?"

"Fine."

"I think walking's very bad for one," said Henry Brampton. "Marilyn used to think out the plots for her books when she went for long walks, and they were all perfectly appalling. Now she does it lying on a sofa. Naturally they're far spicier now. Pour me out another cup of coffee, Marilyn."

And the third very long pause was interrupted by the entrance of Edwin Carson. He had his arm linked in Raoul's, and Freddie Usher followed them into the room.

"Good morning, everyone," said Edwin Carson. "I hope you're all looking after yourselves?"

Everybody was.

"I've just been showing Raoul and Mr. Usher round the grounds. Trying to tell them which were calceolarias and which weren't... I'm afraid I don't know quite as much about my garden as I do about my other hobby."

"I think it is wonderful that you should know of any other thing when all your life is given to your jewels," said Raoul in her deep voice.

(And Jim, recognizing the look in Raoul's eyes, thought to himself: Heavens, another famous actress leaves stage sensation for Mrs. Bertram.)

"What annoys me, Carson," said Freddie Usher, "is the indecent behaviour of one of your guests."

The little man turned and screwed up his face at Freddie.

"What do you mean, Mr. Usher?" he asked.

"Late last night, when I was in no condition to say anything but 'all right, I give in'," said Freddie, "Lady Stone made a date with me. A very early date—before breakfast this morning, in fact.

We were going to have a nice little twelve-mile hike and she was going to tell me all about the aims and objects of the Society for the Prevention of Cruelty to Aged Organizers of Charity Bazaars, or some such title."

"And?..."

"And what happens? I rise at an hour quite three hours before my usual hour. I put on my stoutest shoes. I gird my knapsack on my loins, or wherever it is one girds these things. I am on the appointed spot at the appointed time. And here we are... not a moment earlier than ten-thirty... and no signs of Catherine Lady Stone. Still snorting upstairs in her bedroom, I suppose."

"Cries of 'shame'!" said Jim.

"Well, my dear Usher," said Edwin Carson, "I am afraid that I am somewhat to blame. I should have told you earlier... but then I did not know that Lady Stone and you were having this early morning rendezvous. I'm sorry to say that Lady Stone has had to return to London."

"Return to London?"

"Yes. She had a wire from town asking her to return immediately. In any other postal district but Adderly the wire would have been delivered last night... but here in Adderly telegrams are treated in the same leisurely manner as ordinary letters, and it was not delivered until the first post this morning. She left before eight; I gave her the use of my car."

"Then the Society for the Prevention of Cruelty to whatever-it-was will just have to struggle along without me?" said Freddie.

"I am afraid so. It is a great pity; I asked her if there was any likelihood of her being able to return to-day or to-morrow. But apparently Lady Stone's business will take a few days to transact... some last-minute changes in some of her charity affairs,

I understand. It's most unfortunate. A charming woman, Lady Stone. Most unfortunate…"

And Jim Henderson, as he drank his coffee, thought only of the white circle of light which had shone on the keyhole of Lady Stone's door not twelve hours previously. Of the hand which had slowly turned the key and opened the door so carefully. Of the visitor whom this "charming woman" had entertained at such an early hour of the morning.

"Most unfortunate, as you say, Mr. Carson," he said. "Now who's going to make money for me at bridge?"

XII

"THIS WAY," SAID MARY CARSON. LOOKING AT HER, JIM decided that she was even more attractive at midday than at midnight. Though, of course, the light in the landing had been none too good at midnight. She wore a simply cut costume of tweed which had (if one had the good fortune to be close enough to notice it) that faint, pleasant tang of peat which pronounces the material as genuine Harris. The collar and tie which made so many other women grimly efficient and businesslike, merely made Mary Carson a shade more attractive. The little hat suited her, too, though it was one of those slanting, coquettish affairs which look definitely ridiculous clinging for dear life to the side of most women's heads. Jim Henderson noticed all this as he followed her through the house and out into the back gardens of Thrackley. And found himself rather surprised at noticing such things; for to him usually women's dress was either "not bad" or "ghastly". More often the latter.

The garden at the back of the house was only a narrow strip of neatly planted vegetables and fruit bushes. Behind this the pine-trees reared themselves again all round the house, and there was only a narrow footpath winding itself through the trees to the gate which led to the fields outside. Jim noticed again how extraordinarily self-contained and aloof this house called Thrackley was: ringed in by these tall trees, and then again by this massive stone wall—quite fifteen feet high and with only two possible exits and entrances—the iron gates at the front and this tiny wooden door at the back. A very difficult house to enter and a much more difficult one to leave. He helped Mary Carson to lift back the heavy bolt on the door, and pulled the door open with an effort. And as they stepped out into the field which stretched itself away from the back of the house, a complete change seemed to take place in the atmosphere. A change for the better: decidedly so. Back once more to the ordinary bright shades of greens and blues, with the darkness of the house and its surrounds left for a while behind them. Mary Carson must have felt this way about it, too; she pulled the gate back into position and said: "Thank heavens!"

"Why do you say that?" Jim asked.

"Don't you feel the difference? Don't you feel how splendid it is to get out here into the open after being shut up?"

"It's certainly a bit brighter."

"Brighter? Do you know there are times when I'm so frightened in that house that I want to scream and rush away from it?"

"There's no law against screaming and rushing."

"And then I'm so frightened that I daren't do either."

"But—"

"Come on, Captain Henderson. Feel like climbing that hill over there? If we cross that field and the next one there's a short cut that'll bring us to the foot of the hill in half an hour."

"Splendid."

The long grass was still wet from its morning share of dew, and brushed damply against their legs as they walked through it. It was, Jim noticed for the first time, a glorious morning. Not a cloud in the sky (except for a little white fellow bumping contentedly about, low down on the horizon), and a keen breeze thrusting itself through each tree that it met.

"I hope you don't think that this walk is just an excuse to get an explanation out of you," said Jim.

"An explanation?"

"About last night, I mean."

"Oh, last night…" Mary Carson walked on for some minutes before she answered. "If it were just an excuse, I'm afraid you'd be disappointed. I don't think I'm going to do any explaining, Captain Henderson."

"Really? Then this is walking for walking's sake? Genuine hikery, in fact?"

"Don't look so peeved about it. I'd like to explain a whole lot of things, but I can't."

"May I ask why not?"

"Because I can't explain them to myself."

"A very excellent reason."

He helped her to negotiate a tumbledown stile which led into the next field.

"Suppose, then," he said, "that instead of explaining things you just tell me all about yourself and your life here. I can see that you're wanting to tell someone very much. And if you don't, what on earth are we going to talk about?"

"There's the weather and the government and the scenery and the wireless programmes and the latest murder."

"Thanks. I hear all about them from my landlady."

"Very well, Captain Henderson."

"And—I hate to stop you so early in your story—but the war is over and I am no longer a captain. And the name is Jim."

"Jim?"

"Short, if you really must know, for James. Just call me Jim, though, and possibly, when we get to the top of that hill, I'll be so short of breath that I'll have to call you Mary. Righto… Fire ahead."

"Where d'you want me to start? I'd much rather you asked questions and I answered them. Like an interview with a famous stage star, you know."

"Right. I came across Miss Carson in a corner of her beautiful old-world garden, nestling a dozen of her favourite Pomeranians in her attractive arms. And now, Miss Carson, how long have you been at Thrackley?"

"Just over a year. Before that I was abroad for nearly four years... 'finishing' is the polite name given to it, I think."

"I know. Living in dirty little *pensions* with people who insist on talking English when you want to learn French."

"Exactly. Then my father came to see me—he's always travelling about, you know—and said that he had bought this place in England and I was to go home and assist in the unveiling ceremony."

"Did you choose those etchings?"

"Yes. Do you like them?"

"They show great skill on the part of the etcher and greater taste on the part of the buyer. That sounds like a book-reviewer's sentence, but for all that it's the truth."

"Thanks. They cost four guineas for the lot."

"Business ability as well as taste. Quite remarkable."

"Mind where you're putting your feet."

"Thank you. Extraordinary how careless the cattle are round about here, isn't it. You're not getting on with the life story very fast. You paid your bill and madame of the *pensions* said 'Ta-ta, love,' or words to that effect, and you came back to England... and then?"

"Then I opened up Thrackley. I don't think I realized then how foul and lonely the place was; I suppose I was too busy. My father came down occasionally to see how I was getting on, but I was left very much with a free hand. Any amount of money to spend on the place, and my own ideas about furniture and wallpapers and so on… it was all very good fun."

"Any amount of money is always very good fun. Must we go right to the top of this damned hill?"

"You can see five counties from the top on a clear day."

"My favourite ambition. Come on, Mary."

"Short of breath already?"

"A little."

"Well, after I'd finished and the last of the plumbers had packed up, I was left alone here. At least, alone with Jacobson and another servant."

"I shouldn't imagine Jacobson would be the brightest of companions."

"He certainly wasn't. After a week or so the house got on my nerves, those wretched pine-trees got on my nerves, Jacobson got on my nerves—I felt I should go mad if I stayed at Thrackley a day longer."

"But why—damn this bracken!—why on earth did you stay?"

"My father had told me that I was to remain at Thrackley until he returned from abroad. And I hadn't any wish to have him return and find me away from the house. You don't know him as well as I do."

"Mr. Carson seems to have very well-developed ideas on the is-woman's-place-in-the-home question."

"He's… a little queer. Most people hate him, I know. And I don't blame them, I'm afraid. He trusts very few people and I think he wants to bring me up in the same way… meeting just the people he thinks fit for me to meet, and not coming into contact with anyone outside the selected few."

"I'm very glad I was selected."

"So am I, Capt—"

"Jim. Short, if you remember, for James."

"Sorry. That's why he gets so furious when he learns that I've sneaked out down to the village. I suppose he thinks I'll start telling the proprietrix of the village stores where his precious emeralds and things are hidden."

"Don't you think if we left this path and went over that way it wouldn't be quite so steep?"

"Perhaps you're right. Well, he came back to Thrackley about two months ago and told me he was going to live here for the next few years."

"And were you at home when he turned up?"

"Sitting in the lounge ready to welcome him. He'd had the decency to send a wire saying that he had arrived in England."

"And then?…"

"He pottered about for a week or so, and took down a picture or two that he didn't approve of, and altered the hanging of the lounge window curtains, and…"

"So far as I could see, the only mistake in an otherwise perfect house. I like my curtains straight up and down; not looped up with cords like the painted ones you see on a theatre proscenium."

"That's the way I had them… straight up and down. We're getting near the top now, Jim."

"Praise be to Allah for it. Go on, Mary."

"My father had some workmen in to do some alterations to his study and to the cellars under the house. That's where his collection of jewels is kept… in the cellars."

"Queer idea. Have you seen them?"

"Only once. When they were being arranged before being taken down to the cellars. They're absolutely marvellous—must be worth millions, I suppose. I've never been down to the cellars to see them shown off in their cases; as a matter of fact I wouldn't know how to get down if I tried. Only one person ever goes down there... that's Father."

"Rather a shame that such a wonderful collection should be kept for the enjoyment of one man."

"I don't think he enjoys them. Perhaps in a way he does... I think he's obsessed by them. He can't think of anything but jewels... his conversation is nothing but jewels... he must dream of jewels every night, I should think. Jewels, jewels, jewels... nothing else from morning till night! Do you wonder I gave my one and only string of Ciro pearls to the housekeeper of the *pension* before I left France?"

They had reached the summit of the hill. The downs stretched themselves out on all sides, and far below the house called Thrackley showed itself as a tiny island of dark green and grey. Its compactness and aloofness seemed even more evident when you gazed on it from this point. A secure little stronghold, closed in by that tall stone wall... and in that stronghold in the dip of these hills lay millions of pounds' worth of precious stones. Sparkling things for which the world's dealers and collectors would fight each other and squander their fortunes, which lovely women would covet and rich men wish they could afford to give them... and all in this quiet country house in Surrey, for one man alone to gloat over.

"We'll have a rest before we go down, shall we?" said Mary Carson.

"A very sensible suggestion."

They lay back on the soft grass and allowed the sun to beat down on their faces.

"Cigarette?" said Jim.

"Thanks. Another of the things to which my father has a rooted objection."

"Don't you ever think of clearing out? Running away from it all, I mean? Life down there isn't all raspberries and cream from all accounts. I should have knotted the sheets and scaled the wall of the north wing long before now."

"You don't know how near I've been to doing it... many a time before now."

"Then why?..."

"I don't think you'd understand. For one thing, even if I did wish to get out of it all... it would be a mighty difficult thing to arrange. Look at that house down there..."

Jim looked down at Thrackley and thought of Freddie Usher's plan of vanishing in the early hours of the morning back to London. Yes, he thought: a mighty difficult thing to arrange. Just as well Raoul had been standing at the front door when their car rolled up the drive.

"And I should hate to back out on Father. I know he's got his faults—more than his share, probably—but he's been marvellously good to me. It wouldn't seem right."

"I understand."

"I don't think you do."

"What do you mean?"

"I hadn't meant to tell you this, Jim, but as you've made me tell you so much I might as well finish the story."

"If I've made you tell anything you didn't want to... I'm sorry, Mary."

"You haven't. I've been wanting to talk to someone for months. Do you know I looked over each of my father's guests as soon as they arrived at Thrackley—just in the hope that there would be one with whom I could have a chat like this?"

"What a thrill you must have had when you saw me."

"Sorry—I was still massaging my bike when you arrived."

"Fate all over. Well…"

"Edwin Carson isn't my real father."

Jim Henderson stopped his blowing of small smoke-rings through large smoke-rings. It was one of his most accomplished parlour tricks, but rather more successful in the bar at Graham's than on the top of a hill like this. He turned and stared at Mary.

"Both my parents died when I was young. Edwin Carson was a great friend of my mother… rather too great a friend, I think… he took care of me and got a nurse and clothed me and sent me to school and then to the Continent. He hasn't always been a rich man… it must have meant a good deal of sacrifice for him to do all that he has done for me. Somehow I couldn't just leave him after that."

"I see."

They threw their cigarette-stumps away and started the walk down the hill again.

"I'm terribly glad that Edwin Carson isn't your real father," said Jim.

"Why?"

"I don't really know. But up to now it's been puzzling me to understand how such a lovely daughter could have such a… well, he's not exactly copperplate, is he?"

"Far from it."

"And why did he invite all this delightful collection of London's Bright, if Scarcely Young, Things down to Thrackley this weekend?"

"I think perhaps I'm responsible. He'd realized that I hated Thrackley, and that the loneliness of it was getting on my nerves… naturally he thought of you people to cheer me up."

"Good Lord! Imagine anyone being cheered by Lady Stone and the Bramptons!"

"The choice of the guests was his, not mine."

"And why d'you think he hit on us specimens? Did he prod the telephone directory with a pin and send out invitations to wherever it landed?"

"Not exactly. He's known all of you slightly at one time or another. And have you noticed one thing that you all have in common?"

"Appetites?"

"And jewellery. The same old obsession. Lady Stone with her rubies, the Brampton girl with that rope of pearls, Raoul with her everything. Even Mr. Usher was asked to bring the Usher diamonds with him."

"You mean?…"

"He wants to examine them all. Don't you see that his whole life is devoted to jewels and the study of jewels… he could see no point in asking people down to Thrackley unless they were going to give him some new specimens to stare at and to compare with his own."

Jim smiled. She did not mean what he had meant.

"And would you mind telling me," he asked, "why I was included in this glittering array? Taking care, of course, not to put your foot in what I nearly put my foot in on the outward journey."

"I haven't the slightest idea why you were invited."

"Thanks very much. Could it have been my charm, do you think? Or my looks? Or my little impressions of Clara Butt and the Four Marx Brothers, without which no house-party can truly be called a complete success?"

"Perhaps he thought Mr. Usher wouldn't come without you."

"An unkind thought. But probably quite true. Careful over this stile."

They reached the high wall surrounding Thrackley and opened the little gate, and were swallowed once more in the atmosphere of the place. They threaded their way along the little footpath through the trees, and out into the strip of garden. Instead of going into the house at the back, they walked round the side to enter by the front door. The swing doors of the garage were standing open, and a man in dark blue overalls was leaning over the bonnet of the Lagonda inside. Jim stopped and stared at the man... somewhere, at some time or other, he had seen that face before... now where the devil?... The man in the overalls bent back and unscrewed the two catches which held the bonnet of the car down. As he lifted the bonnet up and turned to examine the engine, Jim got a fuller view of his face. No doubt about it... but where?...

"What's the matter, Jim?" cried Mary Carson. "Want to have a look at the car? It's a beauty."

And at that moment Jim remembered. Remembered a certain morning many years ago, when he and another bright spirit had lathered the chair at the desk where Mr. James Lockhart, M.A., usually sat. Lathered it well and truly with a plentiful supply of soft soap. He remembered, too, that the behinds of himself and of that kindred spirit had been lathered just as efficiently in return. But not with soft soap.

"Ronnie Hempson!" he said.

And the man called Burroughs leapt back from the car he was examining, and the spanner which he held in his hand fell with a crash on the floor of the garage.

XIII

"BEG PARDON, SIR?" SAID THE MAN CALLED BURROUGHS. Jim looked at him. The same thin face, the same jet-black hair and eyelashes, the same slightly hollowed cheeks beneath the high cheek-bones. But the chauffeur had picked up his spanner and was looking at him now without the slightest recognition.

"I'm sorry," said Jim. "Your face reminded me of someone I used to know."

"I used to drive a taxi in London, sir," said the chauffeur. "Maybe you were a fare of mine once."

"Perhaps," said Jim. "There was one delightful fellow who put me safely to bye-bye after a rather hectic night at a Three Arts Ball. D'you think that might have been you?"

"Couldn't say, sir." The chauffeur leaned back over the engine of the car, and then turned his head round to Jim. "Difficult kind of thing to remember, sir," he said. "I was always seeing young gentlemen home to bed."

And the man called Burroughs gave an almost imperceptible flicker of his right eyelid. Almost imperceptible, but a perfectly good wink all the same.

"Come on, Jim," said Mary Carson. "I'm sure it's past lunch time. I'm simply ravenous." And at that precise moment Jacobson the butler lifted the padded drumstick and dealt a hefty blow on the huge brass gong which hung in the hall of Thrackley. Lunch was the only meal at which the gong was used, for then the guests were scattered all over the place (the Bramptons sprawling over the lounge sofas, Raoul in her bedroom varnishing her finger-nails,

Jim and Mary out in the garage, Freddie Usher linked to Edwin Carson's arm and hearing all about the peculiar grouping of the crown jewels of Abyssinia) and no casual intimation that lunch was served would have had the slightest effect. So Jacobson dealt another blow at the gong, and another, and a fourth for luck, and disappeared to the kitchen with the feeling that if that didn't fetch them nothing would, and to hell with them, anyway. And the Bramptons placed their markers in their books, and stretched themselves, and reached the dining-room a clear two minutes before anyone else, and whiled away those minutes by breaking their bread rolls and making rather shapeless ducks out of their serviettes. And Raoul gave a last rub to her finger-nails, and pulled her hair back to its usual anchorage behind her ears, and sailed from the room and down the stairs and hoped devoutly that the repulsive Mr. Carson would not paw at her under the tablecloth at this meal as he had done at the others. And Jim and Mary dashed to their bedrooms, and brushed their hair and washed their faces and put on dry stockings in place of those which had been soaked by their walk, and arrived at the table slightly out of breath and just in time for the soup. And the repulsive Mr. Carson broke off in mid-sentence (just when he had reached the point of his argument about the weight of the three centre diamonds in the Emperor's crown) and said: "Ah, lunch, my dear Usher. Come along now, and you shall sit next to me so that we can continue our little talk." And Freddie Usher said, "My God!" and reached the lunch-table in a very bad temper.

But by the time the chicken and French salad had arrived, Edwin Carson had forgotten all about Freddie and the Emperor, and had transferred all his attentions to Raoul. He hoped that the rest of the company would help themselves, and then he showered Raoul with peppers and salts and mustards and salad creams and second glasses of the excellent white wine and sauces and sugar and cream and a cigarette. And when Raoul's hand slipped under the table, he sent his own down to keep it company, and after a little fumbling his fingers touched it and he squeezed it very slightly. And Raoul looked up over the rim of her wineglass and smiled at him as only Raoul (fortunately, perhaps) can smile. Nice girl, he thought. Exceptionally nice girl. Most unfortunate that she had to return for this matinée of hers on Monday... now why could not this indisposition be continued for a little while? Charming to have her here alone after the others had gone... he might even tell Mary to take a few days' holiday in town, and be left quite alone with Raoul. The thought of it made him squeeze a little harder than before, and Raoul slid her hand discreetly away from his. But she smiled again... with her eyes as well as her mouth... Beautiful eyes... oh, yes, a remarkably nice girl. Must see if it couldn't be arranged.

Jim was in the middle of a very light and airy pineapple *soufflé* when the door opened and Jacobson appeared. At the head of the table, Edwin Carson managed to take his eyes from Raoul's shoulders and to snap out a "Well, Jacobson?"

"A telegram, sir," said the butler. "For Mr. Henderson."

Jim stopped his spoonful of *soufflé* half-way on its journey to his mouth and said: "For me?" Now, who on earth, he wondered, could be sending him a telegram? A month or so earlier, perhaps, and he could have understood it; but now the Derby was over and the Irish Sweep had been won by some wretched employee in a tinned fruit store in Massachusetts, U.S.A. Was it Mrs. Bertram, then?... having read in four of her morning papers that cold and showery weather was expected in all parts, and wishing to know if he had packed his extra under-flannels? And then he remembered:

Freddie Usher! Freddie, evidently bored with Thrackley, had sent this telegram calling him back to town. Of course, that was it… great-aunt Maria seriously ill… urgent call to bedside… and Freddie (ever ready to help a friend in trouble) would nobly give up his weekend and drive him back to town. Quite so. But somehow Jim didn't feel as though he wanted to leave Thrackley in such a hurry. He was beginning to get quite fond of the old place. This morning, for instance, had really been very enjoyable. The blazes with great-aunt Maria, then! He took the telegram from Jacobson and slit the brown envelope open.

"Congratulations good memory try see me alone this afternoon working in garage all day. Hempson," he read.

"Nothing wrong, I hope?" said Edwin Carson.

"No… nothing, thanks," said Jim. "I… I had some friends coming to stay with me next week—they said they'd wire me here and tell me what day they were coming."

"I see," said Edwin Carson.

"Anyone I know?" asked Freddie Usher.

"The Thompsons. No, I don't think you know them, Freddie."

"Well, well, never mind that." Edwin Carson did his smiling act, and patted his lips with his serviette. "For a moment I was afraid it was going to be another of my guests summoned back to London. Like poor, dear Lady Stone. And then I should have thought: I am not looking after my guests, and they are getting their friends in town to help them escape from this dull old place and this dull old man."

"My dear Mr. Carson," said Freddie, "what an absurd idea!"

"Thank you, Mr. Usher, thank you. And now shall we have our coffee out on the veranda? It tastes a great deal better when the flavour of the garden is added to it."

And Edwin Carson pushed back his chair and took Raoul's arm and led his guests out to the painted wooden seats on the veranda of the house. He attended to Raoul's coffee himself, snatching the cup from Jacobson and leering at her as he added cream and sugar. The others were forgotten; and Edwin Carson turned his back on the Bramptons and asked Raoul what she would like to do this afternoon? To laze, or to walk? Or a run in the new car—the very expensive new car, shining in silver and navy, and guilty of seventy-five miles an hour without raising its voice above its normal purr—a run through Surrey, into Kent, with tea somewhere, and home again in the cool of the evening just in time to change for dinner? How did that appeal to Raoul, eh? And Jim Henderson, keeping pace with Marilyn Brampton's conversation and balancing his tiny coffee cup on his large knee and listening to Edwin Carson's mutterings—doing all this at the same time, heard that it appealed to Raoul very much. In about three-quarters of an hour, then? Allowing one's lunch to become thoroughly settled... splendid... he would tell Burroughs to have the car brought round.

Jim laid his cup on the veranda floor. If old man Carson was taking Raoul into the wide open spaces for the afternoon, that meant that now was his only chance of getting a word with Ronnie Hempson. Alias, of course, Burroughs, the chauffeur. Unless Carson drove the car himself and did not require his chauffeur's services. He thought it highly probable that Edwin Carson would enjoy his afternoon with Raoul to a much greater extent if their view were unspoiled by the chauffeur occupying the driving seat. Better not to take any chances, though; for if Edwin Carson did not drive the car, then Burroughs and / or Hempson would be ungetatable until late that night.

"Care for a strenuous single, Freddie?" he said.

"I beg your pardon?" said Freddie.

"A nice little game of tennis? Something will have to be done about this corpulence question, you know. It's really disgusting."

"But, my good man," said Freddie, "tennis—singles tennis, especially—following immediately on a lunch like that is apt to have the most appalling effects on a fellow's constitution. And as for corpulence—"

"Shut up, you blithering fool... do what you're told," said Jim from the corner of his mouth.

"Well, perhaps I am getting a little... yes, now that I look at it that way, I'm sure I am," said Freddie. "Tennis, did you say? What could be sweeter? Remember that time I gave you thirty and beat you six-love, six-one?"

"Eighteen seventy-two, wasn't it?" said Jim. "Or was it seventy-three? Anyway, come on and I'll see if your backhand is still as lousy as ever."

"Lead me," said Freddie, "to the baseline."

They left the veranda and entered the lounge.

"What the blazes," asked Freddie, "do you mean by dragging me from a comfortable chair to hit a nasty little ball with a nasty little racket?"

"Idiot. Remember a chap called Ronnie Hempson?"

"Hempson... I don't think so. Why?"

"Come on, man—think, if you can still do such a thing. Ronnie Hempson... can't you remember a certain match against Oundle when a bloke of that name went in second last man and made seventy odd runs in about twenty minutes?"

"Good God, yes... Ronnie Hempson!"

"Light has dawned in the valley of darkness. Shared a study with me in my second last year at school. Gave a celebrated performance as Mad Margaret in the school operatic's production of *Ruddigore*. Marred only by the fact that his knickers came down in the finale of the second act. Helped me lather old Lockjaw's desk, and landed us in for twelve of the best through keeping the packet of soft soap in his desk. A brilliant scholastic career, in fact."

"All right, all right. I've got him now. Tall, dark specimen."

"Had an aunt who sent him cherry cake once a fortnight."

"That's right. Enormously popular chap—once a fortnight. What about him?"

"He's here."

"Here. At Thrackley?"

"Under this very roof. His name's Burroughs, and he's Edwin Carson's chauffeur."

"Jim, the heat has claimed you as its latest victim. Ronnie Hempson's name is... let me see, now... yes, Ronnie Hempson. And he left school to go into Sandhurst and probably at this very moment he's quelling a rebellion and generally helping to keep the old flag flying in some outpost of Empire. Why, then, this babbling of Burroughs and chauffeurs and so on?"

"Don't talk, Freddie. It gives you away. Just keep quiet and follow me."

They left the house by the French windows which led from one of the side rooms out to the garden. In a minute or so they had reached the garage. The main doors were closed, but a smaller door had been made in them and this stood slightly ajar. Jim pushed it open and stepped into the garage, followed by Freddie. Inside everything was in darkness; there appeared to be no one in the building. The silvered bonnet of the big car could just be noticed shining through the darkness. Jim was about to turn back through the little door when a voice from the back of the garage said: "Shut that door behind you."

Jim felt his way to the door and closed it. The Yale lock clicked into its position, and the garage was now in complete darkness. And then another click came from the back of the building, and the lights from three electric bulbs glared down on them. The man called Burroughs stepped out from behind the car. "Well, well, well," he said. "And who'd have thought of meeting Jim Henderson here?"

"Hempson... it was you, then."

"Me all right."

"This is Freddie Usher... remember him at school? He was the same year as us. But we moved in different circles to him, of course. He was in Tower House, poor fellow."

"Usher... I remember now. Repulsive little rat, always in a dirty collar, highest score in inter-house matches—four."

"That's the chap. The four were really leg-byes, by the way."

"Naturally. How are you, Usher?"

"A bit bewildered, but otherwise all right." They shook hands, and sat on the running-board of the Lagonda.

"Now then, Hempson my lad," said Jim, "we've not got much time for reminiscencing on the old days... Carson's going to get you to bring out the bus in about half an hour. So let's get down to brass tacks."

"In other words," said Freddie, "what are you doing at Thrackley, and why? Last thing I heard of you was that you had passed seventh out of Sandhurst and were off to Chochin-China or Nijni-Novgorod or some such spot to teach the natives how to form fours."

"And now I'm a chauffeur to a crook," said Ronnie Hempson. "Have a cigarette?"

"Thanks."

"You, Usher?"

"Thanks."

"Careful not to drop the match into that petrol tank. I want to get a chance of explaining things."

"There it is safely out, then. Go ahead."

"I gave up the army four years ago. You need a good deal of spare cash to enjoy the army, and I hadn't quite enough. So I turned my undoubted talents to the police force."

"You… a bobby?"

"Mean to say I've been going in danger of having my licence suspended through you and your little stop-watch?"

"For a short while. I was lucky enough to get on fairly well. And at the present time I'm connected—that's the official way of describing it—to the Criminal Investigation Department of Scotland Yard. Which means that I do what someone at Scotland Yard tells me, and never discuss the matter with old school friends."

"Excuse the density," said Jim, "but from the general look of things I should have said that you were a chauffeur to a country gentleman. Not an attachment to the C.I.D."

"I'm a chauffeur, certainly. Not a very good one. But then Carson isn't a very good gentleman. No… I'm here to watch Mr. Carson. To see that he doesn't get into any trouble. To get him into further trouble if he does."

"How d'you manage to get the job?"

"You should see the references that the Yard supplied me with. I'd have got a job at Buckingham Palace with them."

"And what exactly is your job here? Apart from chauffeuring, I mean?" said Jim.

"I've told you. Keep an eye on Edwin Carson. Do you know anything about your host?"

"Not very much. He has an excellent wine-cellar, apparently, and a very charming daughter, and he dabbles in jewels, I believe. That's about all."

"You're right about the daughter. Stone cold with the other two, though. He doesn't dabble... he steals."

"Steals? Good Lord!"

"And he hasn't a wine-cellar... he has a jewel-cellar."

"So his daughter told me this morning."

"She did, did she? She didn't tell you that the reason why Edwin Carson keeps his collection of jewels tucked away in a cellar is that if they were brought out into the open air and shown off to the public, he'd be arrested within an hour?"

"She certainly didn't. But then I've only known her for about twenty-four hours."

"You've been doing fairly well in the twenty-four, though," said Freddie Usher.

"I can't help my sex-appeal, can I? But how d'you know all this about Carson? What exactly have you against him?"

"Nothing definite. But the Yard has had its eye on him for the last two years or so. Before then, so far as is known, Edwin Carson was a perfectly genuine collector of precious stones."

"And since then?"

"Since then... well, the Maharajah of Ralputali discovered a few months ago that the principal stone in a priceless setting of diamonds had been replaced by a marvellously cunning imitation. Three months before, Edwin Carson had been a guest at the Maharajah's palace in India. When the Countess of Bemersly had to sell all her jewels a short time ago, poor old soul, it was found

that the stones in a tiara were practically worthless. A year previ-
ous to the sale they'd been valued at a quarter of a million pounds.
Six months previous to the sale Edwin Carson stayed at Bemersly
Castle for a fortnight's shooting. And so on."

"If that's all you're going on," said Freddie Usher, "I don't think
it's much."

"It's not all. It—"

A bell rang shrilly from the back of the garage.

"That's Carson. Keep quiet while I'm speaking to him."

Ronnie Hempson crossed to the bench which ran along the back
wall of the building, and lifted the telephone-receiver from its hook.

"Yes?" he said. "Yes, sir… Burroughs speaking… yes… right, sir…
at three o'clock, sir… very good, sir… will you want me, sir?… you'll
drive yourself… all right, sir… I'll have it round ready for you…"

He put back the receiver and turned to Jim and Freddie.

"The dear old boss," he said. "Going for a run this afternoon
and won't be requiring my services. Which of the women is it?"

"Raoul… the dancer from the Alhambra. Carson's running
strong in that direction."

"Poor girl. Do you know why she's here? Because she's plastered
with good jewellery given to her by bad men. Do you know why
the Brampton girl's here? Same reason. And you, comrade Usher,
of Tower House? Because the Usher heirlooms have fallen into
your unworthy hands."

"And what have the Usher heirlooms got to do with Edwin
Carson?" demanded Freddie.

"A hell of a lot. There's a lot of damned valuable jewellery in
this house this weekend—quite apart from the wine-cellarful—and
I shouldn't be surprised if some of it stayed at Thrackley after its
owners leave."

"How on earth?..."

"Ask the Maharajah of wherever-it-was and the Countess of Bemersly. They won't know, but there's no harm in asking them."

Ronnie Hempson looked at the watch on his wrist.

"I'll have to be getting the car ready," he said. "Are you two game for a little expedition to-night?"

"As long as you keep it clean," said Freddie.

"I've never had a chance to see those damned cellars of Carson's. It's hopeless trying to get down to them single-handed—someone would have to keep a look-out. I don't see why you two shouldn't assist the C.I.D. in looking into Edwin Carson's affairs."

"What d'you mean?"

"If I could see one of the jewels that have disappeared in the last few years down in those cellars, I'd have the local constabulary up in full force—all two of them—and arrest Edwin Carson on the spot."

"A nice finish to our weekend party."

"Well, what about it? To-night, after you're all safely tucked up in bed—you can meet me in the hall and we'll have a shot at seeing just what the old boy has down there."

"Do you know how to get down?"

"Haven't the foggiest. Which makes it all the more interesting."

"Of course."

"I shall wear my chamois gloves," said Freddie. "Like they do on the films."

"Splendid. Two o'clock, say, if the coast's clear."

"Two o'clock. In the hall."

"Righto."

"Remember that time we staged a cabaret in 'D' dormitory?"

"Yes. This won't be quite so dangerous. Two a.m., then."

"We'll be there..."

And Edwin Carson, who had gone down to the cool of his cellars and lit a cigarette and thought of his afternoon (and why not his evening, for that matter) with Raoul, and phoned Burroughs to get the car ready, and—just for idle curiosity—had pulled back the switch marked "Garage" and put on the padded earphones, and sworn as he listened... Edwin Carson flicked back the switch into its socket and jabbed the stump of his cigarette viciously on the edge of the desk until the glow left the ash.

Then he rose from his chair and congratulated himself doubly. Congratulated himself on having made Burroughs install this admirable system of microphones all over the house. Congratulated himself even more on having himself installed a microphone in the garage where his trusted chauffeur worked. A precaution which, it seemed, had been well worth the trouble.

He crossed the stone floor of the cellar and closed the doors of the lift behind him. And now... Raoul.

XIV

EDWIN CARSON GAVE HIS ARM TO RAOUL, AND SETTLED HER comfortably in the seat beside his own, and tucked the cushion in at her back, and patted a rug of thick fur around her two very shapely legs. It gave him rather a thrill as his fingers touched the smooth silk of her stockings, and he took a great deal longer than was necessary to arrange the rug. Then he asked, three times: "Now, you're sure you're comfortable, my dear?" and when he was satisfied on this point he gave a final pat to the folds of the rug, and closed the door carefully, and scampered round the car's bonnet and into his own seat. He noted with a grunt of pleasure that Raoul's arm brushed against his own as he reached for the self-starter; for he had been just a little afraid that in a big car such as this there would be an unpleasant space between them. But no... the persons who had had the designing of the car to do had planned their spacing perfectly. A pleasant proximity, with no crushing or pressing, but with great possibilities. After a few miles or so, it was only a matter of reaching his left arm long the top of the front seat, and he would have the exquisite Raoul in his arms. No doubt at all, he felt, that this was going to be a wholly delightful outing.

The car swung over the nose of the hill and down into Adderly and through the twistings of Adderly's street. And the few villagers who were about at the time (very few indeed, for taking forty or so winks with a handkerchief over one's face was an almost universal custom in Adderly's afternoons) blinked at the immaculate blue saloon as it passed them, and decided that that was that there Carson bloke from the big house or (if not) then they were

Dutchmen, and hurried in to their various homes to waken their various relatives and tell them the news. And, said the few who saw, not half a bad-looking bit of stuff sitting in front with the old geyser, and no mistake. (Meaning, of course, when they said that, a very good-looking bit of stuff and no mistake.) And the car left Adderly behind it, having so rudely upset its siesta, and accelerated itself as the roads grew wider and the surface of them grew less erratic. The man in the driving-seat turned to the lady beside him, and asked for what was now either the ninth or tenth time if she was sure she was comfortable. He showed her how to press the silver-plated contraption at her elbow to make it present a very expensive specimen of Turkish cigarette. Or, he explained, an equally expensive Virginian if she pressed the little switch this way instead of that. He slowed the car down, and lit a match for the Turkish specimen which she chose, and left the steering-wheel to manage as best it could by itself while he held the match close to her face. And now would she like the roof open? She would. Then there we are... and the sun poured into the car, and the breeze swept over the windscreen and down into their faces, and Raoul took off her absurd half-hat and allowed the wind to play havoc with her hair. Now was she sure that wasn't too much of a draught for her? For she had only to say the word, and he would close the roof again. But no, it was not too much of a draught. Unless, of course, he himself would like it shut. "Not at all, my dear Raoul," said Edwin Carson. "Not at all. Just whatever you say, my dear. To-day, my dear, it is your wish—not mine." And Edwin Carson took his hand once more from the steering-wheel, and gave a series of little pats to Raoul's gloved hands, and Raoul, when the patting was finished, slid her hands under the rug and kept them there. And in this delightful atmosphere the needle of the car's speedometer hovered around the figure sixty, and (with one or two unavoidable lapses when cattle loomed large on the roadway) remained there or thereabouts for nearly two hours.

At the end of that time the car had the very good sense to run out of petrol just opposite those red and yellow and blue and green pumps which are the only drawback to that otherwise excellent establishment, the Haversack Inn at Higher Yelmer. The Haversack Inn (which was the Fisherman's Arms before all this epidemic of khaki shorts and Zipp-fastened shirts and studded boots broke out) is run by one Samuel Fish and his wife Martha. And a very good job they make of the running of it. They will receive their "reggellers" (as Mr. Fish terms those who have been more than once to the Haversack) as old friends, and they will receive their first-timers with a pleasant insinuation that in next to no time (or, at any rate, before the end of the month) they too will be "reggellers". And they set you down in a spotlessly clean parlour, and before you have had time to examine the oleograph of Queen Victoria or the sampler which hangs underneath it (reading "ABCDEFGH Blessed are the Pure in Heart for they shall see God IJKLMNOPQ") Mrs. Fish's face will appear round the door and suggest that if you will be so good as to step along to the back-parlour, there's as nice a tea as ever you saw all laid out and waiting. And that if there's anything else you fancy, just give the bell a push and they will see what they can do. Within the last few years, since the words "Fisherman's Arms" were painted out of the sign over the front door and "Haversack Inn" substituted, and the salmon at the bottom of the sign transformed into a rucksack, the inn has altered a little in character. The petrol pumps, perhaps, were the beginning of it; and there is more grape-fruit than por-ridge eaten at breakfast now; and the number of couples bearing the name of either Smith or Jones who have signed the visitors' book is quite remarkable. But you can still get an admirable tea of freshly-caught trout and home-made bread and scones and cake and jam for the sum of one shilling and sixpence. Which was only one of the reasons why Edwin Carson did not fill up the tank of his car and proceed on his way.

Instead of doing which, he led Raoul from the car through the Haversack's front door, and was met by Samuel (with Martha hovering in the background, the taps of her shining gas stove turned on in readiness for the order) and slipped Raoul's coat from her shoulders and followed Samuel into the front-parlour. And ordered two gin-and-gingers immediately and two of Mrs. Fish's special omelettes in, say, half an hour. And Mr. Fish nodded his head vigorously, and rubbed his hands over each other, and disappeared backwards from the parlour, remarking how nice it was to see Mr. Carson again after all these years and that there was *Punch* and the *Sporting and Dramatic* on the sofa, and that if Mr. Carson or the young lady wanted anything else they had only to ring the bell. Over there, sir, to the left of the mantelpiece. And with a final nod and a last rub, Mr. Fish's head vanished round the edge of the door, and he scuttled off to the kitchen and said to his wife: "It's that stingy old twister, Carson, with a furren-looking kind of a wench. Omelettes, they want. In arfanour." And Mrs. Fish, who had already started on the usual tea of eggs and bacon, said "Hell!" and turned off her gas jets.

When the gin-and-gingers arrived, Edwin Carson lifted his glass and said: "To you, my dear."

"You're very kind to me, Mr. Carson," said Raoul. "Why do you... how is it that you put it?... leave all the other ones and pay so much attention to me, eh?"

"Because you're different from the others, my dear." (Things, thought Edwin Carson, were panning out excellently.) "Very different. They're all... ordinary. Terribly ordinary, compared with you. And you're alone here... you don't know people, you don't understand our English ways—they're very difficult things to understand... you need someone to look after you, Raoul."

"You think so?"

"I'm sure of it."

"Always I have looked after myself. And very well, too."

Edwin Carson sipped his drink and stared at her.

"Never been in love, Raoul?"

"What do you call being in love, eh? I dare not say that I have been so... in England it may mean something so different from in other countries. You understand?"

"But... you've had affairs? Love affairs, I mean? Flirtations?..."

"I am on the stage. Silly boys, they come and give me flowers and rides in their big motorcars and give me great big dinners and good wines. Because, I suppose, I am on the stage."

"Just the sort of things I'm doing to you, eh?"

"No... you are different."

Edwin Carson edged a little farther along the sofa. He took Raoul's empty glass from her hand, and then took her empty hand in his. He was different, was he? Splendid, perfectly splendid...

"How am I different, Raoul?" he asked.

"You? You are old."

Not so perfectly splendid.

"Too old?" he asked her again.

"No, no, no... just—just old. The others, they are too young. You understand?"

"Raoul, I've got a plan. For to-night."

"Yes?"

"After we've had tea here, we'll motor into town... let's see, we could be in by seven or thereabouts... dinner somewhere, and then a show. And then back here... my friend, the innkeeper, will have a supper ready for us. Suppers are his speciality."

"But me—I am supposed to be... indisposed, that is the word they call it, yes? I must not be seen in London."

"We can go to the show late and come out early. You won't be recognized."

"But your guests? What will they think?"

"I will telephone them and tell them what to think."

"But—"

"But, my dear, is such a silly little word."

"I suppose it is."

Splendid again.

He crossed to the door of the parlour, and went out to the hall and closeted himself in the office where Mrs. Fish wrote out her bills and Mr. Fish kept his keys and where a rather ancient type of telephone jutted from the wall. He asked for "Adderly 7" and strummed with the tips of his fingers on Mr. Fish's desk as he waited for the reply.

When the phone rang in the lounge of Thrackley, Jim Henderson was on the point of lifting a cigarette from the table on which the telephone stood. He lifted instead the receiver and said "Hullo." Yes, this was Thrackley. Henderson speaking. Oh, it was you, was it, you old crook? What was that? A tragedy? Raoul had unfortunately met her manager in London... he had taken her into town for a drive... and the poor girl had to appear at the evening performance of *Soft Sugar*. Really? So, of course, Mr. Carson had had to offer to stay in town until the end of the performance, and drive Raoul back to

Thrackley. What else, after all, could he do? A confounded nuisance,
though, and would Mr. Henderson be so very good as to convey
his apologies to the other members of the house-party? Really very
annoying to have to leave them on their own for so long, but there
it was, and what could he do? Exactly, said Jim. He could do nothing, said Jim. And, added Jim, *Soft Sugar*, from all accounts, was a
damned good show. So he would try and be back in Thrackley as
soon as ever he could, and they must all try to amuse themselves
as best they could. And would he tell Mary of this unfortunate
happening? Then she would be able to give all the directions for
dinner, and so on. Thank you very much indeed. It really was most
lamentable, and Raoul, poor girl, was most distressed at having to
play in the show. But there, these managers. Quite, said Jim. Expect
you both back about one o'clock, then? Right… good-bye.

"The dirty old devil," said Jim as he replaced the receiver.

"I beg your pardon?" said Freddie Usher.

"That was Carson. He took Raoul up to town for a run, and
they've bumped into her manager or someone, and her indisposition has had to have a hasty cure and she's got to play in the show
to-night."

"Good. We'll go up and see it."

"We'll do no such thing. This is the chance of a lifetime. We'll
have the whole night—until about one in the morning, at any
rate—to look into old man Carson's affairs. No need to wait until
two a.m. now."

"Of course. I was forgetting that."

"You would. I'm going to find comrade Hempson and tell him
the glad tidings."

And between five and six hours later, in the back-parlour of the
Haversack Inn at Higher Yelmer, Mr. Edwin Carson held Raoul

very tightly in his arms, and his thin, bloodless lips pressed down on Raoul's dark painted lips, and his hands gripped at Raoul's dress until it was crumpled and stained. And then Raoul pushed her body away from this man, who had suddenly become a great deal older and uglier and more repellent than ever she had noticed him to be before, and she stared at him for an instant, and then said: "We will go back to your home, please, at once, you understand?" And a very sulky Mr. Carson pressed the self-starter of a very sulky car, and Mr. Samuel Fish and his wife, Martha, were left with a supper of cold salmon and salad and pineapple fritters and a magnum of champagne standing untouched on the table of their back-parlour, and ended their day by eating and drinking the lot of it themselves. And the car hummed along the trafficless roads, and neither of the two people in the front seat spoke as it hummed. They were within a mile of the village of Adderly when three men met in the hall of Thrackley and set out (with socks over their slippers and electric torches in their hands) on a little expedition. The expedition was progressing very favourably when Mr. Edwin Carson, still swearing inwardly, pressed his foot on the accelerator as he reached the summit of the hill which dipped down to Thrackley.

XV

JACOBSON, SLIGHTLY DRUNK, WAS SITTING ON HIS BED, CLAD in a pair of unnecessarily thick flannel pyjamas and reading the sporting page of the *Daily Observer* when Burroughs opened the door of his bedroom.

"What the hell d'you want at this time of night?" asked Jacobson.

"Have you got the spare bunch of keys, Jacobson? I've left my watch in the garage."

"Why not go on leaving it there?"

"And rely on you waking me up in the morning? No fear. Anyway, I'll have to open up the garage for the boss coming home."

"He won't be home to-night," said Jacobson, launching an attack on his toe-nails with a large pair of scissors.

"Why not? He phoned, didn't he? Said he'd be back about one o'clock."

"When you've known Carson as long as I have," said Jacobson, "you'll know that if he goes out with a bird he don't come back the same night. It's an old Carson custom. Got a pair of sharp scissors on you? These is as blunt as hell."

"Sorry. Get you a pair from the kitchen, if you like."

"Doesn't matter. I wish to blazes there was some women servants in this ruddy house. Wouldn't need to keep cutting my toe-nails if there was someone to darn my socks."

"That's so. What about that key?"

"Over there, on the dressing-table. Bring it back, mind—boss said I wasn't to give those keys to nobody. Go on, take the whole damned bunch."

Burroughs, the chauffeur, took the whole damned bunch. He said "Good night" politely enough to Jacobson and received no reply, for the butler had passed from his manicuring operations to the inspection of a coming corn on the big toe of his left foot. So Burroughs slammed the door behind him, and in the same movement as the slamming of the door he inserted what he devoutly prayed to be the right key in the lock of Jacobson's door, and turned it quietly to the right. Inside the room the butler pulled the sheets up over his body and resumed his reading of April Shower's chance in the 3.15 at Bogside to-morrow. The boss might be out with what Jacobson referred to as a bird, that damned idiot Burroughs might choose to spend the night looking for watches in garages, the rest of Edwin Carson's guests might ring for bath salts or hot water bottles or whiskies-and-sodas until they were puce in the face... Jacobson was comfortably installed in his bed and had no intention of leaving that bed. Even if he had had any intentions of the kind, he could scarcely have carried them out. For in the passage outside, Burroughs, the chauffeur, was slowly extracting what had proved to be the correct key from the keyhole. "That's you settled for the night, you ugly old sinner," said Burroughs, and dropped the bunch of Thrackley's keys into his trouser pocket. A very promising start, he thought.

He ran downstairs and let himself out of the house by the French windows which led from the lounge. Better go to the garage, he thought, in case comrade Jacobson became suspicious. He opened the garage doors with a great deal more noise than was necessary, switched on the light and looked round the shelves at the back of the building. That and that... and possibly that might be useful. He left the garage doors open ("in case," he thought, "friend Jacobson is wronging the dear boss with these aspersions of his") and went again into the house. After which Burroughs, the chauffeur, spent a very busy hour and a half in the study of his employer. He removed his jacket, and worked for a while in the dark. And then he removed his waistcoat, and—after closing the shutters in the one window of the room—he switched on the light. He had only a vague idea of what he was looking for, and an even vaguer one of where he was going to find it. But of one thing he was certain: the only access to the cellars of Thrackley was through this room. Very well, then. At a quarter to one o'clock the panelling of Edwin Carson's study had been completely ruined by much chiselling and boring, and a sweating and very dirty Burroughs knocked on Jim Henderson's door.

Jim had not undressed that night. Instead, he had lain on his bed with a couple of magazines, a stiff and long whisky-and-soda, and a hundred cigarettes grouped around him. His intentions were to stay awake at all costs until twelve o'clock, the altered time of the meeting in the hall. But his choice of the magazine had not been altogether a good one, and after reading Lady Gordon Cliffe-Munro's dissertation on "Chintzes in the Modern Home" and Lucille's account of what was happening to the waistline in Paris, Jim went to sleep. Just, of course, for ten minutes or so... because he would have to be awake to go and rouse that ass, Freddie. Just the sort of idiot who would spend to-night of all nights in dreaming long and sweet dreams.

He was wakened by a very violent shaking at his shoulder. As usual, he prepared to be polite to Mrs. Bertram and not to appear annoyed if it was kippers again. Then he remembered that he was at Thrackley and that it would be the greasy Jacobson doing the curtain-unveiling act. And then he realized again that it was dark. "What the devil—?" he said.

"Shut up. D'you know the time?"

"Hempson! Good Lord, of course... the expedition to the underworld."

"And you snoring like a trooper and likely to go on doing so till doomsday."

"Not at all. I was just getting up. Everything ready?"

"Readier than ever you imagined. I've been down to the cellars already."

"How on earth?..."

"Genius, my boy, sheer genius. No wonder they saw I was meant for higher things than point-duty in Tottenham Court Road. Come and help me wake up Usher."

Waking up Usher took even longer than they had anticipated. When the feat was finally accomplished, Jim and Ronnie Hempson sat on the edge of Freddie's bed and held a council of war.

"Well?" said Jim. "If you've been down to the cellars, what did you find?"

"Nothing. A perfectly ordinary cellar—except that the main part of it has been fitted with a big roll-top desk and a couple of chairs and a snappy little receptacle for holding a decanter and six glasses."

"This expedition," said Freddie, "is beginning to appeal to me."

"That's all very well," said Jim, "but you can't very well arrest a man for having a desk and a drink in his cellar."

"That's all you can see," said Burroughs.

"There's a damned sight more that you can't see. Come on down, if you're ready. It's quite safe. The servants are securely locked in their bedrooms. Jacobson lent me the keys for the very purpose."

"Nice kind fellow, Jacobson," said Freddie.

"Come on, then."

They left the bedroom and went downstairs to Edwin Carson's study. Hempson switched on the light.

"Good God!" said Jim.

"Yes… I'm afraid I've made a bit of a mess. Having done so, I'm also afraid that I'll have to clear out to-night. So we'll have to find out quite a lot about Mr. Edwin Carson before I leave. I want to be able to pay a return visit with a few large police-constables accompanying me."

"Yes… I've a feeling that Carson might notice that someone had been at his panelling."

"Ever been in this room before?"

"Yes. For an hour or so just after I arrived. Carson wanted to have a chat with me about my father."

"And did you notice anything about the room?"

"Can't say I did."

"This is the only room in the house where the panelling's new. All the other rooms are panelled in old oak. This one is in some ordinary soft wood, stained the same colour as the rest. But not quite the same colour. That's what made me think that here was the entrance to the cellars."

"And is it?"

"It certainly is. This room used to be panelled in the same oak as the rest of the house. Carson had it re-panelled in this modern stuff… and he left a couple of feet along this wall between the old panelling and the new. He did the same in the kitchen, but this room was the easier of the two to tackle. And in the two couple of feet which were left he installed a lift."

Hempson put his hand through the hole he had made by removing one of the panels, and half of the wall slid sideways in front of the other half.

"There's some way of pressing something or other in the pan-elling which must release a catch inside and open up the way to the lift. But I hadn't time to find it, so I just hacked a way in with a chisel."

"Carson will be pleased."

"Won't he? Come on, let's go down."

"Do you know how to work the thing?"

"Ordinary lift controls. Unfortunately I couldn't get the doors to open when I did get down. Had to chisel my way out as well as in. Carson'll be tickled to death at that as well."

"Second floor, boy, please," said Freddie. "The banqueting-hall."

"Certainly, sir… banqueting-hall, sir… there you are, sir."

Hempson had left the lights on in the cellars, and the three stepped out on to the stone floor. The place was bare with the exception of the big desk, the chairs and the little closet, all at the far end of the cellars. Jim walked across the room until he came to the desk.

"Got those keys, Hempson?" he asked.

"Yes. I don't expect they'll fit that, though. These are really just the house keys."

"I expect you're right. No harm in trying, though."

Six of the keys on the bunch were small enough to fit into the keyhole of the desk. Two went in too far, two not far enough, one turned a quarter of a circuit, one nearly half. "Hell!" said Jim.

"No need to swear about it," said Hempson. "Trust in little Ronald and his tame chisel. Safes, panels and desks opened in strictest confidence for a ridiculously small fee."

"Get on with it, then," said Jim.

"Certainly. Though I don't really think we'll find anything of importance in here. After all, what we want to find to-night is evidence that Edwin Carson's been pinching jewels on a large scale for the last few years. He'd hardly keep the old tiaras in here."

"I know. But I'd rather like to know what all these wires that lead up the side of the desk are connected to. My 'satiable curiosity again."

"Good heavens! I never noticed them. Where the blazes is that chisel?"

"And while you're getting on with the good work," said Jim, "Freddie and I will prowl around."

"I know where I'm prowling to," said Freddie. "I hope to heaven this little cocktail cabinet isn't locked. I'm hopeless with a chisel."

"Come on and see," said Jim, and crossed to the wall where the cabinet stood. Then he stopped and peered at the wall above it.

"What's the matter?" said Freddie. "Aren't you thirsty?"

"Listen to this, Hempson," said Jim.

"What is it?"

Jim tapped the wall with the knuckles of his hand—tapped it about a foot above the cabinet, and then a couple of feet higher.

"That's odd," said Hempson.

"Not odd at all. This isn't a solid stone wall at all. Sections of it are imitation stone—painted steel, by the sound of it. Now, what d'you think is behind those sections? Carry on with the chiselling operations, Hempson my child. We're getting hot."

"I'm getting dry," said Freddie. "This wall-tapping and chiselling's too much for me. Have a drink, Jim?"

"No, thanks. Help yourself, though. Don't mind me."

"I wasn't going to."

And Freddie opened the cabinet, revealing a decanter of the excellent brandy which he had sampled after various meals at

Thrackley. And six glasses of cut crystal. And a very efficient-looking .32 revolver.

"Thanks," said Jim. "I'll take charge of that. You're too young, Freddie. Now carry on and enjoy your drink."

The chisel which had done so much good work already braced itself for a final effort. Hempson slid it into the narrow opening he had made near the lock of the desk, and worked it backwards and forwards... and the lock gave after a short struggle, and the top of the big desk rolled back with a snap as it revealed the scattered contents inside.

"Well!" said Hempson. "You were right about the wiring. No jewels in here. No secret papers. No compromising letters or last wills and testaments. But any amount of switches. All sizes and all shapes."

"Try one," said Jim.

Hempson put his fingers to one of the switches at the back of the desk. As he pulled it back, a section of the wall at the other end of the cellar slid upwards, revealing a square of plate glass through which the brilliant electric light shone on to a background of blue velvet.

"Good God!" said Jim. "We've found it!"

"You might at least have waited until I finished this drink," said Freddie.

"Damn your drink! Come and have a look at these."

Rubies. Twelve of them, all enormous, their facets catching the light in an amazing beauty. In the middle, a perfect specimen, slightly larger than the others.

"Poor old Lady Stone!..." said Hempson.

"What d'you mean?"

"That's the centre stone in that hideous necklace thing she wore. And now she's back in London with a dud in its place."

"I think," said Freddie, "I'll try some more of those switches. I'd very much like to know if I've still got those damned diamonds of mine."

"Go ahead."

Freddie went ahead. With each movement of his hand a fresh square of light shone out into the room. In five minutes the drab grey of the cellar's walls had been changed into a frame for an amazing glittering collection. Diamonds in one section… pearls in another… emeralds on pure white velvet in a third.

"That's enough," said Hempson. "Quite enough. Some of those trinkets are recognizable enough to get Mr. Edwin Carson removed from Thrackley to another part of the country for a good many years. Now I'm clearing out."

"What about us?"

"Get back to your rooms and behave as though nothing had happened. Carson need never suspect you… it's me he'll be after. That's why I'm doing a bunk. And I promise you faithfully that I'll be calling again to-morrow."

"What if Carson tries to get away himself?"

"I don't think he will. If he does, try and get in touch with me in Adderly… or with Scotland Yard direct. In any case, we'll have someone ready to trail the old boy if he does attempt a getaway."

"This is getting too much like one of those gangster films for my liking," said Freddie. "And there are still two more of these jolly little switches to be tried. What about it?"

"Why not?"

"Why, as you so aptly put it, not?"

He pulled one of the switches towards him.

"I don't see anything," said Freddie.

"You wouldn't," said Jim. "It's behind you."

"Good Lord! What the blazes?…"

"The entrance to the room where Carson makes his imitation jewels, I suppose… yes, a very nice little plant. All the latest ideas in mechanism. Now try the other one, Freddie."

The last of the switches was pulled back in its socket. At the far end of the room, to the right of the entrance from the lift, three bolts shot back simultaneously.

"Lord!… I never noticed that. Wonder where this Sesame leads to?"

They crossed to the other end of the cellar and swung open the door which the bolts had released. It swung easily, though it was fully four inches thick.

"Can't see anything," said Jim. "Fetch your electric torch, Hempson."

"Here you are."

Jim switched on the torch and played the circle of light through the doorway and into the room. He stopped it for a moment as it passed over something on the floor, and then he felt at the side of the door for an electric light switch.

And when he found it and flooded the little room with light, they saw that the something on the floor was Catherine Lady Stone.

XVI

EDWIN CARSON SWUNG THE NOSE OF HIS CAR THROUGH THE open doors of the garage, and switched off engine and lights. He was still in a very unpleasant mood. Mr. Carson had been accustomed all his life to get what he wanted. There had been only three occasions when he had not got what he wanted; and to-night had been one of the three. He groped in the darkness for an electric torch, and switched it on when he found it. The beam fell on the legs of Raoul as she felt her way out of the car, and the very shapeliness of those legs seemed to aggravate his annoyance. What insufferable fools women were. Here (referring to himself) was a man with unlimited wealth, a splendid house, a certain amount of fame, ready to give himself and all these to a slip of a girl whose life at present consisted of performing nearly naked dances thrice nightly in a not too brilliant revue. And what did the slip of a girl do? She slapped his face. Damned hard, too, thought Edwin Carson as he rubbed his hand over his cheek... damned hard for a slip of a girl like that. He locked the doors of the garage with his own keys and led the way to the house.

He found the lock of the front door with a certain amount of difficulty, and stood aside to allow Raoul to enter. The hall was in darkness. Evidently the servants had gone to bed as he had ordered. Then he spoke for the first time in an hour.

"Drink, Raoul?" he asked.

"No, thank you. I'll go right up to my room, if you please."

"Just as you wish. I'll see you up."

"That is all right, Señor Carson. I know the way now."

He shrugged his shoulders, and crossed to the sideboard to pour out a drink.

"Good night, then, Raoul," he said.

"Good night, *señor*." She paused at the foot of the stairs. "And I am sorry that you have had a wasted evening, *señor*."

"So am I. Let's forget, shall we, my dear?"

"I have done so."

"Good night."

"Good night, *señor*."

He watched her go until she vanished round the bend in the stairs. And then he drank his whisky at a gulp. It made him feel a trifle less disgruntled with the world. He crossed the floor of the hall, switched off the light, and entered his study. And what he saw made all the soothing effects of his drink collapse like a playing-cards castle.

The three tall panels which had been so very expensive to install were slid aside, leaving the black opening which he had so often used to reach his cellar. All round the opening the panelling had been hacked and destroyed. Two of the panels had been removed altogether from their framing and lay on the carpet of the study. He stared at it for a minute, and then crossed to the opening in the wall and listened carefully. And then he removed his thick glasses and mopped his sweating face with his handkerchief. His fingers were shaking as he put on his glasses again.

In a few minutes the dream which Jacobson, the butler, was dreaming (a horsey affair, in which the Ascot Gold Cup was being unaccountably run round and round the grounds of Thrackley, with Jacobson and Edwin Carson neck-and-neck on a pair of shaggy pit-ponies) was rudely interrupted by a loud knocking on the bedroom door. The pit-ponies took a last convulsive swerve through the pine-trees, and then vanished as Jacobson blinked himself awake.

"Who the hell's that?" he asked.

"Me, you fool. Come and open this damned door."

Jacobson was surprised. Firstly at the idea of his employer returning at this hour of night; and secondly at the idea of his employer being so drunk as to be incapable of opening a perfectly simple door. He threw a pair of thin, hairy legs out of the bed-clothes and crossed to the door, swearing at the meanness of an employer who lays thick carpets in the guests' bedrooms and iced linoleum in the rooms of the staff. Then he turned the handle of the door, and saw that there was something in Edwin Carson's failure at opening it. Which, thought Jacobson, was extremely odd, for he had never locked his bedroom door since that unfortunate evening when only that door (or one very like it) stood between a getaway and a three years' detention in one of His Majesty's prisons.

"It's locked," he said.

"I can see that, you blasted idiot," said the voice on the other side. The boss, Jacobson told himself, was in one of his moods.

"Jussaminute. I'll get the key."

"A very sensible idea, Jacobson. Would you mind being as quick as you can about it?" Jacobson crossed to his dressing-table. He looked over the conglomeration which was scattered over it—the cheap solidified brilliantine, the double set of teeth floating serenely in their glass of water, the six and fivepence in small change, the watch and chain. Where the devil... And then suddenly he remembered. Burroughs!... Opening up the garage. Damn the man.

"Listen, boss... Burroughs got my keys. He'd left something in the garage. Wanted to go and get it. I lent him the bunch."

"My God! Of all the... wait a minute. I'll get mine. They're downstairs."

Jacobson, having no alternative to waiting a minute, sat on the edge of his bed and thought. Burroughs had locked the door, had he? Now why, in heaven's name? Queer chap, Burroughs. A bit dippy, thought Jacobson. Not quite—

The noise of a key scraping its way into the lock made him give up his debating on the dippiness of Burroughs. Edwin Carson opened the door and walked into the room. Looking, in Jacobson's eyes, like hell warmed up.

"Back early, boss," said Jacobson.

Edwin Carson snorted.

"You think so, do you? Personally I think I'm back a damn sight too late."

A tiny trickle of sweat fell from his brow on to one of the thick lenses of his glasses.

"Anything the matter?"

"Anything the matter? Oh, no! Nothing except that the entire staff have been fools enough to be locked in their rooms. Nothing except that my study has been broken into and the entrance to the cellars burst open. Nothing except that several of my so-called guests are having a tour of inspection of the cellars at this moment. Oh, no. Nothing's happened."

Jacobson allowed his jaw to drop several inches. He said, "What?"

"You heard. And it's all through you, you brazen-faced nitwit. Didn't I tell you definitely not to give your keys to anyone? Why on earth can't I get hold of someone I can trust? Someone who wouldn't be quite fool enough to give the keys to every room in this house to the first person who asks for them."

"But Burroughs—"

"Good God, man, what do you know about Burroughs? And Burroughs apparently knows a great deal too much about me to be presented with the keys of my house."

"But—"

"Shut up, will you!"

And Edwin Carson raised himself on tiptoe and brought the palm of his hand across Jacobson's cheek, so that for an instant the cheek turned white and rushed into a crimson outline of Carson's fingers.

"My God, you little swine!"

"Don't speak to me, Jacobson. There are three men down in my cellars just now. You know what that means. We're caught. Come and let the others out of their rooms. And take that."

"That" was a revolver, black and shiny. Jacobson took it slowly out of Carson's hand.

"Now go and unlock Kenrick and Adams. Bring them here to me at once."

The butler disappeared in the folds of a thick grey dressing-gown, and stooped to pull a pair of felt slippers on to his feet. He stopped as he reached the door.

"What about the girl?" he asked.

"I've tried her door—it's locked. Owing to your thoughtfulness, Burroughs was able to do his job thoroughly. You'll leave her where she is. Much better for her door to remain locked to-night. Now, for God's sake, hurry."

In five minutes Carson and his three servants were down in the study. With the exception of Carson, they were all a slightly bleary and ill-dressed collection. But from the pocket of each of their not too fashionable dressing-gowns the hard barrel of an automatic protruded in a businesslike manner.

"All right?" said Carson.

The three men nodded.

"Very well, then. We'll just go down and see what these guests of mine are up to. There is no necessity to use those revolvers except as… a little persuasion. Come on, then."

The four crowded into the narrow lift. The machinery whirred almost inaudibly, and the lift lowered itself smoothly to the level of the cellar. When it had stopped Carson bent close to the doors of the lift and listened for a minute. Then he pressed the button at his side and the doors parted silently. The flood of light which came from the cellars blinded him for an instant. He blinked, and then saw that, so far, things were in his favour. The three men, Jim and Freddie and Burroughs, had their backs to the lift entrance. They had evidently not heard the whirr of the lift. They were bending over a large object sprawling on the floor. He saw between their legs that the large object was Catherine Lady Stone.

"Good evening," said Edwin Carson.

The three swung round. Burroughs, the chauffeur, said "Carson!" Freddie muttered "My God!"

"I'm sorry," said Edwin Carson, "if I have interrupted you. I had no idea that you were so interested in precious stones as to break into my private collection. Adams… Kenrick… just step out of the lift and keep your revolvers levelled at these gentlemen. Jacobson, you might remove that ugly-looking object from the chair at Captain Henderson's side, will you? I have a feeling that Captain Henderson might wish to play with it."

The butler, somewhat shapeless in his dressing-gown, laid his hand on the revolver and stuck it in his other pocket.

"Now then," said Edwin Carson, "it is really time that we were all in bed. Don't you agree, gentlemen?"

The three stared at him. He had obviously recovered his humour, and stood before them pulling at his nose and choosing his words carefully.

"Kenrick, you will escort Mr. Usher to his room. I am sure you must be tired, Mr. Usher, after such an exhausting evening. Personally I always find housebreaking a much more tiring way of spending an evening than, say, a quiet game of bridge."

"Really?" said Freddie. "But I should have thought you must be quite used to it by now."

"Thank you, Kenrick. You know Mr. Usher's room? See that he is comfortable, please, and lock the door, won't you? And, Adams... will you do the same to Captain Henderson?... Thank you. I shall see Burroughs to his room myself... I'm afraid I shall have to dispense with your services after this, Burroughs... a pity... but you were never really a very good chauffeur. And Jacobson... will you see Lady Stone to her room? You always had a way with the ladies, hadn't you, Jacobson?... otherwise I would have escorted her myself. I see that she has recovered from her unfortunate... er... experiences... no doubt these gentlemen have been doing all they could for her. A pity, isn't it, that you found Lady Stone? You might have been quite a long way from Thrackley by now if you hadn't wasted so much time over her. You'll find, I think, that women are scarcely ever worth the trouble one takes over them... good night, then, gentlemen."

The three moved over to the lift, a dressing-gowned attendant behind each.

"Oh, just a minute, gentlemen." Edwin Carson had crossed to his desk. He peered back at the group at the lift doors. "I see that you have been playing with these switches. Interesting, aren't they? I'm afraid you missed one of them, though... quite an important one, too. This one..."

He pulled back a panel at the side of the desk, revealing a single switch on a base of ebonite.

"I'm going to switch this one on. It's a burglar-alarm that up to now I've always regarded as a great waste of money. Perhaps I was wrong. In any case, I should not advise you to touch any of your windows this evening. You will not repeat the experiment, I think... good night, gentlemen... good night, Lady Stone."

The doors of the lift closed with an effort behind Lady Stone's limp body. The slight whirr went on for a moment and then stopped. Edwin Carson listened to the footsteps crossing the study floor above his head. Then he pulled back the switches one by one, so that each brilliant square of light vanished in turn and the cellar was left finally in a darkness broken only by the single light at the desk. He sat down slowly in his chair and poured himself out a very large brandy.

Not, after all, such a terribly dull evening, he thought.

XVII

AT A QUARTER TO SIX IN THE MORNING CATHERINE A LADY
Stone decided that she could stand it no longer. Catherine
Lady Stone had been twice in her life to the films, and the extraordinary behaviour of the people on the pictures was the only thing
to which she could compare this weekend at Thrackley. The
annoying thing about the weekend was that the other members
of the house-party seemed to think that it was a quite ordinary
house-party. She sat on the edge of her bed and reviewed the situation. She decided at once that Edwin Carson was mad. But not
pleasantly mad; very dangerously mad. Lady Stone, in her capacity
as Chairman of the Society for the Care of the Mentally Deranged,
had come across a good deal of madness in her time. But it had all
been of the harmless variety. Bank clerks under the impression that
they were Julius Caesar, and housemaids imagining themselves to
be Boadicea, and so on. Edwin Carson's madness was not of the
Caesar-Boadicea type. Definitely not. In addition to being mad,
Catherine Lady Stone decided, this man Carson was also a criminal.
Possibly at one time a quite normal collector of precious stones…
but now a man who had become so obsessed by his hobby that he
would stop at nothing in order to add to his collection. Not even
at attempting to steal the jewels of one of his guests. Not even at
ramming a very nasty-smelling handkerchief down the throat of
that guest when she fortunately wakened at the time of the theft.
Not even at keeping that guest under lock and key for two days
in a dismal cellar, six feet square, with very little ventilation, light,
food or drink. Very well, then.

Catherine Lady Stone got up from her bed and crossed to the dressing-table. She was on the point of switching on the lights at the side of her dressing-table, when she remembered that what dressing there was to be done had better be done in the dark. A very difficult job, for Lady Stone was accustomed to have her corsets laced around her by an efficient French maid, and consequently was rather lost when she had to do anything by herself, even in the broadest of daylight. But at last she was ready, and Lady Stone looked around her and felt along the top of the dressing-table to see just what should be taken and what left. Her fingers came upon her note-case and her jewel-case—the first full, the second empty. She groped further to find her handbag, and stuffed the note-case and a few odds and ends inside it. Catherine Lady Stone had one idea only: to get out of Thrackley as soon as possible, to reach (even if she were forced to do so by walking) the nearest police-station, and to get, if necessary, the flying squad itself to pay a visit to Thrackley and to put Edwin Carson exactly where he belonged. It was, she decided, no use talking about this to the other members of the party. This was a job that needed someone with initiative and organizing powers. The others, poor souls, would be quite hopeless at it. She realized that Captain Henderson and Mr. Usher and that smart young man who was Edwin Carson's chauffeur must have become suspicious about her absence and made their way to the cellar and eventually found her. But what good would it do to get in touch with them now? They were probably locked in their bedrooms, anyway (she tried her own door at the thought; unlocked, heaven be praised!), and in any case one woman with all her wits about her had a much better chance of getting out of this damnable house than three outsized, heavy-footed males. Catherine Lady Stone was secretly beginning to enjoy herself. This was, she felt, a situation made to measure for a woman like herself. And, to tell the truth, Catherine Lady Stone's first thought was to remove her own body as far from Edwin Carson and his house in as short a time as possible. She did not hold with hosts who placed chloroformed handkerchiefs over the mouths of their guests.

She opened her bedroom door slowly and peered out. The light of the sun's rising was effectively hidden by the trees outside, but there was enough light coming through the big staircase window to enable her to see her way across the landing. She made her way slowly down the stairs, thanking heaven that Edwin Carson had laid these heavy carpets over his floors. She reached the lounge, and steered her way between the furniture to the big French windows. And here Lady Stone stopped, and regretted that her knowledge of burglar-alarms was so small. Did the wretched things go off as soon as one touched the window? Or did one have to actually open the window before they worked? For an instant she thought of creeping back upstairs to waken Captain Henderson and employ him as an accomplice. Such a nice, sensible young man. The very man who would know all about things like burglar-alarms. And then Catherine Lady Stone decided, no: to blazes with the men in this house. A spineless lot, more than likely all quaking in their bedrooms at this minute, with not a single idea of getting out of Thrackley among the lot of them. No, if she couldn't get the better of a little thing like a burglar-alarm, then she (Catherine Lady Stone) was not the President of the Women's Council of Charitable Workers. She reached out a hand gingerly to touch the pane of the window in front of her. The lounge remained quite silent. She felt her way along to the bronze handle of the window. Now this was where she must be careful. Many a woman would have muttered, "To hell with the thing!"; would have tugged at the

handle and trusted in Providence. But not Catherine Lady Stone.
Providence, where burglar-alarms were concerned, was not altogether reliable. She felt the handle with the tips of her fingers, ran
them up the frame of the window until they stopped at a small
metal box, followed the frame up again as far as she could reach.
Splendid, thought Catherine Lady Stone. Now, all that needs to
be done is to find something to cut this wire and Edwin Carson
and the rest of them will be in Vine Street, or Marylebone, or
wherever it was, before breakfast time. She saw it all as she ran her
fingers along. the thin wire which might have been so efficiently
damning in the hands of anyone else: "Country house sensation.
Well-known charity worker foils dangerous gang of crooks". And
now for something to cut this damned wire.

A knife. Or a pair of scissors. Catherine Lady Stone dived into
the handbag which she had brought with her. Her fingers rattled
through its contents. There was a welter of keys, odd change, a
pair of ear-rings, a dozen letters in envelopes, even a nightdress
rammed into the bag on the assumption that a woman, even one
escaping from a lonely house at six in the morning, cannot be
wholly lost if she has with her her nightdress. But the little pair
of nail scissors for which she was searching was not to be found.
"Damn!" said Catherine Lady Stone, a member of the Council of
the Society for the Purification of the English Language. She felt
her way around the room. There must be something, somewhere,
which would cut its way through this ridiculous piece of wire. She
felt the tops of two tables, nearly upsetting a vase of geums in her
hurry. Nothing there. She crossed on tiptoe to the bureau which
she knew stood against the opposite wall. Locked. How like Edwin
Carson to lock his bureaux at night. She felt the top of the grand
piano. Two framed pictures and another vase of flowers. There

was nothing for it—she would have to go back upstairs and get the pair of scissors. Catherine Lady Stone repeated the word "Damn!"

The sun was feeling its way through the pine-trees now, and the landing at the top of the stairs was lighter. The door of her bedroom was open as she had left it... she crossed the room to her dressing-table and felt once more over its glass top. Her fingers touched at last on the scissors... wretched little things which even the lightest strand of wire would ruin... but at least they were sharp. Then her hand touched something else. She felt it and gave a little gasp of astonishment. Her choker necklace of rubies. Impossible that she could have missed it before... yet how in heaven's name was it here? She rammed it deep into the folds of the nightdress in her bag, and crept out again to the landing.

In a few minutes Catherine Lady Stone was very busy trying to coax a pair of scissors whose forte had always been finger-nails to do a spot of work on wire. It was an annoying job. The wire had been fastened tightly down to the style of the window, and it was a difficult matter to force the scissors in behind it. And, having done so, the scissors behaved in a most perplexing manner. Having led, up to now, a comparatively easy life in helping to keep Lady Stone's hands presentable, they protested very strongly at being set to cope with a length of exceedingly tough wire. Lady Stone perspired freely, a thing she had not done since the Henley Regatta of 1897. The scissors, instead of getting to work on the wire, cut into the flesh of her hand and made a thin trickle of blood run down the window-pane. But at last the wire snapped and Lady Stone stood back and mopped her forehead. Now then, thought Catherine Lady Stone. She gripped the handle of the French windows, tucked her handbag under her other arm, and prepared to make a bolt for it. The thought flashed across her mind that she might quite easily have cut a wire which had nothing to do with the alarm. Part of the electric light wiring, for instance. No time to worry about that now, though. She turned the handle slowly downwards, and listened for the sound of a hundred or so electric bells and buzzers. The lounge remained silent. She pulled the French windows inch by inch towards her, and still there was an entrancing lack of noise. And then Catherine Lady Stone flung open the window and stepped out on the veranda with an air of something attempted and something done which none of the other poor goofs in the house would have had either the sense or the courage to attempt to do. She looked round about her at the garden and the pine-trees, and took a satisfying gulp of the morning air. She had done it! Only the front gates of Thrackley to negotiate now, and she was out of this appalling place and ready to get the arm of the Law to reach out to the equally appalling Mr. Carson. Catherine Lady Stone, feeling a great deal more satisfied with herself than she had done for two days, stepped briskly off the veranda and on to the grass at the edge of the gravelled drive. The "Society woman foils crook" posters seemed nearer and clearer than ever at that moment.

Only for a moment, though. For Catherine Lady Stone had gone no further than three steps along the narrow grass edging when the large and unpleasant form of Jacobson, the butler, appeared from behind a bush of ghostly white broom and laid a heavy hand on the back of Lady Stone's neck. "Now, what the bloody hell," said Jacobson the butler, "do you think you're doing at this time of the morning? Got up to see the sunrise, did you?"

Catherine Lady Stone, President of (*inter alia*) the Women's Council of Charitable Workers, fainted for the second time during her weekend at Thrackley.

XVIII

WHEN JIM, HAVING FIRMLY EXPECTED TO FIND HIS BED-room door locked, tried the handle and found that this was not the case, he promptly put the previous evening's events down as a particularly bad nightmare. Secret passages to jewel-laden cellars... sensational discoveries of half-drugged women... dispatching of guests to bed by servants wielding revolvers in their hands... no, definitely no. He decided that he had been reading far too many of these detective novels recently. Or possibly it was that slightly over-ready Gorgonzola with which he had rounded off last night's dinner. Yes, all blame to be attached to the Gorgonzola. He had had much too much, anyway.

By the time he had bathed and dressed and arrived downstairs in the lounge there was no doubt at all that the evening's excite-ment had taken place in his dreams. The rest of the guests were already at breakfast. One glance at them was enough to satisfy Jim that the whole affair... the jewels in the cellar, the finding of Lady Stone, the revolver in Jacobson's fist... had been part of the scenario of a Gorgonzola-flavoured sleep. Such a perfectly ordi-nary house-party, munching their eggs and bacon in the middle of a perfectly ordinary country like England. Catherine Lady Stone chatting with Henry Brampton on the possibilities of the weather breaking down. Raoul, sleek and immaculate as ever, listening more or less attentively to Marilyn Brampton's discus-sion on the misunderstood depths of D. H. Lawrence. Freddie Usher reaching out his third cup of coffee for Mary Carson to refill. Quite absurd, all these detective-thriller notions! Damn

that Gorgonzola! And then Jim took another and a more careful look at the occupants of the breakfast-table. And noticed
that Catherine Lady Stone's complexion had changed from its
usual expensive blush to an unpleasant shade of ash. That both
Marilyn and Henry Brampton were talking in high-pitched, excit-
able tones. That Mary Carson looked worried, almost tearful.
He walked across the room and helped himself to grape-fruit
from the sideboard.

And, as he settled himself into the chair next to Mary Carson,
the door at the other end of the lounge opened and Edwin Carson
walked to his place at the head of the table. He was looking a great
deal more unpleasant than usual. His forehead frowned down over
the thick lenses of his spectacles. The fringes of his grey hair stuck
out untidily about his ears. He had not shaved. Jim decided that he
had not been to bed. Or that, if he had, he had eaten even more
Gorgonzola than Jim. As he sat down in his chair the conversation
at the table petered out and stopped completely. Lady Stone, reaching for marmalade across the table, gripped the jar with a rather
shaking hand. The spoon fell from it with a clatter on to one of
the plates. Then there was silence.

"I must apologize," said Edwin Carson, after a moment's pause,
"for leaving you to yourselves last night. It was most unfortunate.
But quite unavoidable. As you know, I had taken Raoul out for a
short drive in the afternoon. Unfortunately, we came across Mr.
Edwards, who is Raoul's manager. Mr. Edwards insisted that Raoul
should perform at the evening show of her delightful little play...
I can quite well understand that the absence of Raoul would have
a very serious effect on the success of the performance. And on
the box-office receipts. So we had no option but to remain in town
until the end of the show... and most charming it was, especially

to one who had not been inside a theatre for nearly ten years. I hoped you looked after our guests, Mary? But then you would all probably have a much more pleasant time in my absence than you would have had if I had been here to bore you with my conversation. Captain Henderson, you are eating nothing... please help yourself..."

Jim looked across the table at Lady Stone. She had laid down her knife and fork and was fumbling in her handbag. From the bag she took a small crystal bottle of smelling-salts, waved it for an instant under her abrupt little nose, replaced it in the bag.

"Three of the occupants of the house, I know," continued Edwin Carson, "had a much more satisfactory evening than would have been possible if I had been here at Thrackley."

He paused. The heavy lenses swivelled round the table. He reached in front of Mary for the pewter coffee-pot and poured himself out coffee in silence. Then he went on talking in his quiet, monotonous voice.

"I am going to tell you exactly what happened when Raoul and I returned to Thrackley last night. I am going to tell you a great deal more than that... I hope you will not be too bored or uninterested to listen to me. But please continue with your breakfasts. There are more eggs on the heater on the sideboard... Lady Stone, you have no coffee..."

"Thank you," said Lady Stone, in the kind of voice which may accurately be described as still and small. "I have had quite sufficient, thank you."

"Very well, then. Raoul and I got back here about one o'clock. We would have been home sooner, but unfortunately we were held up on our way down from London by a belt of that annoying variety of fog in which this part of the country specializes.

I say unfortunately, because perhaps if it had been a clear night some of the rather distressing events of last evening would not have occurred."

("Rather distressing events?" thought Jim. Gorgonzola, after all, detached from all blame.)

"When Raoul had gone to her room, I had a drink and then went to my study. You all know my study... not a very elaborate room, but small and—in my opinion, at least—tastefully panelled in a very cheap imitation of a very expensive oak. When I opened the door of my study last night, I found that that panelling had been ruined. I do not think I have ever told you that part of that panelling conceals a lift which descends to the cellars underneath this house. I will tell you the reasons for that later. Someone, in any case, had been extremely anxious to find the entrance to that lift. Up to a point, they were not very successful. They had to use force, chisels, saws—all of which would have been quite unnecessary if only they had thought of using instead a little intelligence. But the point is that they found the lift. And, having found it, they gained access to the cellars of Thrackley."

Jim looked across the table at Freddie Usher, and found him staring open-mouthed at the ceiling. He wondered how Burroughs was getting on with his breakfast in the kitchen. Edwin Carson had paused for a moment. He was stirring his coffee slowly, looking in turn at each of his guests as he stirred. Then he laid the spoon back in its place in the saucer and went on speaking in the same quiet voice.

"Now, why should anyone wish to get into the cellars of this house? I will tell you. The cellars of Thrackley are not quite ordinary cellars. There are, in those cellars, round about four and three-quarter million pounds' worth of the most marvellous collection of precious stones existing in Europe to-day... four and three-quarter millions..."

He had raised his voice slightly now, and his hand, as he lifted his cup of coffee to his mouth shook just a little. "Now," thought Jim, "we are getting warm."

"Nearly all my life has been spent in getting together that collection. Apart from myself, no one, up to last night, has ever seen the whole of it. Those jewels were intended for my eyes alone. Partly because there are very few... I might almost say there is no one... who understands those jewels as I do. And partly because, if the police of Europe were to see even a few of the stones in that collection, I should be arrested within an hour and probably spend the rest of my days on the wrong side of a prison wall. Which I have not the slightest intention of doing..."

He paused again. There was absolute silence in the room. Two small beads of sweat appeared on Edwin Carson's forehead and ran slowly down his brow. He ran his hand over the deep forehead and across his bald head.

"You are probably thinking that I am a fool to tell you this. But I am no fool... you will find that out, my friends. You are my guests. You are also very much in my power. You will find that until I choose to let you do so, not one of you can get away from the grounds of this house. And I do not choose so yet. When you do go, you may be quite certain that I shall have gone before you... that I shall be very far away from Thrackley. It is not such a terribly difficult matter to get out of England overnight if one has money. And once I am on the Continent... then my hospitality to you will be over, the gates of Thrackley will be opened, you may go out and tell your stories of stolen jewels to the first policeman you meet, to Scotland Yard, to the Sunday newspapers... I shall not care. I hope that they will believe you... for when they come to search the cellars of Thrackley they will find very little. A little wine, perhaps... a stack of logs in one corner and a pile of coal in another... but jewels? I am afraid not. You see, my friends, it is you who have been the fools."

The quiet voice had vanished now. Edwin Carson quivered with excitement, almost shouted each word as he glared round the table.

"Yes... you, not I, are the fools," he repeated. "Why do you think each of you was invited to stay with me in this house? For my pleasure or entertainment? I am afraid I must disillusion you if that is what you thought. You came here to add to my collection... to fill just a few gaps which were spoiling the effect of that collection. Some of you have obliged already. Others will do so before they leave this house. Will you look for a minute at that exquisite ruby in the centre of the necklace which Lady Stone is wearing? I cannot imagine why she should wear a choker necklace at breakfast... unless perhaps she thought that the safest place for such a thing in Thrackley was round her neck. That ruby is worth... perhaps fifteen shillings. Probably less, certainly not more. The original stone is lying on white velvet in the cellars underneath this room. For that, my friends, was my original idea in bringing you to Thrackley. You were to contribute unknowingly to my collection. It was not to be discovered until you had safely left Thrackley behind you that the delightful jewels which you brought with you had been replaced by equally delightful but quite worthless imitations. Perhaps such an unfortunate discovery would not be made for years... until, shall we say, some of you fell on hard days and were forced to dispose of your priceless jewellery? But unfortunately that scheme of mine did not work out as I had planned. Lady Stone is a distressingly light sleeper... you should do something about it, Lady Stone... there are excellent cures for insomnia. And so Lady Stone had to be kept quiet for the remainder of her stay at Thrackley. She was admirably quiet until last night, until Captain Henderson and Mr. Usher and one of my servants so ungallantly disturbed her. A great pity…"

Five pairs of eyes stared across at the red centrepiece of Catherine Lady Stone's necklace. It shone vividly, catching a fresh glint of light with each motion as Lady Stone breathed. Yet not one of the owners of those five pairs of eyes doubted for an instant that the stone was made of glass. And somewhere, not very far away, the real stone was shining a little more vividly.

"Now, what is to happen? Well, I think I have told you. You are to stay here until I please to let you go. I do not think any of you will be so foolish as to attempt to leave this house… I can almost promise you that you will not make a second attempt. Excuse me for just one moment…"

He rose from his chair, folded his serviette neatly on his plate, crossed to the French windows which looked out on to the strip of garden and the pine-strees outside.

"This, of course," he said, "is one of the obvious ways of leaving the house."

He laid his hand on the handle of the French windows. As he pulled it down to open them, the clanging of an electric bell sounded deafeningly from each corner of the room. The door at the end of the lounge shot open.

"All right, all right, Jacobson," said Edwin Carson in his quiet voice, "I was just explaining this little contraption to our guests. I see it is working again perfectly… it was put out of commission by a very adventurous lady at an early hour this morning. That will do, Jacobson, thank you. And please do not point that revolver at my guests. Lady Stone's heart is not all that it might be."

And Edwin Carson took his hand off the bronze handle and walked back to the table. The room seemed uncannily silent after the few moments of din. The door shut quietly behind Jacobson and his revolver.

"You see?" said Edwin Carson. "In perfect working order. And that is not all. For the front door of this house is unconnected to the wiring of the alarm. You are perfectly free to walk in and out of that door as you please. What then?... I am afraid that you will find that both the gates in the wall which surrounds this house so efficiently have been equipped with the same little device. And have you noticed that wall, my friends? It is, I think, sixteen feet high, and very difficult to scale. Difficult, but not impossible. But, as you may have noticed, at the top of that wall there is a row of iron prongs. They were put there originally to keep small boys from stealing fruit from the trees near the wall. There is no fruit there now, I'm afraid, but the prongs are still there. And they are wired to the distressingly loud alarm which you have just heard. And... in case there might be one of you who would try to scale that wall, trusting to luck that you would be able to get over the top before the alarm took very much effect... just in case of that, there is an exceedingly strong electric current running right through those prongs, through the bolts in the little gate at the back, through the iron gates at the front of the house, running through them all at this very minute. I would not say that it is strong enough to kill a man... but I should advise you, when you are planning how to get yourselves out of Thrackley, to think of some other way than through the gates or over the wall."

He crossed to the foot of the staircase, and paused as he placed his foot on the first step.

"Oh… I forgot to tell you. The telephone is, I'm afraid, out of order. And now please do whatever you wish for the remainder of your stay at Thrackley. And so shall I…"

And Edwin Carson walked slowly up the wide staircase, and the five people seated at the table followed him with their eyes until he turned at the landing and disappeared from their sight. Then Jim turned and stared out of the French windows… stared through a gap in the pines at a glimpse of the high wall which was only one of the barriers which held those five in the house called Thrackley. As he looked, a cat walked slowly along the top of the wall, silhouetted against the blue of the sky beyond. He watched it, fascinated. It stopped, looked down at the garden below it, then stretched a thin paw out towards one of the iron prongs which stuck out from the rim of the wall, trying, apparently, to catch hold of a leaf or something dangling from the prongs. And then the cat leapt high in the air above the wall and its body fell on to the grass below. It lay there, stretched out, quite still. Jim took a drink of his coffee. He had left it untouched all the time Carson talked, and it was now quite cold. He shivered a little… not because of the coffee's temperature. Edwin Carson had been right when he said that his wiring was in perfect order.

XIX

For the few seconds which followed immediately upon Edwin Carson's disappearance there was complete silence in the lounge. But only for those few seconds. And then:

"God bless my soul!" said Catherine Lady Stone.

With which remark the other occupants of the breakfast-table burst unanimously into conversation. Even the Bramptons threw aside for once their air of aloofness and boredom with everything and everybody and added their share to the mêlée. But it was Lady Stone's voice which predominated (as it had done at many hundreds of committee meetings, garden fêtes, and political gatherings). After all, felt Lady Stone, she had a right to say her say, having been implicated in this affair more deeply than the rest.

"No doubt about it," said Lady Stone's shrill soprano. "Not a bit of doubt that the man is mad. Quite, quite mad. A dangerous lunatic."

"Did he really lock you up in his cellar?" inquired Henry Brampton.

"My good man, if you are under the impression that I have spent the last two days in a small stone room, with no light and very little air and with my meals pushed through a disgusting—If you are under the impression," said Lady Stone, becoming thoroughly warmed, "that I have done all this of my own free will, then you are very much mistaken."

"I never thought so," said the sleek Mr. Brampton. "But I should be the last to say that Edwin Carson is mad just because he locked you up, Lady Stone."

"This," said Lady Stone, "is neither the time nor the place for attempted cleverness, Mr. Brampton."

"And d'you really believe that's not your original ruby?" asked Freddie Usher.

"Of course, it isn't. I'm perfectly certain of that. Mind you, it's a very clever imitation, but not clever enough to deceive me. I happen to know something about jewellery."

"In addition to which," said Jim, "you happen to know that you found one of Carson's servants rummaging about your bedroom late on Friday night. And when you had a word with him on the subject, you were very promptly made to swallow a handkerchief, and only returned to the fold at an early hour this morning. Yes, quite apart from your own very excellent knowledge of precious stones, Lady Stone, you can bet your Sunday corsets that Carson has changed that ruby for a dud."

"Well, if he's done it with Lady Stone's," said Marilyn Brampton, "what about the other jewels in this house? How do I know he hasn't my pearls down in his damned cellar?"

"Not having Lady Stone's knowledge of these things," said Jim, "you just don't know. Annoying, isn't it?"

Raoul, the dancer, made her first contribution to the discussion.

"He has not had my jewels, this Carson," she said slowly. "In each link of my bracelets, in a corner of my emeralds, somewhere on each piece of my jewellery, there is a monogram… a little R… so very little, perhaps only I could see it."

"Old man Carson seems to have all the equipment for putting little Rs on your knick-knacks," said Freddie Usher.

Raoul smiled at him as though Mr. Usher were a particularly distressing painting which she had been asked by the painter to admire.

"See, I show you all," she said.

Her brown hands reached up to her ears; she slipped the ear-rings from beneath her jet-black hair. They were of platinum, with a small but exquisite turquoise set in each. She laid them on the table in front of her and peered down at them for a moment.

"Well?" said Lady Stone, somewhat irritated at being side-tracked by this dancer person and her little Rs.

"Too late," said Raoul slowly.

"What d'you mean?"

"The setting is mine... the stones have been changed. There is the little R on the link of the setting—you see it?—and none on the stone..."

The pair of ear-rings fell from her fingers with a tinkle on to her plate.

"Well, now," said Lady Stone in her most businesslike of voices. Inwardly Lady Stone was a little relieved to find that she was not the only person at Thrackley who had had the misfortune to be fooled by Edwin Carson. And now it needed someone blessed with a fair amount of intelligence, common sense and gifts of organiza-tion to take command of the proceedings. Catherine Lady Stone, in other words.

"Well, now," repeated Lady Stone, "I think you'll all agree that Edwin Carson means what he says about the jewels belonging to his—er—I suppose we are still his guests—yes. He has managed to come into possession of my own very valuable ruby... only temporarily, I hope. He has also—er—stolen some little things of Raoul's. For all we know, other members of this house-party may have been treated in the same way. The question is, does he mean the rest of what he says?"

"What do you mean?" asked Henry Brampton.

"My good man," said Lady Stone, "you don't honestly mean to say that you believe that we can be kept here as prisoners until this man Carson sees fit to let us go?"

"I don't see why I shouldn't believe it. And I am not, and have no intention of becoming, your good man."

"Really, Mr. Brampton!... but the thing is so ridiculous! Here in the heart of England... I mean, one can quite well understand this sort of thing taking place in Russia or Chicago or some of those places, but here in a peaceful old country house in England..."

Lady Stone paused, rather from lack of breath than lack of desire to go on with her monologue.

"Well," said Marilyn Brampton, "take a flying run out of those French windows and see what happens."

Lady Stone cast a rather quivering eye on the bronze handle of the French windows, and subsided into her chair.

"All this talk!" said Raoul suddenly. "So stupid! Why do we not talk to someone who knows about this place?" She stared across the table at Mary Carson. "The daughter of this man who is so mad, so dangerous, such a criminal... why does she not speak, eh?"

Five pairs of eyes turned to Mary Carson. She was sitting at the end of the long table, next to the vacant place which Edwin Carson had left. She had stared at him all the time he was talking, and stared again from one to the other of the guests as they talked after he had gone.

"Why, of course," said Lady Stone. "How silly of us! Now come along, my good girl—"

"I can't tell you anything. I don't know any more than the rest of you. If you're all prisoners at Thrackley, then I'm just as much a prisoner as any of you."

Lady Stone ran the tip of her tongue around her lips, and placed her elbows firmly on the table. Obviously an ally of Carson, this girl. Probably not his daughter at all. And quite obviously under orders to shut her mouth and keep it shut. Right, then.

"You don't expect us to believe that, do you, my dear? After all, you are Mr. Carson's daughter? You must know something about the—er—the habits of your father..."

"What's the use?" inquired Henry Brampton from the other side of the table. "She's in with the gang. Don't expect her to give anything away, do you?"

"Shut up, Brampton," said Jim. "If it's of any interest to you, Mary is not Edwin Carson's daughter." ("Quite," said Lady Stone to herself. "Quite so.") "And I believe she knows no more about this mess than the rest of us."

"Thank you, Jim," said Mary. She rose and leaned over the back of her chair before crossing to the door under the stairs. "I tell you I'm in this just as deep as you are—just as deep, and no deeper," she said; "but until you've quite made up your minds that I'm not a crook, you can talk the matter over without me."

"Some day, Brampton," said Jim after she had gone, "something very messy will happen to you. And I hope I'm driving the car that does it."

"But, damn it all—"

"Oh, go to hell!"

Mr. Brampton shrugged his shoulders and went, if not to the place suggested, to the French windows at the end of the room. He stared moodily at the bronze handle.

"And what happens now?" said Raoul.

"Heaven and Edwin Carson presumably know the answer to that one," said Jim.

He felt in his pockets, found his case, and lit a cigarette.

"We're in a hole. No doubt about that. I think Lady Stone's right when she says that Edwin Carson is mad. But he's also a criminal… a clever one and a dangerous one. Obviously he brought you all here with the intention of adding to his collection of jewels. He's rigged up all the latest apparatus downstairs for the making of imitation stones. All he had to do was to get hold of your jewellery, remove the specimens he wanted, put a dud in their places, and say 'God speed' to the lot of you on Monday morning. If the scheme had worked properly, the deception would probably not have been found out for years."

"But it didn't work properly."

"No," said Jim. "Thanks to you, Lady Stone, eating perhaps just a little too much quail at dinner, the scheme didn't work out according to plan. But Carson isn't the man to be put off by a little thing like quail. And now that he's been found out, he intends to carry on with the whole plan as arranged. Except that he's doing it now by force instead of by cunning. Yes, brothers, we're in a hole. Good and deep."

"It's all very well," said Lady Stone irritably, "to go on saying that we're in a hole."

"There's no other way of describing Thrackley," murmured Henry Brampton.

"But," continued Lady Stone, ignoring Mr. Brampton, "what do we intend to do about it? We must have a plan. It's perfectly obvious that we must have a plan."

Lady Stone spat out the word in such a way that all who heard it would realize that it was spelt with a capital P.

"I have several acquaintances at Scotland Yard… we must get in touch with them. Then we must have Edwin Carson put under arrest… though no doubt the man will be certified insane. And then we must arrange for the return of the jewels."

"It sounds," said Freddie Usher, "just too simple for words. Yet I suppose you've got about as much chance of doing it as a drunk man with St. Vitus' dance has of getting to the top of Ben Nevis on a pair of antiquated rollerskates."

Lady Stone, subdued by this flight of oratory, said weakly, "What do you mean, Mr. Usher?"

"Well, for one thing, your plan starts with the words 'get in touch with'…"

"Well?"

"You try it, Lady Stone," said Jim. "I'm sure we all wish you luck."

He pressed out the stub of his cigarette. Then he rose and walked away from the table.

"And where might you be going?" said Lady Stone.

"I don't expect Edwin Carson has any objections to our moving our limbs occasionally. After all, he can't expect us to stay sitting round this table until he's ready to let us out. If you're really interested, I'm going to have a talk with Mary."

"Not a bad idea," said Henry Brampton. "But you'll need all your tact to get anything out of the enemy. The female of the species, remember…"

Jim turned as he reached the door of the lounge.

"I hope I'm not in that car when it hits you, Brampton," he said. "I hope it's a six-ton lorry."

And the door slammed behind him as a punctuation to this remark.

He found Mary standing at the front door of the house. She looked back over his shoulder as he came out of the lounge.

"You can come out here," she said. "It's not against the rules. I've just tried it, and not a single alarm went off."

Jim smiled and walked to the doorway beside her.

"Come on out to the garden," he said. "I suppose that's all right? The raspberry canes aren't wired up with dictaphones and electric currents, are they?"

"How should I know? It's not by any means impossible."

"Let's risk it, shall we?"

"Of course."

They walked round the corner of the house until they reached the strip of vegetable garden which ran along two sides of Thrackley.

"Cigarette?" said Jim.

"Thanks. It'll do me good."

"The Prince of Wales," remarked Jim, "was reported once to say that he knew of nothing more soothing than a good cigarette."

"Well, I could do with a spot of soothing; couldn't you?"

"Yes... I'm terribly sorry about what that ass Brampton said."

"That doesn't matter. It's only natural that they should think I'm in with the gang, isn't it?"

"I suppose so. But if ever I meet that man alone in a dark street I'll give him one of the snappiest socks on the jaw he's ever experienced."

"Thanks very much, Jim."

"Mary... we've got to get you out of here."

"Why me? What about the rest of the party?"

"Oh, they've got to get out, too, but..."

"Well?"

"Well, I can't stand the idea of you being mixed up in all this. Living here with Carson and all the rest of it. I... I'm too fond of you, Mary."

"Yes. I suppose that is the trouble."

"Trouble? What—"

"There's no use wasting time talking this sort of talk just now, Jim. Not that I don't like it, you know. I do. Very much indeed, thank you. But dear old Lady Stone was right when she said we must have a plan. We've got to get the police in on this before Edwin Carson pulls it off."

"You think he's in earnest when he says he's going on with the business?"

"Of course he is. That man's life has been wrapped up in the study of jewels, Jim. He's obsessed by them... so much obsessed that now he'd stop at nothing to make an addition to his collection. He's mad, Jim..."

"If only we could get in touch with Hempson..."

"Hempson?"

"Burroughs, I mean. The chauffeur. Of course, you don't know. He's our one chance. He's no ordinary chauffeur. Scotland Yard have had their eagle eye already on your—on friend Carson. And Burroughs is the man they've put on the job of looking after him."

"But that's not much use now. Carson probably has him under lock and key. I suppose he knows now that Burroughs is a policeman?"

"I don't know."

"Even if he doesn't, he'll be keeping him well watched after last night. I wonder..."

"What?"

"We'll try the garage, Jim. I don't expect for one minute that we'll find Burroughs or Hempson or whatever his name is... but we might find something."

"How are you going to get in?"

"I've got a key. The only key I was ever allowed here. I used to take the car out myself sometimes to run up to town—after promising Carson faithfully that I'd stick to the country lanes and not even go near Adderly. Wait here a minute—I'll get it."

She was back in a minute, the key in her hand.

"How are things in the house?" asked Jim. "Any signs of Carson?"

"Not a vestige. They're still talking nineteen to the dozen round the lounge table. Lady Stone has decided to write to the *Daily Express* about it all."

"There'll be quite enough in the papers without any voluntary contributions from that old hen. Come on, let's try the garage."

"Don't hurry—just walk slowly. Carson has probably put Jacobson or one of the servants to watch us from the house. We're all right once we get to the garage. I don't think you can see it from the house through these trees."

They reached the small cement building. Mary put the key in the little door set in a corner of the big swing doors.

"Come on in," she said, "and close the door behind you. Then no one will get suspicious."

"Right," said Jim. He groped about in the darkness. "Where the blazes is that damned switch?"

"Up to the right... in that wall in front of you. Got it?"

"No... yes I have... here we are."

He switched on the electric light and filled the garage with a blaze of light. Then he turned and looked round the building.

"Jim!..." said Mary.

"What's the matter? My God!..."

The big navy-coloured Lagonda had been run into the garage with its bonnet right up against the back wall of the building.

Over that bonnet sprawled the limp figure of a man. His hands fell loosely over one of the mudguards. A narrow rim of bluish-black ran around his neck, just above his collar.

Ronnie Hempson, alias Burroughs, the perfect chauffeur, was very definitely dead.

X X

EDWIN CARSON LOOKED UP FROM THE PAPER OVER WHICH he had been poring when a knock sounded on the door of his study. He folded the paper away in a drawer of his desk and lifted the receiver of the telephone at his elbow. He bent down over the mouthpiece of the receiver and whispered into it.

"There's someone at the door of my study, Jacobson. Just see who it is…"

He waited for a minute, drumming his fingers on the oak top of the desk. The person at the other side of the door knocked again. A louder, more emphatic knock than the first. The sort of knock, it seemed to Edwin Carson, which definitely meant business.

"Well?… indeed… well, just stay outside my study until he leaves, will you, Jacobson? Thank you…"

He put back the receiver on its stand, and opened another of the many drawers in the desk. He took out the revolver which lay in a mass of papers and envelopes, and walked to the door with it gripped firmly in his hand. When he reached the door he stood for a moment, then slowly turned the key in the lock. A well-oiled lock, one of those in which keys could be turned silently and smoothly and without effort…

Poor Burroughs!… he had always been very attentive about these things.

And Edwin Carson walked back to his desk and sat in the chair behind it. He laid the revolver in front of him and covered it with a few sheets of notepaper. And then he said: "Come in, Captain Henderson."

It was evident from Jim's manner as he entered the study that he was not in the best of moods. His lower lip was drawn tightly over the other lip, the small, dimple-like affair between his eyebrows was twitching very slightly (a danger signal, if only Edwin Carson had known it, common to the Hendersons as a clan), and his jaw was thrust out much in the manner of the bows of a ship cleaving its way through a particularly nasty sea. Edwin Carson surveyed all this through his thick-lensed glasses, and felt rather more comfortable when he remembered that under the two sheets of quarto paper in front of him lay a very businesslike weapon.

"Well, Captain Henderson," he said, "this is indeed a pleasure. Not having your usual game on the tennis court this morning, eh?"

Jim looked round the room and finally settled what he hoped was his most aggressive stare on this very unpleasant specimen seated at the desk.

"You can cut out the social stuff, Carson," he said. "I don't think you need worry about keeping up the perfect host attitude any longer now. It must have been a bit of a strain."

Mr. Carson looked hurt.

"You are still my guest, Henderson. And, after all, what have I done to you since you came to Thrackley? Haven't I kept up what you choose to term the perfect host attitude as far as you are concerned? There may, perhaps, be room for complaint with the other members of this little party, but I don't think that you can have anything against me."

"You haven't snaffled my dress studs, if that's what you mean. I can't understand why the hell you asked me here, seeing I haven't anything worth stealing."

The little man at the desk looked a shade more hurt than before.

"Really, Captain Henderson—" he began.

"Oh, for God's sake stop trying to fool me. Let's get down to brass tacks."

"By all means. What is the reason for this visit, Captain Henderson? Some complaint about the food or the servants? Or are you merely homesick like the others?"

"Ronnie—I mean Burroughs—your chauffeur..."

"Yes?"

"He's dead. I suppose you killed him."

Edwin Carson gripped the edge of the desk and leaned forward towards Jim. For a moment Jim dallied with the idea of landing what is commonly referred to as a sock on the jaw. Then he dismissed the proposition, attractive though it was. For what good, after all, would a sock on Edwin Carson's jaw do to him? In any case, Carson probably had a brace of his servants ready behind the desk to deal with sockers. Which was very nearly true, for, in the corridor outside, Jacobson was on the point of opening the study door and taking a hand in the proceedings. He had only a limited view of Mr. Henderson's back through the keyhole, but he did not like the look of that back at all. A nasty, purposeful, hundred-per-cent action back. And if Mr. Henderson's back view looked as bad as that, what (thought Jacobson to himself) would Mr. Henderson's front view be like at the moment?

"Well?" said Jim. "Do you deny killing Burroughs?"

Edwin Carson did not answer. Instead, he reached forward to an oblong box of ebony wood which lay on the desk. He drew out a Turkish cigarette and tapped it on the desk-top, rather to Jim's disappointment, for he had expected the ebony box to contain something more melodramatic than a hundred cigarettes. A revolver, perhaps, or a dangerous-looking dagger. He watched Carson light his cigarette in silence.

"Will you have one?" said Carson, pushing the box over to Jim.

"No, thanks," said Jim. A few thousand magazine stories and films and stage plays in which the hero had been drugged by one of the villain's special brand of cigarettes loomed up in his mind. And then, telling himself to be not quite such a damned fool, he said: "Yes, I think I will."

"Splendid," said Edwin Carson. "Now, I'll tell you quite frankly. I did not kill Burroughs. But I told Jacobson to kill him. He was dangerous. He knew too much. You others—the guests, I mean— you are so helpless in the matter. You don't know enough. But Burroughs—he was different. He knew everything. I'm afraid I trusted him completely. The only man, I think, who ever fooled me. And so he had to go."

"You're a little swine, Carson."

"Thank you."

"I suppose you knew that Burroughs was a detective?"

"Only recently. He told me so himself."

"He told you?"

"Well, not exactly. But he told you, when you and Mr. Usher met him and had your charming talk on your old schooldays in the garage. I had to fit the microphone installation in the garage myself... Burroughs could not see the necessity for one there. And he was so thorough about the other installations all over the house... did the whole thing without a single mistake. Even when you found the microphone in your bedroom, Captain Henderson, he was the first to suggest a more suitable hiding-place for it. Yes, I knew Burroughs was a detective... not a very good detective, do you think? Really good detectives do not employ stray guests at house-parties for their assistants."

"Never mind that. Burroughs is dead. What are you going to do about it?"

"About what? About the body?... that will be disposed of quite easily, Captain Henderson. No need to worry yourself on that account. And the rest is in your hands. The question is—what are *you* going to do about it?"

"I'm going to get you hanged," said Jim.

"I don't think so. Just consider the situation. When you get out of here I shall be safely on the Continent. It is very easy to get lost on the Continent. One lies low for a week or so, and grows a beard perhaps, and then one may walk down the Rue de Rivoli and ask the way to the Gare de Lyons from any gendarme without the slightest fear. And you... what will you be doing?"

"We," said Jim, "will be making a hell of a row. Especially Catherine Lady Stone. We'll have every newspaper giving your pedigree, every police force in Europe learning your description by heart, every jewel merchant and fence in England and the Continent ready for you and your rotten collection of sparklers."

"Interesting. Very interesting. But I wonder?... When you leave Thrackley, what will you do? Go and tell the police, and perhaps the newspapers. And they will come to corroborate this fantastic tale of yours. And what will they find? An old house, deserted. A very ordinary cellar with none of the cunning machinery for converting old stones into new which you will have described. And certainly," said Edwin Carson, "they will find no dead bodies at Thrackley."

"I sincerely hope," said Jim, "that they will have the pleasure of finding yours."

"I wonder if you would have said that thirty years ago?"

"What do you mean?"

"Nothing... nothing at all. Good morning, Captain Henderson. I have a great deal of work to do. Passport to arrange... 'plane to charter... everything to get ready for leaving this delightful spot. Good morning."

"Of all the bloody little swine I've met," observed Jim as he walked to the door of the study, "you are the bloodiest."

"And probably the littlest," said Edwin Carson, reaching for another of his excellent cigarettes.

Jim slammed the door noisily behind him. He had not got the best of that interview, he thought.

"Now what the hell do you want?" he asked.

Jacobson, the butler, smiled his very distressing smile and picked up a tray which lay on the table beside him.

"I was on my way, sir," he said, "to sound the gong for luncheon. Any objections, Mr. Amateur Detective?"

"None whatever, Mr. Professional Murderer," said Jim.

The company which gathered for lunch was in very much the same state of mind as that which had collected itself round the breakfast-table. Catherine Lady Stone still monopolized the conversation. She had, it appeared, remembered an intimate friend at Broadcasting House who would be the very man to help them out of this dreadful affair. Though, when pressed on the subject, Catherine Lady Stone had to admit that she had not the slightest idea how any official, high or low, of the British Broadcasting Corporation could be of much practical value in getting the Thrackley guests out of Thrackley: Freddie Usher and Henry Brampton still looked on the affair as a temporary tragedy to which a solution was bound to turn up sooner or later. And Raoul and Marilyn Brampton were both frankly frightened. Raoul because she saw herself out of favour with Mr. Cyrus T. Crammstein, whose latest venture, *Soft Sugar*, was just recovering from a rather unfavourable first night and could certainly not be expected to stand the absence of any of its principals on more than two consecutive evening performances. And Marilyn because she had unfortunately happened to go to the garage shortly after Jim and Mary had left it and had seen Burroughs, the chauffeur, lying dead over the bonnet of the Lagonda.

Two of the house-party were absent from the dining-room, Jim noticed. The host ("Thank God that little rat has had the decency to stay away from this meal," as Lady Stone put it) and Mary.

"Well," said Freddie Usher, "do we squat the bodies? No sense in waiting for Santa Claus, is there?"

"He's probably foraging among my cuff-links at the present moment," said Henry Brampton.

"Let's start."

"Where's Mary?" asked Jim.

"You ought to know, if anyone does, Captain Henderson," said Lady Stone. "Haven't you been in the garden with her all morning?"

"Yes… she left me about an hour ago to go to her room."

"Probably assisting with my cuff-links," suggested Mr. Brampton.

"If it weren't for the fact that we were just starting lunch, I should kill you quite cheerfully, Brampton."

"Well, we are just starting lunch, so that's quite out of the question," said Lady Stone. "And we've got quite enough to put us off our food without anything more. Come along—let's sit down."

"Perfectly right, Lady Stone. The Geneva attitude every time," murmured Freddie Usher. "There, now, boys, behave yourselves. Jim, pass Mr. Brampton the salt, there's a good fellow."

The five guests at Thrackley sat in their places around the big table. Jim unfolded the serviette which lay on his plate. It crackled as he did so. Yes, crackled: no doubt about it. He prodded it on his lap... the thing crackled again. And (being unaccustomed to serviettes which behaved in this way whenever you touched them) he felt in its folds and brought to light a half-sheet of notepaper. He laid it out on his knees and read:

> I'm down in the cellars, Jim, safely locked in. Don't worry about me, and please don't do anything or tell anyone about me. I've found that Carson is making a bolt for it to-night—either he's got all he wants in the way of jewels or else he's got the wind up. Keep a look-out from your bedroom window, Jim, but don't do *anything* until you see Carson get out of the grounds. I think with me down here we've got a pretty fair chance of coming out top in this after all. Don't let anyone see this note—tear it up after you've read it.   MARY.

Jim looked up from the note into the unpleasant face of Jacobson, the butler, poising plates around the back of his chair.

"Soup, sir?" Jacobson inquired.

"Yes, damn you," said Jim.

XXI

A T SEVEN O'CLOCK EDWIN CARSON REMOVED HIS JACKET AND rolled up the sleeves of his shirt. There was a great deal to be done and none too long a time in which to do it. He hung the jacket neatly over the back of one of the chairs in his study (for on even the busiest of busy evenings there is no need to spoil a perfectly good jacket by flinging it on the floor) and he telephoned to the kitchen of Thrackley and asked Jacobson to present himself immediately. When the butler arrived, Edwin Carson pointed to the jacket... and Jacobson smiled, took off his own rather antiquated tail coat, detached the detachable cuffs from his shirt, and rolled up his sleeves to the same businesslike heights as those of his master. And Edwin Carson locked the door of the study, put the key in his pocket, crossed to the shattered panels which had once hidden so effectively the entrance to his cellars, said "Come on, then!" and both he and the butler disappeared from view.

And from seven-five, when the lift deposited them in the cellar, until a quarter to two on the following morning, Edwin Carson and Jacobson worked extremely hard.

"We'll close up the machinery first," Carson had said. And within an hour the door which led to the little room at the end of the cellar was giving a very creditable impersonation of a substantial stone wall. There is no better way of closing a gap in a wall than that of using the stones you have removed to make that gap. Edwin Carson realized this. When he had had that door knocked through the thick wall of his cellar ("Just a little storeroom... I shall be keeping bulbs and things like that here," as he had explained to the two well-paid and consequently uninquisitive workmen who had done the job) he had given very definite orders that the stones should not be removed from the cellars... no necessity at all to drag them all the way up through the house and into the garden:a much more simple matter to lay them neatly in a corner of the little-room. So, after an hour's fairly heavy loss of perspiration, the entrance to the little room had almost disappeared. Only a couple of the big stone slabs to go into position now at the top of the opening... and then the apparatus on which Edwin Carson had worked so long, the clever little lathes and polishers and cutters which had turned out a twin to so many precious stones... all lost from view, perhaps for ever. Preferably for ever, thought Edwin Carson. He stood on tiptoe on one of the remaining stones and peered into the room... the square of light which was all that now filtered through fell on one of the benches. A tiny file and a few coloured pearls lay in the light. A pity that he had had to leave everything in such disorder, but that could not be helped. He stepped down from the stone and helped Jacobson to hoist it in its place. The last slab fitted exactly into the space behind it. "Now," said Edwin Carson, "if you will just touch up those little spaces between the stones, Jacobson... not too much, you understand?... just a little bit, to give the impression of old cement that has worn away... that's right... and remember to sweep the floor round here, won't you?... all this dust off the stones might make people think, mightn't it?" He was rather enjoying the evening already; rather revelling in the thought that, where almost every other man would have left some clue or have forgotten some tiny but important thing... he, Edwin Carson, was going to make another perfectly flawless exit.

He crossed to the desk, pulled out its many drawers, ran his fingers through their contents. Then he pulled towards him, one after the other, the switches which lay in the panel at the side of the desk. The oblong cases all around the cellar walls came slowly into view... the brilliant electric lights reflected once again on the different stones lying in their beds of velvet. And Edwin Carson took the stout Gladstone bag which he had brought down from the study, and went slowly round the walls, stopping at each case. He produced a ring of tiny keys from his pocket, opened first the wire protection and then the plate glass covering of each case. He ripped the pale blue velvet cloth out of the first case, arranged it at the foot of the Gladstone bag, spilled the dozen diamonds which had lain on it into a corner of the bag much as though they were the beginnings of a weekend's packing. In half an hour the Gladstone bag was filled with a sparkling collection of jewels... and the cases around the walls seemed particularly dull and lifeless without their contents. Another length of velvet from the last of the cases folded neatly on top of the bag's contents, a minute's searching for another ring of keys, and the double lock of the Gladstone bag fastened with two satisfying clicks. Edwin Carson walked back to the desk. He pushed back the switches in the panel... the wall was once again just a wall.

"Now, Jacobson," he said, "you'll remove this panel of switches, please... be very careful not to damage the desk while you're taking it out... you have your tools?... that's right... an ordinary screwdriver will do the turn, I think... and I'll attend to the wiring while you're busy with that."

The wiring of the cellar took rather longer than Carson had expected. It had been, after all, very thoroughly wired. Wires to each of the cases in the walls, electric light wiring to nearly a dozen bulbs in the main cellar and the little rooms which led off it, wiring to the machinery in the ante-room which was now blocked up, ordinary telephone wiring to the house and the garage. Edwin Carson perspired a great deal more freely than ever before, swore at the pair of pliers in his hands, cursed the idiots who had stapled down the wires so firmly in position. But, for all the swearing and the perspiring, he made fairly steady progress and by midnight only the electric lights in the main cellar remained to be disconnected.

"What d'you want to take them down for?" said Jacobson. "Nothing suspicious in having electric light in a cellar, is there?"

"Something very suspicious in having twelve high-powered points, don't you think, Jacobson?... and besides, if ever anyone does investigate this part of the house, I should prefer them to have as little light as possible to help the investigation... get on with your work, Jacobson, and talk a little less... you can burn all the papers in the desk, if you've nothing better to do... put them in the middle of the floor and set a light to them... all except those in the pigeon-hole at this end... this end,-mind you... and bring me that other case across to put this damned wire into..."

"You're not taking all that much away with you?"

"What do you think?... leave it all here in a heap in the middle of the floor for the first person who comes down here to trip over and start asking questions?... really, Jacobson, you have no imagination... none at all."

The unimaginative Jacobson shrugged his shoulders and turned to the heavy oak desk. He emptied each of the many drawers and pigeonholes until there was quite a satisfactory pile of papers lying on the stone floor of the cellar. Only the little bundle in the pigeon-hole at the left of the desk remained untouched.

"Got a match?"

Edwin Carson tucked the last strand of wire into the case at his feet, brought a booklet of matches from his waistcoat pocket, struck one and threw it on the pile of papers. The match hesitated for a minute, decided to go out, thought better of it, and in a very short time the cellar was lit up with the flames. Carson looked at the fire as it lowered.

"You haven't touched anything in that end pigeon-hole?" he asked.

"Not a thing."

"Good." He crossed to the desk, putting his hand to shield the eyes behind the heavy spectacles as he passed the fire. "No… all here. I'll take care of this little bundle myself, Jacobson. A very important bundle… very important indeed."

He untied the string around the papers in his hand and laid them out on the top of the desk. A photograph of a young, attractive-looking man. Three diaries, held together in a rubber band. A very long typewritten letter. Another long document, a legal one by the look of it, witnessed and sealed on its last page. He stood for quite a while gazing at the photograph of the young man… and then he remembered that there was still a great deal of work to be done, and that this was neither the time nor the place for becoming sentimental…

"Right, then, Jacobson… I think we are nearly ready now… just have a last look round, will you?… No, come over here and help me push the desk back against this wall… that's right… and take those chairs up to the study—and that little cabinet over there… don't leave any furniture down here at all except the desk… we can't very well take that out…"

Jacobson collected the two chairs and the small cabinet, placed them in the lift, pressed the switch which sent the lift whirring smoothly up to the study.

"Jacobson!… just a minute!…"

The lift stopped half-way on its journey. The feet of the two chairs, the cabinet, and Jacobson were all that could be seen from the cellar.

"The dust-sheets," said Edwin Carson. "Bring them down while you're up there... and some dust—a lot of dust, Jacobson."

"Dust?"

"Yes, you fool... dust. I told you to collect some, didn't I? We have to leave this place looking as though it hadn't been opened up for years."

"You're doing the thing properly, aren't you?" said the voice of Jacobson.

"It is the best way to do anything, Jacobson."

"All right... I'll get your damned dust."

"And hurry, for God's sake... it's after one o'clock already."

The lift whirred again and Jacobson's feet disappeared upwards. Edwin Carson looked round. The fire of papers was almost out now and the dull red glow of it was the only light in the cellar. He crossed to the desk, felt along the top of it, found his electric torch and switched it on. He played its beam around the walls. He made it stop for a while on the built-up door to the machinery room, and smiled in satisfaction at the solid piece of stone wall which he saw. Then he crossed to the other end of the cellar and tried the door of the little room in which Catherine Lady Stone had spent her very uncomfortable Friday and Saturday evenings. It was locked, though the bolts on the outside of the door were back from their catches. He stood back, pulling at his nose in annoyance. He could not remember having locked that door... yet he supposed he must have done so... anyway, the keys were upstairs in the pocket of his jacket and he had no time to worry about that now... there was nothing in there to give anything away, anyhow. He walked back to the desk, collected the papers which he had taken from the pigeon-hole, tied the string around them and patted them untidily into his hip pocket. And then he placed his finger on the only two switches left fitted in the desk, and pulled them back in their sockets. He smiled again at the thought of his guests lying more or less peacefully in their beds, quite convinced that they were imprisoned in a house surrounded by burglar alarms and powerful electric currents. Whereas, from that moment onwards, any of the people inside Thrackley were able to walk out of the house and past the high wall which ran around the grounds without the slightest fear of raising an alarm or receiving a shock. A very satisfactory situation indeed.

He walked to the lift, pressed the switch in front of him, waited until the cage came to rest opposite him, and stepped in. Jacobson was in the study when he stepped out of the lift and through the broken panels.

"Dustcloths," said Edwin Carson, surveying the butler. "Dustcloths and dust... very good work, Jacobson. Just go down and do what I told you, then... spread the cloths over the desk... and just scatter all that mess about the place to make the cellar look something like a cellar... and don't take all night about it, Jacobson, for God's sake... Hurry, now... we're ready to go, Jacobson... ready to go!"

The butler stopped before entering the lift with his load of dustsheets and his bucketful of dust.

"Good many hurried getaways we've made—you and I, Carson," he said.

"A good many, Jacobson, as you say. And I'm not so sure that this one isn't going to be the most successful of the lot. Come on, man, get down and get that done... let's get out of here."

"I won't be sorry, Carson."

He looked back over his shoulder at the little man busy foraging through the papers on the study table.

"What about Adams and Kenrick?" he asked.

"Don't you worry about them, Jacobson," said Edwin Carson. "I'm looking after them all right."

"And the girl?"

"She… she'll just be left behind, Jacobson."

And the butler smiled and vanished behind the panels with his dust and dustcloths. Edwin Carson put his finger to the switch—the lift went smoothly down to the cellars again.

"All right, Jacobson?"

"All right… I could do with a light, though."

"Just a minute. I'll bring down my torch."

And then Edwin Carson did a very strange thing. He threw the light of his torch on to the switch which operated the lift, pressed for a moment on the small ebonite panel in which the switch had been built. And a section of that panel slid back, showing a second socket into which the switch might go if anyone chose to make it do so. He pressed on the switch with his thumb until it shot with a click into the socket. And the lift from the cellar came slowly to half-way between the cellar and the study floors. And stayed there.

He turned off the light of his torch and listened in the darkness.

Very faintly the voice of Jacobson could be heard… miles below, it seemed:

"Carson!… Carson!… what the hell are you doing with this lift?… Send the damned thing down, will you?… Carson! Carson, you bloody little swine!…"

And in the study Edwin Carson leaned over the shaft of the lift and said quietly:

"The dustsheets over the desk, Jacobson, and spread the dust about carefully… all over the floor, you understand?… I want it to look as though no one had entered that cellar for years…"

He knew that Jacobson could not possibly hear him. But it was rather satisfying to be able to say these things to a man whom he had just fooled so successfully. And Edwin Carson put on his jacket and began to hum contentedly to himself. A pity that he had not got Jacobson to dust the jacket before he went down to the cellars. But still—another very good night's work, he thought.

XXII

THERE ARE MANY WAYS OF SPENDING AN EVENING MORE pleasant than lying quite still on the stone floor of a small, unlit room. Mary had found this out early in the evening, and by one o'clock the truth of it was painfully evident. She lay flat on the cold floor of the room which led off the main cellar and listened at the gap between the floor and the bottom rail of the heavy door. They were still there, and still busy. The smell of smoke, which had puzzled her a short while ago, had almost gone how; the lights of the cellar had evidently been turned off, for the thin streak of light no longer came under the door. Now they were moving furniture... she could hear the big desk being dragged across the cellar floor, and the other chairs and things being collected together. And one of the two persons who had spent so busy an evening within a few yards of where she lay was carrying something to the lift and taking whatever it was out of the cellar. The shaftway of the lift ran up the wall at her side... she could hear the whirr of its machinery. And whoever had been left in the cellar was walking slowly round the walls; she could make out the sound of his feet as he came nearer the door in front of her. She lay very still when the feet stopped in their walk and someone tried the handle of the door...

He tried it again, giving the lock a hefty shove. She recognized the muttered "Damn the thing!" as Edwin Carson's voice, and lay back against the wall, holding her breath in the silence. The footsteps sounded again in the cellar outside... going slowly away from the door. She put her hand to her forehead and found it wet and very cold. And what was Edwin Carson going to do now?

She listened again. Evidently something else being dragged across the floor towards the lift. A second's silence, then the sound of the lift coming down from the floor above. She heard the two bumps as Edwin Carson placed his very valuable luggage on the floor of the lift cage. And then up again, more slowly than usual this time. She waited for nearly five minutes… had almost decided to turn the key in front of her and step out into the cellar when the lift whirred down again. Not finished even yet, apparently… only one pair of feet on the stone floor this time, though. And almost as soon as the feet had stepped from the lift, the cage shot up the shaft again. Quickly… more quickly than ever she had heard it before. Another silence, and then, echoing through the cellar, so loud that it seemed to deafen her:

"Carson!… Carson!… what the hell are you doing with this lift?… Send the damned thing down, will you?… Carson!… Carson, you bloody little swine!…"

Jacobson!… She listened for an answer and heard none.

"Carson!… My God, I'll kill you for this!… You filthy swine… let me out of here… let me out, do you hear?… Carson, for God's sake…"

Mary felt on the floor of the little room for the electric torch which she had brought, found it, raised herself on her knees, and slowly turned the key in the lock of the door. The door opened easily, without the slightest noise. She stepped out into the big cellar. Pitch darkness everywhere. She could hear Jacobson's breathing a few yards in front of her. She pressed down the switch of the torch, flung the circle of light full in his face.

"What—who the hell's that?"

"Put that revolver down, Jacobson."

"You… Miss Mary… what the—?"

"Never mind how I got here, Jacobson. I've been here all night. Carson's tricked you, has he?"

"Looks like it... the dirty little blackguard..."

"Sounds good, that, coming from you. Come over here. And lay that revolver down somewhere. Any lights down here at all?"

"Not now. Taken them all out not an hour ago."

"Well, this torch will last for an hour or so. Now you do some talking, friend Jacobson. What's been happening here to-night?"

"Mind your own damned business."

"And let Carson get away scot free, with you left to explain a dead man and a wholesale theft of jewellery? Come on, now, Jacobson, think again."

Mary waited a minute before he answered. Jacobson apparently had thought again.

"You're right, Miss Mary. By God, you're right. I'll tell everything I know about that damned crook... I will, honest to God... I don't care what the hell happens to me... but, my God, I'll do my best to get something to happen to him."

"Now," said Mary, "you're talking sensibly, Jacobson."

"You know what's been going on here, don't you, miss? You know what the boss's game has been these last two or three years?"

"I could make a pretty good guess."

"Well, this here cellar has been where the dirty's been going on. There's a room in there—at the end there—same kind of place as the one you came out of... God, you didn't half give me a turn, miss..."

"Never mind your turns. What about this room?"

"That's where he kept all his doings. For turning out dud jewels. Worked there all night, he did. Never went to bed. He got me or one of the other lads to snaffle the stuff... said at first he wanted to borrow the goods for experimenting on… that went a long way down with me, I must say… and by the morning he'd have a dud fixed up to put back in place of the real ones. Regular wonders, they were, too… couldn't tell the difference if they was standing side by side…"

"I know. I've seen them."

"That was in there. He's had me block up the doorway to-night. Wanted everything to be left as if it was just an ordinary cellar. Dustsheets over that desk and everything. Even got me to bring dust down here… the lousy little swine!… If ever I so much as…"

"All right, all right! What else have you done to-night?"

"Taken down all the electric lights and all the wiring."

"Wiring?"

"Yes, miss—the whole place has been wired up so much you couldn't move without tripping on something. Telephones, dicta-phones, microphones, this burglar-alarm of his… he did the thing proper, I'll say that for him…"

"You've disconnected everything? Nothing's left wired up?"

"Not a thing… except the alarm and the wires to the current round the walls. Had to leave that, you see, to keep all you people inside. If you'd tried to open them gates while that current was on, you'd have had a nasty surprise all right."

"And that's still connected up?"

"Yes—he switched it off just before he went up to the study. Then he sent me down with this damned dust. Dust!… I'll dust him if ever I get my eyes on him again. That's what he'll be, Miss Mary… just dust…"

"Jacobson! Where's this switch?"

"The one he's left? Over there… inside the desk."

"Come over and show me."

They crossed to the other end of the cellar. The butler pulled open the top of the big desk. Mary shone her torch inside it.

"There… that switch in the black panel."

"D'you realize what's happening, Jacobson, at this moment? Carson is getting away. Getting clear of this for ever, if he's at all lucky. He's probably in the garage now, getting that stuff into the car. In a few minutes he'll be going down the drive, through the gates, out into the world. D'you realize, Jacobson? *Through the gates!*"

"My God, Miss Mary…"

"That little switch is the one thing that can stop him. It's at 'Off' just now, Jacobson…"

Jacobson peered down into the desk. His head showed up as a huge shadow on the cellar wall.

"Off… quarter… half… full…" he read. "Clear out without me, would you, Edwin Carson? Get away after making me do all your filthy work for you… bringing down dust to the cellar to put your ruddy finishing touches to it… Well, good-bye, you dirty little swine…"

Mary turned off the light of her torch. In the dark she heard the three clicks as the switch was pushed along the panel.

"What do we do now?" asked Jacobson.

"Just wait, I think," said Mary. "I don't think we'll need to wait very long."

XXIII

THE THRACKLEY HOUSE-PARTY MADE FOR THEIR BEDS THAT evening at the early hour of nine-thirty. Their day had consisted entirely of sitting opposite one another, talking to one another about one another, and eventually looking at one another in a peevish silence... just the sort of programme which is apt to have a fraying effect on the stoutest of nerves. Catherine Lady Stone was the first to go. Lady Stone had not spoken for the last two hours (which, as Henry Brampton remarked, made the situation seem all the more unreal), and when she suddenly shot from her chair and said loudly: "I can't stand it another minute!" the effect was much the same as if a lorry-load of milk-cans had collided with a double-decker bus in the middle of the Two Minutes' Silence. The door of the lounge slammed behind Lady Stone, and the rest of the house-party stared at the door as though they were seeing it for the first time. "You don't think she's going to risk the alarms?" said Marilyn Brampton, who had reached the stage when she would gladly have seen Lady Stone electrocuted if only it would enable her to walk over the dead body and out of the grounds of Thrackley. "No," said Freddie Usher, "I think she's gone to bed. And as it's the first sensible thing she's suggested to-day, I think we might do much worse than follow the old dear."

So the Thrackley guests walked silently upstairs to their rooms. If one had been able to snatch a glimpse in those rooms one would have noticed that the guests behaved very differently from their first night at Thrackley. Catherine Lady Stone lay on her bed, fully clothed. She had tried to make her day's entry in her diary and had been much annoyed to find that on this day of all days, when so much might have been written down, her hand shook so violently that even she herself could not make out the writing. Marilyn Brampton paced the carpet of her room, lit one cigarette off the stub of another, and jumped at least six inches every time the wind knocked one of the pine branches outside against the panes of her window. Henry Brampton did his best to forget the awkwardness of the situation by a nice use of the decanter of whisky and the siphon of soda water which he had tucked under each arm as he left the lounge. Freddie Usher, who had noticed Mr. Brampton's armfuls, spent an unhappy hour wishing that he had either Mr. Brampton's foresight or the courage to go downstairs alone and find another decanter. And Jim sprawled across the settee in his room and read, for the fiftieth time, the note from Mary.

"I'm down in the cellars, Jim, safely locked in... *don't do anything* until you see Carson get out of the grounds... with me down here we've a pretty fair chance of coming out top in this..." All of which sounded very much as though Mary had what Catherine Lady Stone kept on demanding—a Plan. But he didn't like it. The idea of Mary being alone down in those cellars... where Carson and the rest of the gang were bound to spend at least part of the evening before making their getaway... an odds-on chance that Carson would examine the cellars mighty carefully before leaving... would discover Mary... and then God alone knew what might happen... No, he didn't like it at all. And, for all the way Mary had underlined that "don't do anything" in her note, Jim felt that a certain amount of co-operation was called for. Besides, he argued to himself in the mirror, if you didn't do anything until Carson had got clear of Thrackley, what the hell could you do after that? No... one thing he could have a shot at doing, anyway, and that was to make Edwin Carson's exit as difficult a job as possible. And the obvious way to set about that was to pay a visit to the garage and remove the sparking-plugs of the Lagonda. Remove the sparking-plugs of Freddie Usher's car, too, if necessary, since Mr. Carson did not seem to be at all the kind of gentleman who would have any scruples about pinching another man's car when his own was out of action. Right, then. He crossed to the corner of the room where he had laid his suitcase. He felt the hard lump at the bottom of the case where his old Army revolver rested. Move Number One, then: to get a little ammunition for the revolver from Freddie Usher, to pay a visit to the garage and remove all available sparking-plugs and throw same as far into the pine-trees as possible. "What," said Jim to himself, pulling a pair of golf hose over his shoes, "what could be simpler?"

He knocked at Freddie's door and walked in. Mr. Usher was brushing his teeth. "Even though we are cluttered up in a lousy electrified prison by a nasty little maniac," said Freddie through a great deal of lather, "there's no sense in allowing one's pyorrhoea to get away with it, is there? What are you after?"

"A few cartridges, please. I brought the old gun, as you told me, but I hadn't any ammunition. And nothing improves a gun so much as ammunition. Thanks, that's enough. At least, I hope so."

"Who's the victim?"

"Just anyone. I don't feel at all particular at the moment."

"Can I be of any assistance?"

"No, thanks. Except by keeping out of the way."

"Thanks very much."

"You don't mind if I ruin the engine of your car?"

"Why on earth—?"

"I'm going to do a spot of plug-removing. I'd better do yours as well as Carson's. I know you wouldn't like him to go off in your nice clean Rolls. Good night."

And Jim opened the door and stepped out once again into the corridor. He started to walk to his own room, when the sound of voices from the staircase made him stop. Opposite the door of Freddie Usher's room was one of Thrackley's immaculate and up-to-date bathrooms. He stepped in quickly, closed the door, and sat on the floor with his ear to the keyhole. The owners of the voices were on the landing now. The other two members of the Carson beauty chorus—Kenrick and Adams. He heard a door being quietly locked. "That's 'im, then," said Kenrick. A few more steps along the corridor and another key turned in another lock. "And little Freddie—that's the lot, isn't it?" said the unpleasant baritone of Adams. Jim waited for nearly five minutes after the two pairs of footsteps had gone downstairs again, then stepped out into the corridor. He tried his own door. Locked! Hell!... the cartridges in his pocket were of no great use now. He walked to Freddie's room and tried the handle of his door. Equally locked. There was this to his advantage, anyway—that Carson and Co. now thought that the entire house-party of Thrackley was safely under lock and key, whereas one member was very much out and about, even with a useless pocket of ammunition and no gun. He knocked lightly on Freddie's door. "Come in," said Freddie.

"Sorry, I can't. You've been locked in, old boy. So have I, but I wasn't in the room when they locked it. Just go to bed like a good fellow and I'll tell you all the news in the morning."

"What about the gun?"

"Have to do without it. Unless you can get yours below the bottom of the door. Have a shot."

But Mr. Usher's door was one of those sensible affairs which refuse to allow the slightest draught to come sweeping in below the bottom rail, and the tip of the revolver's barrel was all that could be wedged through the narrow space. "Hell!" said Jim.

"Quite," said Freddie from the other side. "Hell!"

"Well, good night, Freddie... sweet dreams."

When Jim reached the foot of the staircase he was relieved to find two things. The lights in the hall had been left on, and the front door of the house had not been bolted and barred in its usual secure fashion for the night. Mercifully so, he thought; for there seemed no other way of reaching the garage than through the front door of Thrackley. He walked out into the garden, keeping on the grass borders and avoiding any steps on the gravel drive which might give him away. The night was cloudy and windy; there was an incessant swaying and swishing and creaking in the pine-trees all around him. He reached the garage, took a look round, and walked towards the small door at the end of the building. Since he had no keys, there would have to be another lock broken to-night. The thing was becoming quite an epidemic at Thrackley. This was a small, delicate affair, though; one or two good heaves from the shoulder ought to do the trick, provided that they did not attract the attention of anyone inside the house. He gave the first of the one or two heaves. The door gave without the slightest argument and he careered wildly through and into the darkness of the garage, coming to a sudden stop by crashing into the bonnet of Edwin Carson's Lagonda. Splendid... apart from the bump on his forehead where he had met the Lagonda. The little door must have been unlocked all the time. So far, at any rate, the gods were on the side of the righteous.

He searched up the wall to his left for the electric light switch. Last time he had found that switch he had found also a very unpleasant surprise... he wondered if the limp body of Burroughs, the chauffeur, would still be sprawling across the car's bonnet... or had Edwin Carson already disposed of that little reminder of his tenancy of Thrackley? He found the switch eventually and turned it on. And another surprise, almost as unpleasant, met his eyes in the glare of the electric light.

He was not alone in the garage. Far from it. Right at his feet, to the side of the Lagonda's running-board, lay the still figure of Burroughs. And sitting quietly in the driving-seat of the Lagonda was Edwin Carson's accomplished cook-general, Mr. Adams. Mr. Adams sat quite still at the steering-wheel of the car. He looked as though he might easily drop off to sleep at any moment. But in his right hand he gripped a revolver. And the barrel of that revolver was pointed exactly at that part of Jim's anatomy where up to the present moment his heart had always beaten with a fine regularity.

"What the hell do you want?" said Adams.

Jim took another look round the garage. He saw that there was not much point in answering Adams's question. Part of what he had come to the garage to do was already done: the sparking-plugs and a good deal more of the innards of Freddie Usher's Rolls-Royce lay in disorder on the cement floor. And the possibilities of carrying out the rest of his little de-plugging plan seemed rather remote with Adams and the revolver sitting so snugly in the Lagonda. No... a graceful exit was what was called for at the moment, he decided. If such a thing were possible under the circumstances. He backed gingerly to the little door of the garage.

"Come on—what's the game, eh?" said Adams.

Still Jim did not answer. Try as he did, he could think of no suitable reply to the persistent queries of friend Adams. And then friend Adams made his big mistake of the evening. He was determined

to get something out of this ruddy man, Henderson, and equally
determined not to let the ruddy man, Henderson, out of the garage
until he had finished with him. He opened the door of the Lagonda
and stepped out. As he did so, things began to happen to Mr.
Adams with a dreadful suddenness. The first and most important
of these things was that what seemed an indecently long leg shot
out towards him with the speed of a greyhound who has yet to
discover that an electric hare is not at all good for the digestion. For
one horrible second Jim thought that his leg had been a few inches
inadequate; but the revolver shot out of Adams's hand, crashed
against the corrugated iron roof of the garage, and fell on the floor
at the back of the building. And before it had fallen Jim had followed
up his leg-theory work with a wholesale plunge at friend Adams.
For a moment the garage seemed to be filled entirely with feet,
arms and legs all in an advanced state of St. Vitus's dance. Then
Adams lost his balance, and the two men crashed to the floor of
the garage. As they rolled on the floor Jim realized that they were
fighting actually on top of the dead body of Burroughs'. For a split
second his cheek touched the cold back of one of the chauffeur's
hands. It was not a pleasant sensation. The man Adams was small,
but wiry, and (so it seemed to Jim) specially oiled for the occasion
to make him ten times more elusive than the most slippery eel.
He wrenched himself out of Jim's grip, squirmed between his
legs, had himself raised on his knees before Jim could turn round
to get hold of him again. Only a second passed before Jim was
standing upright and ready to perform another Rugby tackle. But
in that second he saw that Adams had managed to get a large and
unpleasant-looking spanner into his right hand, and had it raised
above his head in what seemed to Jim a very determined way. He
jerked himself to one side as the spanner crashed down, grazing

his right shoulder and arm. And at that Jim saw red. He had kept himself admirably under control, he told himself, during all his weekend at Thrackley, and now the time seemed exactly ripe for letting someone know that he possessed such a thing as a straight left. The straight left flashed out. His fist landed exactly on Adams's jaw. The crack which it made when it landed was by far the most satisfying sound Jim had heard since he arrived at Thrackley. Adams could not have thought it so. He gave an unhappy little groan, his knees buckled up under him, and he fell—spanner and all—on to the floor beside the dead body of Burroughs. His head bounced smartly on the running-board of the Lagonda as he fell, and a steady trickle of blood oozed out from the gash in the side of his scalp. Jim felt his own hand and attempted to waggle his fingers. He realized with a further sense of satisfaction that at least two of his fingers were broken. He might not have done much good towards stopping Edwin Carson's exit, but he felt a great deal more contented with life than he had done during the past twenty-four hours. Now for Mary... He picked his way over the bodies of the two men on the floor and crossed to pick up the revolver which he had kicked from Adams's hand. It seemed exactly the sort of thing that might come in very useful on a night like this. He was just stooping to pick it up when the little door of the garage opened and the hard, unpleasant voice of Edwin Carson rapped out the two words: "Don't move!"

For a moment Jim stayed absolutely still in his half-stooping position. Then, disobeying Carson's order, he looked back over his shoulder at the latest arrival in the garage. It was evident that Carson was in no playful mood at the moment. For the second time within a quarter of an hour Jim experienced the unenviable position of having a magnificent view down the barrel of a revolver.

He noticed that Edwin Carson wore a heavy overcoat, a scarf and a cap pulled well down on to his thick spectacles. Cue for exit of principal character, apparently. He wished devoutly he had followed the instructions in Mary's note, "Don't do anything"... and at that moment it looked as though he had done, and probably undone, everything he possibly could.

"Stand up straight."

Jim stood up and turned to face Carson. He found himself noticing that Edwin Carson was sweating while he himself was cold—exceedingly cold.

"You've been a bit of a damned nuisance to me, Henderson," said Carson slowly. "I suppose I was a fool to bring you down here. If it was anyone else but you who was standing there just now I'd pull this trigger and put a bullet in their brain. I'm going to pull the trigger, anyway... but seeing it's you, that's all you're getting..."

Jim had a confused impression of a surprisingly quiet report, a sudden shoot of flame, a stinging pain somewhere in his left leg. He would have fallen had he not gripped the edge of the bench which ran along the back wall of the garage. After which he did not see things too clearly. But he realized the astonishing fact that Edwin Carson had crossed over to him, had lifted him bodily on to his back with an ease which was amazing for so little a man, had carried him out of the garage and was now labouring with him through the garden and into the house. With each uncomfortable jolt Jim's brain became, if anything, a little more foggy... yet he knew that he was being taken up the wide staircase of Thrackley, along the corridor which led to his bedroom, that the man who was carrying him was opening his bedroom door, that he was inside the room now and had been laid more or less carefully upon his bed. The pain in his left leg twitched damnably.

He tried to raise himself on the bed… he had a faint recollection of Edwin Carson standing at the door and saying: "Now, I don't think you'll be any further trouble. Good-bye." And an even fainter recollection of the key turning in the keyhole after Edwin Carson had left the room.

It seemed to Jim that he lay without moving for hours after the door closed. Actually it was less than ten minutes. He got up slowly and put his leg down gingerly on the carpet. The pain shot through the leg with the renewed vigour of a rugger team after the half-time lemons, but he managed to limp across the room to the dressing-table. He took a long drink of cold water, filled the wash-basin with a further supply of the same liquid and plunged his head into it. He came up, gurgling and short of breath, but with his brain considerably cleared. He stood and listened for a minute in silence. Had Carson made his getaway while he was lying on his bed? He crossed the room to the windows and listened again.

Behind those trees down there, if his geography had not deserted him at this crucial moment, lay the garage and the block of small outside building beside it. He strained his ears for what seemed an unending length of time without hearing anything more important than the scratching of an itinerant strand of ivy against one of the panes of his window. And then… a nasty, scraping noise, made much nastier and much more scraping because whatever was the cause of the noise was being done slowly and stealthily and in an effort to make as little disturbance as possible. Diagnose that nasty, scraping noise, thought Jim, and what have you? And the only answer to that was that the heavy swing doors of the garage were being heaved open. A very obstinate, annoying set of doors to open, too. It looked as though the principal character was still on the stage.

And in another five minutes a further sound added itself to the swishing of the pine-trees and the scratching of the errant piece of ivy. A low, rich purr... that sort of purr which is in itself one of the best possible advertisements for the very powerful and very expensive variety of car which responds to the slightest touch of the self-starter at any hour of the day or night. Jim waited while the purr continued... a little louder, then a slight pause, then louder again, then back to the first steady note. The trees, though they resembled most Society débutantes in that they were as dense as they were beautiful, might as well not have been planted in their position as far as Jim was concerned. He could see the whole of the manoeuvres through listening to those expensively sounding notes of the long navy-blue saloon car in the garage... the slow backing out between the garage doors, the little run in reverse up the slope to the left of the garage entrance, the changing of gear and then the gradual speeding up of the car as she ran down the drive. In thirty seconds now it would come into view where there was a gap in the trees.

Jim watched it with difficulty as it slid down the drive to the big iron gates. One person alone in it—Edwin Carson, the host of the house-party—and in the back of the car a piled-up mass of cases was just recognizable. Lady Stone's choker necklace... Raoul's turquoises... heaven knows how much more precious cargo... all somewhere in the back of that silently moving car. And Edwin Carson making his getaway, calmly and collectedly, just as he had had the effrontery to tell them. Hell!...

The car was within a few feet of the gates now. It stopped, and Edwin Carson got out from the driving-seat. He looked around him, then up at the house... Jim drew back behind the mullion between the two windows... and then, apparently satisfied, the little man walked to the big iron gates to open them and leave his guests and his house to look after themselves.

Even from his viewpoint, where he could see everything in the opening in the trees, Jim hardly realized what happened to Edwin Carson in that next minute. He saw him carefully remove the white gloves he was wearing, place his hands on the heavy upright bars of the gates in an effort to pull them open. And then the back of Edwin Carson twitched suddenly, his arms straightened out like piston-rods, his whole body squirmed in convulsions. He dropped on the gravel path at the foot of the big gates... one hand still clung to the iron bar which it had gripped. He lay quite still.

Jim stood at the window for fully a quarter of an hour before he could take his eyes from the still, cramped figure. Carson's face was turned towards the house... Jim could just make out the glint of his spectacles in the glare of the car's headlights. Something had happened to the little man's mouth... something unpleasant...

The low purr of the Lagonda went steadily on.

XXIV

MARY SAT IN THE DARKNESS OF THE CELLAR AND STARED at where she imagined Jacobson, the butler, to be standing. Neither of them had spoken for some time. The light of Mary's torch had gradually weakened and she had switched it off at last in case some light on the subject might be needed later on. But without its beam the cellar seemed a great deal darker than anything she had ever known before, and the only bit of furniture left in it—the big oak desk pushed into the far corner—was not the most comfortable thing to sit on for any length of time. She gripped the revolver which she had quietly annexed from Jacobson while he was busy with the switch at the side of the desk. It made her feel a little more comfortable—but not much. She thought... if Jim or somebody doesn't come down that lift in the next ten minutes I'm going to start screaming... as if I hadn't had quite enough lying still in the dark already this evening... wonder if Edwin Carson's tried to get out through the big gates yet... suppose Jim tried to stop him... wish Jacobson would move and let me know he's still there... can't stand this silence and the dark much longer... another minute and I'll switch on this torch just to get my nerve back... come on, Jim... for God's sake, come on...

And Jacobson stood very still, leaning against the stone wall of the cellar a few yards away from Mary. He thought... well, Carson must have got it by this time... only wish I'd been there to see the rat die... no, couldn't have been down here then... wonder how much longer they'll be before they come down... suppose this is Amen for comrade Jacobson... why the hell did I get into such a panic when this damned wench stepped out of the little ante-room into the cellar?... and why the hell let her get hold of that gun?... no hope of getting away now... cornered in a cellar with a gun pointed at you... police in it in a few hours now... murder, suppose that's what it'll be... murder!... when they ought to give the freedom of London to anyone that put an end to Edwin Carson... if only I get out of this damned cellar there might be a chance... easy enough to get clear of the house... all the guests would still be locked up... once get hold of that gun and keep this dame quiet—only a matter of pushing back that lousy little switch and hacking a way up through the lift and then out... but the dame's sitting pretty tight across there with that revolver... hell of a risk... and yet...

Jacobson hoisted himself away from the cellar wall. He knew exactly where Mary was sitting. If she hadn't changed it since she switched off her torch, the gun was in her right hand. The hand nearest to him. He put one foot forward, leaned on it, brought the other one inch by inch in front. He stopped and listened. He could hear the girl breathing, less than six feet from him. He took another silent step forward and listened again. Then he jumped. His left arm crashed down on Mary's right hand, jamming the hand and the revolver against the top of the desk. The revolver went off with a report which echoed through the cellar. From the direction of the quick shoot of flame he knew that the bullet had buried itself in the cellar floor. He twisted the hand that held the revolver over the top of the desk as far as he could make it go... until at last the grip round the gun loosened and he jerked it into his own hand. The torch had fallen from Mary's other hand on to the floor. He kicked it away from the desk and stooped to pick it up, keeping the revolver levelled at where he heard the sound of Mary's breathing. Then he stood up, sweating, and switched the weak ray of light on to his companion in the cellar.

"Come over here," he ordered.

He walked backwards to the desk, keeping both Mary and the barrel of the revolver in his hand in the circle of the torch's light. The switch at the side of the desk clicked back thrice to the position marked "Off"—he did not care now if Carson had yet to make his getaway—all he saw was the much more important sight of Jacobson making his. He ripped the dust-sheets from the top of the big desk. Going to be useful, after all, these dust-sheets. He laid the torch on top of the desk so that its beam still lit up Mary crouched against the opposite wall. "Now, then, my lady," said Jacobson in an unpleasant voice. He pulled the dust-sheets into an improvised rope, whipped it over Mary's head and round her waist. The girl seemed to develop at that moment a great number of hitherto unknown arms and legs. She kicked, struggled, lashed out with her arms, and once came very near to biting a juicy piece from Jacobson's ear. Jacobson stood back and brought the barrel of the revolver to within a foot of her face. "Try that again, miss," he said, "and I'm going to plug you. Understand?" Apparently Mary understood only too well. She allowed Jacobson to carry on his work with the dust-sheets without any further attempts to damage his hearing. "That's a good girl," said Jacobson, knotting the sheets tightly round her wrists and ankles. "Now try and get a kick out of that."

He watched her for a minute, saw her stagger slightly, trip in the folds of the sheet which bound her feet, and fall heavily on the cellar floor. Fainted, eh? All to the good... keep her quiet for a bit. He snatched the torch from the top of the desk and ran across the cellar to the smashed lift entrance. The torch would last another five minutes or so at the most… after that he would have to do his stuff in the dark. He took a look at the lift. The floor of the cage had been stopped a foot or so beneath the level of the cellar's ceiling… He jammed the torch in his pocket, stood back and jumped. His fingers caught the cage and he hung to it desperately, jerking his body up and down in an effort to bring the cage down with him. His hands ached until he was on the point of letting go his grip… and at that moment something gave in the lift hoists and the cage crashed to the level of the cellar floor, throwing Jacobson down with it. He stood up, wiped the sweat from his forehead with the back of his hand, and jumped again. In a minute he was on top of the roof of the cage, inch-deep in dust and the oil of the lift controls. He switched on the torch again and saw above him the gap through the broken panels which would take him into Carson's study. He put one foot on each side of the shaftway, worked himself up inch by inch until he was able to grab hold of the panelling and heave his body out through the jagged opening. He stood up and leaned against the table in the study, gasping for breath. And then he walked to the door and opened it slowly.

The lights in the hall were still burning. He walked on tiptoe to the front door and found it unlocked and unbolted. Edwin Carson hadn't worried much about his usual lockings-up to-night—probably the first night since he came to Thrackley that Jacobson could have had free access to the whisky after the guests were finished with it. But for once Jacobson's thoughts were not inclined to such things as whisky. He pulled the front door open, gave a last look round the hall, and stepped noiselessly out into the garden of Thrackley. He would cross the drive at the corner, at its narrowest part, where there would be the least noise from the crunching of his shoes on the gravel. Only that to do, and to plunge himself into

the blanket of the pine-trees and then take his time to get to the
gates and get out. Get out for ever, thank God. He had done it!...

★   ★   ★

When Jim stepped back at last from staring at the sight of Edwin
Carson lying stiff at the foot of the big iron gates, he was reminded
that his host had at least left a visiting-card in the shape of a bullet
wound in his left leg. He pulled off his shoe and sock and turned
up his trouser leg to investigate the damage. A flesh wound only;
the bullet had grazed the side of his calf, removing a neat chunk
of flesh. Jim hopped across the room on the remaining efficient
leg, rummaged in the wardrobe until he found the oldest and most
tattered of the shirts he had brought to Thrackley, tore it into a
long, untidy bandage and bound it tightly over the wound. And
now to get out of here.

He walked to the door of his bedroom, tried the handle, and
took a dissatisfied look at the strength and thickness of the door's
mahogany panels. No use trying that. He turned back to the windows, stared again at the unpleasant yet fascinating sight of Edwin
Carson's body, twisted and still hanging to the iron gates, lit up in
the beam of the car's headlights. Very conclusive proof there that
the Thrackley electric current was still functioning. And if that was
so, then it was a hundred to one chance that the burglar-alarms
would still respond if anyone took it into their heads to open a
window. But that, so far as Jim could see, was the only way of
getting out of the bedroom. And in any case, however loudly the
alarms might ring, the Carson gang had been lessened by fifty per
cent—Carson himself lying stiff at the foot of the big gates outside,
and Adams lying almost as stiff on the floor of the garage. Only

Jacobson and Kenrick to cope with. Unless Carson had already coped with them himself before attempting his exit, which was very likely. The window, then, alarms or no alarms.

But before he pulled the window open he walked back to where his suitcase lay, disturbed the revolver from its resting-place at the bottom of the case, and filled it to capacity with the ammunition which he had borrowed from Freddie Usher. It felt much better to be gripping that firmly than to go about with one's hands empty. He jerked back the snib of the window sash and pulled the casement open. Yes… alarms still in excellent working order. From all over the house he could hear bells clanging in angry, urgent tones. He looked over the sill of the window—a fifteen-foot drop ending in a neat bed of gloire de Dijon roses. In ordinary circumstances he would have thought nothing about it (there had been an equally high wall at school which had to be negotiated every night when travelling fairs pitched their caravans a mile or so out of bounds), but with only one leg functioning properly it was an altogether different matter. He selected a landing-place between two of the gloire de Dijons, uttered a brief prayer to heaven that he would land on the right leg, and dropped.

Jim's opinion of Euclid, or whoever the fellow was who said that any heavy body would fall perpendicularly through space, dropped, too. Either (a) he took a decided list to starboard half-way on his journey between the window sill and the rose-bed, or (b) the two gloire de Dijons shifted their positions out of sheer spite immediately after he jumped. In any case, he appeared to land fairly accurately on both of the rose-trees. They were by far the finest and most thorny trees in the bed. For the first time in his life Jim knew exactly how a pin-cushion felt when full. But if they did nothing else (which they did), the rose-trees, at any rate, broke his fall and he picked himself up and extracted a score or so of elderly thorns from the seat of his trousers.

He limped quietly along the side of the house and was turning the corner to go and tackle the front door when he realized from the widening strip of light thrown on to the gravel drive that the said front door was being slowly opened. He stepped back against the wall, thanking heaven that it was a rhododendron bush and not a rose-tree this time in which he was hiding. He heard the slight but unmistakable sounds of feet stepping carefully on the drive and coming towards him. He stood perfectly still and watched from the corner of his eye as the owner of the feet appeared round the corner of the house. Jacobson. With a gun in his right hand. He saw the butler walk past the end of the house and cross the drive to the flower-beds on the other side. And with no regard at all for the feeling of the Coltness dahlias in the beds (which could scarcely have recovered from their encounter with the tyres of Freddie Usher's car at the beginning of the weekend), Jacobson stepped over the bed and into the jet blackness of the pine-trees farther on. Jim waited a minute and thought out this latest development. Was Jacobson after Carson? If so, he was in for a disappointment, being just half an hour too late. Or had the wanderlust got hold of the butler?—was this to be another attempted getaway? In any case, there was no point in standing here behind a moist rhododendron bush—much better follow Mr. Jacobson and see exactly what was in the air. And, thought Jim as he stepped out on to the drive, one body hanging dead to those damnable gates was quite enough to be going on with. He pushed his way on between the pine-trees, stepping as carefully as he could with his damaged leg. Jacobson must have been twenty yards or more ahead... he stepped silently from tree to tree, peering into the darkness to try and catch sight of the butler. He was within a dozen yards of the high stone wall when he did so.

Jacobson was standing beside the gates, in the glare of the Lagonda's headlights. He stared down at the twisted figure at his feet. The unpleasant grin on his face, which was the first thing that Jim noticed, changed almost at once to an expression of real fear. And Jacobson stretched out his hands, grabbed hold of the other half of the iron gates to that where Carson was lying, and pulled it towards him. Jim opened his mouth to shout… and then realized in amazement that the gates were not having the same grim effect as they had had on Edwin Carson. The butler had the half-gate open now and took a last look round at the house, the empty car, and the body of his former employer. And at that moment Jim's left leg gave a twinge of pain rather more angry than usual. It may have hurt badly, but it made up Jim's mind for him in a fraction of a second. He raised his revolver, took careful aim, and plugged Jacobson in as near a spot as possible to that chosen by Carson in his own anatomy. Jacobson fell with a grunt to the ground. "A few more," thought Jim, "and we'll have to close the gates and put up the 'House Full' notices."

It took him five minutes to heave Jacobson into the back seat of the Lagonda, truss him up and lock the doors of the car on him. In another couple of minutes he was inside the house and rummaging through Edwin Carson's study. He gave a grunt of satisfaction as he found the big bunch of keys lying deep in the mass of papers and rubbish which Carson had left heaped on the table. He forgot the pain in his leg once again and took the stairs three at a time to reach the door of Freddie Usher's bedroom. It was, naturally enough, the last key on the bunch that opened the door. He marched into the room and said, "Good morning, Freddie."

"Oh, it's you, is it? How's the massacre going?"

"Not too bad. One death, two wounded legs (one of them mine), and a Grade A sock on the jaw."

"Death, did you say?"

"Mine host… killed by his own dirty invention. He opened the gates to leave us all in the lurch… unfortunately for him he either forgot to turn off his damned electric current or someone else turned it on again after he'd left the cellars. At any rate, he's dead… good and stiff."

"Good God!"

"Well—now I want you to get busy, Freddie. I think I've done enough work for one night. This blasted leg is beginning to hurt like hell."

"At your service, James."

"Good man. Get hold of this bunch of keys, then, and go round the house and let all the family out of their bedrooms. You may find Kenrick, the servant, is locked up in his room; he's the only one I haven't met to-night. If you do, let him stay put. Get them all down in the lounge in ten minutes. I've got a little speech to deliver."

"And what about you?"

"I'm going to get hold of Mary, if I can. She'll still be down in those ruddy cellars. It may be that she's responsible for stopping Carson's getaway… and also causing that very nasty death of his… and if that's the case, it's going to be kept as quiet as possible."

"Righto. I'll go and unveil the bodies. Nothing else?"

"Yes. I want you to get into Adderly village as quick as you can, knock up the local bobby and bring him back to this godforsaken house just as fast as his size elevens will carry him. And put a call through to Scotland Yard—there'll be a phone where the bobby stays, I expect—and get them to send a man down here right away.

Tell them that both Hempson and Edwin Carson are dead. That'll fetch them. And for God's sake, Freddie, don't waste any time in the Hen and Chickens."

"Swifter than the eagle in its flight, old boy," said Freddie. "Greased lightning simply left at the post. Oh…"

"What's the matter?"

"It just occurred to me… how do I get to Adderly? Carson's car?"

"No——we'd better leave Carson and his car and what's in it just as they are."

"Well… if you've taken out all the plugs of my bus, it looks as if I'd have to walk."

"No—wait a minute. Remember the day we came to Thrackley? When you in your wisdom insisted on driving down a side road and hit a girl on a bicycle?"

"Yes. But of course it was you who said that—"

"That bicycle's in the garage. The front wheel's a bit out of sorts, and both tyres looked pretty fed up last time I saw them. But it'll go, Freddie."

"Me? Go three whole miles on a push-bike?"

"Why not? The finest thing on earth for developing the calf muscles. Freddie, get going."

And Jim slammed the door on an extremely worried Mr. Usher and (this being the most sensible way of getting downstairs with a bandaged leg) slid recklessly down the banisters and landed neatly outside the study door. He crossed the room and peered down the lift through the opening in the broken panels. He yelled twice… "Mary!"… and imagined that he heard a faint answer to the second of the yells. He pressed desperately along the moulding at the side of the panelling… why the blazes hadn't he watched more carefully when Burroughs demonstrated how the lift was worked? But at last

there came the pleasing sound of the lift whirring up towards him…
but not with the usual smooth whirr, but as though something had
gone sadly amiss with the works. Thank God it worked, anyway!…
In a couple of minutes he had the limp, trussed-up. figure of Mary
deposited safely on the study carpet. He ought, he knew, to have
set about immediately on the job of undoing the sheets tied round
her. Instead of which he indulged in a long and very satisfying kiss
as a reward for his evening's excitements.

When he reached the lounge he found that Freddie had already
performed his unveiling act. Catherine Lady Stone sat on the
extreme edge of a chair, fully dressed and with her handbag stuffed
to overflowing under her arm—ready, apparently, to make another
bolt for it. Marilyn and Henry Brampton had evidently decided that
there was no sense in remaining fully dressed in their bedrooms all
night and were now clad in dressing-gowns of such vicious tones
that they made Freddie Usher's pyjamas seem pale and anaemic in
comparison. Raoul had not changed from her evening gown… she
looked as sleek and immaculate as ever. Jim saw Mary comfortably
settled in a chair, then turned and addressed the other members
of the house-party. "I'm very sorry to disturb you at this hour of
the morning, ladies and gentlemen," he said, "but there are one or
two things which I feel you might be interested to know."

Catherine Lady Stone rose rather shakily from her chair. "Mr.
Usher gave me this to give to you," she said. "Where he is now,
and what he is doing, I have no idea."

Jim took the note from Lady Stone. "Kenrick's in his room all
right, and swearing like a sergeant-major," he read. "Where does
a bicycle keep its brakes, anyway?"

"Thank you, Lady Stone," he said. "Well, now… the most
important thing to tell you is that our—er—host, Edwin Carson,

is dead. He was killed an hour ago—killed by his own unpleasant device for keeping us inside Thrackley. I'm sure none of you will be very sorry to hear of his death."

"Then… then we can get away from this detestable place at once?" said Catherine Lady Stone.

"Of course, Lady Stone. But I'm sure you'll see the necessity of staying here until the representatives of the law arrive. They won't be long, I can assure you. That is, if our methods of getting in touch with them don't… fall flat on the way."

"Wait here?" said Lady Stone in her shrill soprano. "Not a minute longer, my good man. If we can get ourselves out of this house without the risk of being killed when we do so, then I for one intend to leave this very minute."

"I'm not lingering round the old place any longer than is necessary, either," said Henry Brampton.

"Where do you propose to go, then?" asked Jim.

Lady Stone gave a second snort. "I have a perfectly good pair of legs, Mr. Henderson," she said. "They are, I hope, quite capable of taking me into Adderly village. I've no doubt there is some way of getting to London from there—even at this hour of the morning. But if you think you can keep me in this house a minute longer, then I'm afraid you're very sadly mistaken."

"Me, too," said Marilyn Brampton. "Henry, get me some clothes out of my bedroom."

"And what about you, Raoul?" asked Jim.

"I go with Lady Stone," said Raoul in a quiet but very determined voice. "I stay here too long already—much too long."

"Very well, then," said Jim. He crossed to the door, leaned against it and faced the other guests. "If you lot think you're going to disappear and leave me here to explain this weekend's happenings to a lot of nit-witted constables you're very much mistaken. Our job is to stay here at Thrackley until the police have settled this business. And that's exactly what we're going to do."

"And how do you propose to stop us clearing out if we want to?" said Henry Brampton. "Same way as Edwin Carson, eh?"

"Exactly," said Jim.

Catherine Lady Stone turned a shade paler—a thing which one would not have thought possible a minute earlier.

"What in the name of heaven do you mean, Mr. Henderson?" she said.

"Edwin Carson's hanging dead to the front gates of Thrackley at this minute," said Jim. "Go and have a look at him if you like. The gates are still closed. And the current that killed Carson is still running through those gates. And the only person who knows where the switch is to turn off that current is yours truly, James Henderson. And he's not turning off that switch yet. So that, dear friends, is that."

"Oh!" said Catherine Lady Stone. Only once had she felt similarly thwarted, and then by a heckler (at an annual general meeting of the Council for the Repatriation of Destitute Bulgarians) who had asked her in a loud voice from the back of the hall if she could tell the meeting where exactly Bulgaria was, anyway. "Oh!" she repeated, and flopped back into her chair with the air of an early Christian martyr who was being kept for the last, largest, and most ferocious of the Romans' troupe of performing lions.

Catherine Lady Stone estimated the time that the six persons in the lounge sat and stared at one another in silence as being not a single second under three hours. Actually it was ninety-five minutes. At the end of which time the noise of a high-powered car coming up the drive and stopping at the front door shattered the silence and made the Thrackley house-party dash from the lounge to see what exactly was happening now. From the high-powered car stepped, in order of precedence, one large constable, Freddie Usher, one large constable, one large constable, a short elderly man in plain clothes and a trilby hat, one large constable, and one extremely large constable. Lady Stone stared at Mr. Usher as though Hamlet's ghost had suddenly appeared in front of her in bright mauve pyjamas.

"Mr. Usher," said Lady Stone, "would you mind telling us where you have been during the last few hours?"

"Adderly," said Freddie. "Collecting the arms of the law."

"And how did you manage to get in and out of the grounds of this house, pray?"

"Through the old gates, of course. Why?"

Lady Stone made a faint gasping sound deep down in her throat.

"I'm sorry, Lady Stone," said Jim, "but it seemed the only way of keeping the bunch of you inside Thrackley until the police came. The wanderlust got hold of you, I noticed. And really it's much better to wait and see the thing through instead of dashing off at three in the morning without saying 'Thank you for having me' or anything like that. Good morning, inspector... come and I'll introduce you to the house-party..."

And for the first time in the weekend (and for that matter in her entire life) Catherine Lady Stone was completely speechless.

XXV

M R. WILSON FROM SCOTLAND YARD CLOSED THE LOUNGE door deliberately behind him and surveyed the Thrackley house-party at length. A large and stolid man, this Mr. Wilson; a man who thought and moved and spoke at what seemed an annoyingly slow pace. But Mr. Wilson from Scotland Yard rather prided himself on the fact that he obtained better results than did most of his colleagues without losing either his temper, his wind or his perspiration. Of which three things, as he pointed out to these colleagues of his, they lost an unnecessarily large amount.

"Well, we're all here, are we?" said Mr. Wilson at last. And receiving only silence in reply to this, Mr. Wilson slowly produced a cigarette paper and a tiny pile of tobacco, rolled the cigarette with tremendous care, ran his tongue along the edge of its paper, and searched in each of his nine pockets for matches. Then he said: "All here. That's fine. Could one of you gentlemen oblige me with a match?" (Provoking man, thought Catherine Lady Stone. The idea of the Yard sending a man like that down here... a great lumbering halfwit. She must write to the Chief Commissioner about it. Absurd. Did ever a man take so long to light a cigarette?...)

"Well, now," said Mr. Wilson, "just make yourselves comfortable, will you? There's one or two things I want discussed before any of you leave this place. You'll not be sorry to leave it, I expect? Though it's a fine old place... yon watercolour up there must be worth a pretty penny, I should say... not that I'm a judge of these things, mind you. But—"

"It is a very valuable Turner, inspector," said Catherine Lady Stone. "Now would you mind telling us what you have to tell us, and let us get out of this detestable house as quickly as possible?"

"Certainly, Lady Stone," said Mr. Wilson. He blew a couple of neat smoke-rings, watched them until they lost their shape and became vague blots of smoke. Then he said: "Your host—Mr. Carson... he's dead."

"I don't think any of us are particularly sorry," said Henry Brampton.

"Maybe not. Would you like to know how he died? I'll tell you. It's a pretty long story, though. Just you sit back in your seats and light your cigarettes... I suppose you've all realized by now that Edwin Carson was a man who wouldn't have any scruples about how he got hold of precious stones as long as he did get hold of them. I can't understand a man being like that... a string of half-guinea pearls looks the same to me as a sixpenny string from Woolworths or a thousand-pound rope from some of these posh shops... but there it is. Some men are like that."

Raoul settled unhappily in her chair. Not the slightest use, she decided, to expect being in town in time for her matinée. At this rate, not the slightest.

"That's why he asked you all here to Thrackley. He managed to steal your necklace, Lady Stone, and your pearls, Miss Brampton, and some jewellery of yours, Miss—er—Raoul. It's all right... they're all here in this case. You'd better have them back now, I suppose."

Lady Stone put her fat fingers around the ruby which had once been the centre stone of her necklace and allowed Mr. Wilson to go very slightly up in her estimation. A good, reliable man, no doubt; but still a slow-witted idiot.

"I've been speaking to that butler fellow… Jacobson, isn't that what he's been calling himself? He's in a very talkative mood this morning. He's told me just how Carson managed to get these jewels away from you without causing the least bit of suspicion. A genius in making imitations of these things, old Carson was. It just goes to prove my theory that a half-guinea string of pearls is as good as a thousand-pound rope any day. Better, maybe. Well, anyway, Carson got away with nearly all the stuff he wanted—I think you had some bits of things that he was after, Mr. Usher, but he hadn't time to collect them—and he planned to leave you all here last night. Made very thorough preparations for getting away, too. I suppose he'd go off to the Continent and lie low for a while… and then come back and take another house and another name and another set of easily fooled guests… no offence meant, of course, ladies and gentlemen… and repeat the performance. He made a bad mistake last night, though. He left our friend, the butler, behind… locked him in the cellar… left him in the lurch to face all these awkward questions that I've been asking him this morning. A pity, that… an awful pity… to spoil a perfectly thought-out plan, just through thinking of his own miserable skin first…"

Mr. Wilson took a last puff at his cigarette and jabbed the stump out on the ashtray beside him.

"He locked friend Jacobson in the cellar. That was really the best room in the house, you know. I suppose Carson demonstrated just how difficult it was for any of you to get out of Thrackley? I've been taking a look round this place this last hour or so: that burglar-alarm's just about the neatest job of its kind that I've seen. And I've seen a good few in my time, I may tell you. And just to make matters worse, there was an electric current which could be put through all the ironwork around the walls… all those prongs on top of the wall, all through the big gates at the front of the house and the small gate at the back. Yes, it was no easy matter to leave this place in a hurry if Edwin Carson had set his mind against your leaving. But you know all this, don't you? There's no need for me to explain it to you."

"None whatever," said Catherine Lady Stone.

"That's fine. Well, old Carson was ready to leave. He'd done friend Jacobson in the eye, he'd switched off the electric current and all he had to do was to drive the car through the gates and get away to wherever he pleased. It's a terrible pity none of you thought of getting away yourselves about three o'clock this morning. You'd have had a mighty pleasant surprise when you found that the burglar-alarms didn't work and you could open the big gates without risking your life. That was what Edwin Carson expected to do, of course. Unfortunately for him this young lady was rather too clever for him."

Jim looked across at Mary. Amazing how a girl could still be looking as lovely as ever after a night like the last.

"She was down in this cellar of Carson's, too, you see. She'd gone down to investigate a few things, and very sensibly decided that she'd be of more use down there than in her bedroom. A risky thing to do, miss, but it was worth it. And when the old butler fellow found himself locked down there, this young lady came out from where she was hiding and the pair of them talked things over for a little while. They'd been taking for—about five or ten minutes, would it be miss?—when the switch that Edwin Carson had turned to the 'Off' position was turned back again to the 'Full on' position. And a minute or so later Carson tried to open the big gates to let his car through. If ever a man deserved to have a nasty death, he did. And we can't grumble. He got it."

Jim leaned forward in his chair. "Those other two servants of Carson's," he asked. "What about them?"

"Both quite safe and sound, sir. We found one locked in his bedroom suffering from an overdose of chloroform, and the other lying on the floor of the garage with a jaw about three times as big as it should be."

"Really?" said Jim.

"They're under lock and key now. A pair of very ordinary crooks."

"Well, inspector," said Catherine Lady Stone, "thank you very much. A very lucid explanation. I'm glad the Yard sent a man like you down to settle things up… some of you men are so officious and bombastic. I shall certainly mention how very capable you've been when next I see Lord Turner. I meet him fairly often. Quite an intimate friend of mine."

"Thanks very much, Lady Stone," said the large Mr. Wilson. "Very kind of you, I'm sure. Though, of course, Lord Turner's retired from the Yard now."

"Oh," said Catherine Lady Stone. And, feeling that the subject might do with a little changing, she added: "Well, are we free to go now? Nothing more you want with us, inspector?"

"Nothing at all at the moment. If you'll just leave your correct names and addresses with one of the men I've brought with me. There's bound to be a certain amount of inquiry into all this, but it'll be kept as quiet as we can. If you'll do the same it'll be a great help… Thank you, ladies and gentlemen… Oh, Mr. Henderson!…"

"Yes?"

"Would you mind just staying a few minutes after the others have gone? There's one or two things I'd like to have a word with you about."

"Certainly."

Jim walked to the door and caught Mary's hand before she went out of the room.

"Wait outside for me, Mary, please," he said. "The inspector wants me for something or other. Don't go away, now. I've got a lot of things to say to you."

"I'll be waiting, Jim."

"Fine."

He walked back to the table at which the inspector was sitting, lit a cigarette and wondered what the devil this peculiar, stodgy little man could want to say to him.

"We'll have the door shut, eh, Mr. Henderson?" said Mr. Wilson, after going through the ritual of rolling another cigarette.

"Well, what's the mystery, inspector?"

"No mystery, sir. Bit of a surprise, maybe, but certainly no mystery. I want you to look through these things. They were found on Carson's body when I searched him this morning. I oughtn't to let you see these, sir. It's only because they're things that concern you and because I think you'll keep quiet about them that I'm doing this. I'd get flaming hell from the Powers that Be if they knew I was doing this."

"Very good of you," said Jim.

"Here they are. Three things… all that was found on Carson… bar a wallet of notes and a little matter of a few million pounds' worth of jewels. That's the first thing we found." He handed Jim a photograph, fairly large, unmounted. Jim looked at it and then:

"Good God!"

"Recognize it?"

"Of course I recognize it. It's me."

"Ungrammatical but quite correct," said the large Mr. Wilson. "And very good of you, too. Taken some time ago, though, wasn't it?"

"Ages ago. At least, about fifteen years or so... I remember having it done—just a short while before my mother died. But what the blazes was Edwin Carson doing with my photograph?"

"Exhibit B, Mr. Henderson. No need to read it all, though you'll have a chance of doing that before long. It's Carson's diary. Read the entry on the page where I've slipped in that bit of paper."

He tossed the leather-backed book across the table to Jim, rose from his seat and walked across the room to the window. Jim picked up the diary and opened it at the page which the inspector had marked. He read:

> June 23rd. Arrangements complete for next weekend. All accepted except Wensley. Jim wrote me this morning to say that he was coming. Think of seeing him again after twenty years! His address, which I found by the merest chance, is in Ardgowan Mansions—a dirty little boarding-house. He must be hard up, poor lad. Determined not to let him find out who is his host next weekend, however great the temptation. It must be very seldom that a son comes to stay unknowingly at his father's house. Jacobson is an idiot. To-day, when I was testing the lathes in the workshop...

Jim laid the diary on the table. The stolid Mr. Wilson stopped his investigation of the two flies who were sunning themselves on the window-pane, came back to the table and said:

"When was your father supposed to die, Mr. Henderson?"

"When I was quite small—about three or four, I think. I never knew him. Saw him occasionally, I suppose. But he was in South Africa when I was a kid."

"Yes. Been in South Africa a good long time. I.D.B., from all accounts. And then a few years as a guest of His Majesty. And then back to England—back here to Thrackley…"

"Do you honestly mean—?"

"Ever hear anything about your father? Anything you can remember? His appearance… any peculiarities… distinguishing marks… think, now…"

"Yes… my mother told me often about an accident they both had. He nearly lost his sight—both his eyes were cut terribly. She used to say that the scars were like frames round his eyes."

"That's good enough for me," said Mr. Wilson from Scotland Yard. "Come in next door, will you, Mr. Henderson?"

Jim followed the large frame of the inspector through to the little room off the lounge. He stopped as the inspector pulled back the sheet which had been thrown over Edwin Carson's body. He stared down at the little man's face; they had taken off the big, thick-lensed spectacles…

"No doubt about it, I suppose."

"No doubt about it, as you say, Mr. Henderson," said the inspector. "Edward Henderson, alias Edwin Carson, alias ten or twenty other damned names." He drew back the corner of the sheet over Carson's face. "That's why you were asked down here. Not to get hold of any of your knick-knacks. Sentiment. Just pure sentiment. Killed many a man before this one."

They walked slowly back to the lounge.

"I wonder," said Jim, "if he'd mind us having a drink? I don't think so… and, my God, I could do with one at the moment."

"A very sensible idea. Know where it's kept? Splendid."

"You'll join me?"

"Thank you, Mr. Henderson. A small one. The Chief always holds a breath-smelling parade when we get back from these country-house jobs. Thank you, sir."

"Good luck, then."

"And to you, sir. Not that there's much point in wishing you that now, sir."

"What d'you mean?"

"Exhibit C, sir. I shouldn't try to read it now. It's rather long. It's Carson's—your father's will. A very queer will. I know I shouldn't tell you anything of this—shouldn't have read the thing myself, perhaps—but having gone so far there's no sense in stopping, is there?"

"Well, what's in the damned thing?"

"The first couple of pages are most interesting… especially from a police point of view. They settle up a whole lot of things that needed settling. You see, it's only within the last few years that Carson started to add to his collection by stealing. These first two pages are really a list of every jewel he's stolen since three years ago… names, description of stones, date on which the things were pinched, and so on. He's leaving them in his will to their original owners. That was like Carson. Extraordinary fellow… mad, you know, Mr. Henderson, but clever… terribly clever."

"And after the first two pages?"

"The third page is mostly about you. You see, Mr. Henderson, even before Edwin Carson started this rather unorthodox way of adding to his collection, he already had got hold of specimens that must be worth a good many hundred thousand pounds. All collected in a strictly legal fashion… bought at sales, from other collectors, a few discovered in out-of-the-way places, and so on. A very nice little lot indeed. He leaves all that and all his other worldly goods to you."

"Do you mind," said Jim, "if I have another drink? Just before you tell me anything more."

"Nothing more to tell, sir. You'll be sent these things as soon as we've settled up this affair. I've got your address in case we want you again. But that's all for the present, sir… I've tried to tell you it as briefly as I could, sir. I rather thought you wanted a word with the young lady."

"What brains you detectives have! Damn the drink! Have one for me, Wilson, and thank you terribly for what you've told me."

"A pleasure, sir, I'm sure," said Mr. Wilson, from Scotland Yard, and produced his third roll of cigarette-paper and his third tiny pile of tobacco.

"Mary," said Jim. "I've got a lot of things to talk to you about. A lot of very important things. Things that can't be discussed here… What's that shiny-looking thing at the front door?"

"Mr. Usher's Rolls-Royce," said Mary. "He's spent the whole morning putting its entrails together again."

"And where is he now?"

"Upstairs. Packing. He's promised to take Lady Stone back to town."

"Isn't that just splendid? Freddie always took a long time to pack. Usually he forgets his shaving stuff. Jump in, Mary."

Mary jumped in.

"What about Lady Stone and Mr. Usher?" she asked.

"I don't care a hoot in hell for Lady Stone—and Freddie Usher and I went to the same school, which can usually be trotted out as an excuse for pinching another man's car."

"Splendid."

"Splendid it is."

He pressed the self-starter. The car's nose swung round and the tyres made a satisfying crunch on the gravel of the drive. The two occupants did not speak until the car was through the big, open gates of Thrackley and out on to the main road. Then Jim removed one hand from the steering-wheel, placed it around the neck of the girl beside him, drew her into a closer and much more comfortable position.

"Now," he said, "I'm going to talk all the way to London, so just lean back and prepare yourself for a good listen. There was one thing I wanted to ask you, though… what the devil was it, now?… Oh, yes, I know—will you marry me, Mary?"

"Yes," said Mary. "I think I will."

"That's very satisfactory. You say the nicest answers. Kiss me, will you?—and then I'll start the recitation."

"For heaven's sake mind that hen!"

"Damn the hen. Kiss me, please."

"The hen!"

"Kiss, please."

"Oh, very well," said Mary.

And the Wyandotte in question caused a sensation among its family and friends by clearing the hedge at the side of the road with a good three feet to spare. A thing it had not done for years.

XXVI

MRS. BERTRAM, PROPRIETRIX OF THAT EXCELLENT BOARDING-house (or, rather, "establishment") at number 34, Ardgowan Mansions, N., looked over the top of her spectacles to see that things were progressing favourably on her gas stove, and settled herself in the wicker armchair beside her kitchen fireplace for her early-morning scanning of the newspapers. Really there was far too much in the papers nowadays. Mrs. Bertram could remember the time when the people in Fleet Street were quite pleased with themselves if they dished up one murder or, at the most, two society weddings and a suicide in a single issue of their day's paper. But look at this morning's crop, for instance: Prime Minister Flies to Save Conference, Famous Film Star Files Divorce Proceedings, Hunger-Striker Dies in Prison After Ninety-seven Days' Fast, Fierce Riots in Cuba, Government Defeated in Guatemala, Martial Law Declared in Barcelona, American Flyer Beats Long Distance Record, Ipswich Girl Found Dead in Hedge, Missing Jewels Recovered in Country-House Sensation, Nudist Colony Attacked by Indignant Women, Yorkshire Bowler Takes All Ten Wickets, Gateshead By-Election Result, Stage Favourite Re-marries, Bank Clerk Battered and Robbed. Now, what chance had a working woman to cope with all that lot? Especially when there was also the woman's page, the racing column and the serial to get through. Mrs. Bertram pushed her spectacles up her nose and sifted out the best of the day's sensations. The country-house business would just be another of these society how-d'you-do's, she decided, and there was no longer any interest in the hunger-striker if he was now neither hungry nor striking. Mrs. Bertram ran her eyes swiftly through the Prime Minister, the famous film star, the Ipswich girl, the Nudists and the battered bank clerk. Really, the goings-on nowadays... The P.M. was hurrying across to Geneva to assure the successful and indefinite adjournment of the latest conference; the famous film star gave as grounds for her divorce the distressing fact that her husband picked his teeth in company; the Ipswich girl (photo on back page) had been stabbed through the heart with a joiner's chisel; the Nudists had had to bolt for it into an adjoining wood; and the battered bank clerk... now, this was really meaty, this was. "The unfortunate victim of the outrage was carrying a leather bag containing..." At which moment one of the many bells in the corner of the kitchen clanged out suddenly in an impatient din. Mrs. Bertram took her spectacles off and her eyes away from the battered bank clerk and peered up to see who it was that was making all that row. Number Six: Mr. Henderson. Now, what on earth did Mr. Henderson want with his shaving-water at this time of the morning? Really, if a hard-working woman couldn't get a minute to glance at the paper, it was a bit thick and no mistake. Mrs. Bertram rose and poured a quantity of boiling water from the large pan on her gas stove into one of her blue enamelled jugs. Mr. Henderson up, and it not yet gone eight o'clock... something sadly wrong here. But then Mr. Henderson had slumped rather badly in Mrs. Bertram's estimation during the past twenty-four hours. Chiefly because of this here girl. Never so much as looked at a girl before, Mr. Henderson hadn't. And then suddenly ("without," as Mrs. Bertram explained to the lady over the fence, "without so much as an excuse-me or a by-your-leave") in he walks arm-in-arm with this here girl. Nice, refined-looking girl, of course. Nothing against her as far as looks go. But Mrs.

Bertram had very well-developed ideas about the running of her "establishment". No commercials (the late Mr. Bertram had travelled for soap). And definitely no couples. She had spent the last three years telling Mr. Henderson that it was high time he went and got himself a nice girl to look after him, but now that the idea seemed to be on the verge of fulfilment Mrs. Bertram was not nearly so enthusiastic. Particularly as it looked very much as though she was about to lose one of her lodgers. Always right on the dot at the end of the month, Mr. Henderson was. A nice, reliable young man. She gave a violent knock at the reliable young man's door.

"Come in, Mrs. B.," said Jim.

Mrs. B. came in and received another jolt. Mr. Henderson was up and half-dressed. Such a thing, at two minutes to eight in the morning, had always been looked on almost as sacrilege in Number six bedroom of Number 34, Ardgowan Mansions. This here girl again, thought Mrs. Bertram to herself. She poured the hot water into the basin on the dressing-table and flung one of her morning papers on to Jim's bed.

"Good morning, Mr. Henderson. Up with the lark, aren't you?"

"I'm turning over several new leaves, Mrs. B. Going to get up and bring you breakfast into bed every morning after this."

"What sort of a time did you have when you were away, sir?"

"Not bad, Mrs. Bertram. Not at all bad."

"Quiet, I'll bet, down there in Surrey miles from anywhere. My, the goings-on you've missed here this weekend. Right in front of my own eyes on Saturday afternoon, Mr. Henderson, that there little brat of a message-boy of Parkinsons, the fruiterers, near as tuppence underneath a great hulking motor-lorry. And Mr. Jackson tells me—"

"Is Mary—Miss Carson up yet, Mrs. Bertram?"

"She is. Been up this last half-hour. Borrowing face cream and brushes and combs and Lord knows what else. Seems to have come away without nothing at all, she does. Did you leave in a hurry, the pair of you, Mr. Henderson?"

"In a whale of a hurry, Mrs. Bertram. What do you think of her, eh?"

"As far as looks go, sir, full marks. But I must say—"

"Well, you'd damned well better like her, Mrs. B. Because she's going to be Mrs. James Henderson just as soon as we can get someone to ask a few necessary questions."

"Mr. Henderson! You don't say!"

Jim crossed to his bed and picked up the copy of the morning paper which Mrs. Bertram had brought. He turned to its centre page and searched along the headlines. Yes... all here, full details, long and exclusive interview with Lady Stone. "Read your paper this morning, Mrs. B.?" he asked.

"What I could before you started pealing your bell, sir. Some sort of a to-do in Cuba, it seems, and—"

"And that. Page eight, col. six: 'Country-House Sensation. Famous Missing Jewels Discovered. Dangerous Crook Killed. Thrills for House-Party Guests. Exclusive Interviews.' Go on, get your specs. on that. Full details of my quiet weekend in Surrey."

Mrs. Bertram grabbed the paper and stared at the column with her mouth open. "But... Mr. Henderson—" she gasped. But Mr. Henderson had left her alone in the room with the exclusive interviews.

He walked along the corridor until he reached the door labelled "9" in neat black lettering. He knocked and waited for Mary's "Come in".

"'Morning, darling," he said. "Sleep well?"

"Better than for months. No pine-trees to worry about."

"Fine. It's all in the papers, dear. Two and a half columns of Lady Stone, some heavy publicity stuff by Raoul's manager, close-up of Raoul's legs on the picture page, all my grimy past, and a very attractive photo of you with the title, 'Girl Who Helped to Outwit Dangerous Criminal'. I think a long journey to somewhere where they don't get the newspapers is indicated."

"Looks like it."

"Oh—and it's out of the question to hope for breakfast here now, I'm afraid. Mrs. Bertram's just found the Thrackley story in the *Daily Observer*. She'll be beyond the pale and unable to think of anything like bacon and eggs for a good hour at least. We'll go out and feed at a restaurant, shall we?"

"Right. I'll be ready in a minute."

"When do they open, anyway?"

"Restaurants?"

"No… registrars' offices."

"I've no idea."

"We'll go and find out, shall we?"

Which they did.

BRITISH LIBRARY CRIME CLASSICS

ALSO AVAILABLE

Many of our titles are also available in eBook and audio editions